Bully Route Home
Literary fiction

Blue Water, Red Blood
Historical fiction

The Cross on Cotton Creek
Historical fiction

A Place No One Should Go
Suspense/mystery

The Hangin' Oak
Suspense/mystery/mainstream

September on Echo Creek
Woman's mainstream

Story Time-R
Short story collection

The Bait Man

by

DL Havlin

ISBN: 978-1-986-762-366
Copyright 2017 by D. L. Havlin

This book was printed in the United States of America by Taylor and Seale Publishing, LLC, Daytona Beach Shores, Florida, 32118.

Taylor and Seale Publishing, LLC
2 Ocean's West, Suite 406
Daytona Beach Shores, FL 32118

All Taylor and Seale books are available through bookstores and on line at Amazon, Barnes & Noble, and Books a Million.

Dedication

This book is dedicated to Linda Kay Solinger.

If we're all very, very lucky we'll have the opportunity to acquire friends that are always there for us in the special times of our lives.

In times of need and sadness they support us, and in times of success and celebration they share their joy for our good fortune.

The Solingers are such friends and Linda Kay is one of the reasons *The Bait Man* is now a published novel. Linda possesses the rare ability to be entirely honest and is willing to share her opinion in a way that is up-lifting and constructive. Linda knows books, having been in the business. She is one of my most valued critics.

DL Havlin

Acknowledgements

For years I read acknowledgements in books with little or no appreciation of what they represented. After over twenty years of writing, I read them with understanding and reverence. Anyone who writes has had others make contributions to their successes and mitigate their failures. I've benefitted greatly from *many* peoples' assistance in *many* different ways.

I owe a continuing debt of gratitude to my mentor/editors, Robert Fulton, PhD. who forged some raw material into a writer, and Babs Brown who has been and continues to be my watch dog, barking loud and long when my work lacks in any area. Authors Bev Browning, Veronica Helen Hart, and Robert B. Parker, agents Mary Sue Seymour and Anne Hawkins provided me with encouragement when my confidence was waning and kept me at the keyboard.

I owe special thanks to Taylor & Seale Publishing and to its Editor-in-chief, Mary Custureri and to V.H. Hart, her Senior Editor. Their belief in my work and encouragement is greatly appreciated. Obviously, you wouldn't be reading this book without Mary and Taylor & Seale.

I've been blessed with many excellent "test pilot readers" during my career. The list has grown too long to mention them all, but there are several that have been with me for a long time. Chet Collins, Linda Kay Solinger, Paul Owens, Carol Robb, Nancy Rogge, Gloria Andrews, Linda Hilliard, and Pat Cole don't spare criticism or praise … if it's earned.

Finally, I reserve my largest, most heart-felt thank you for my loving wife, partner and do-all assistant—Jeanelle. Without her support, encouragement, understanding and tolerance I'd have abandoned writing long ago.

The
Bait Man

One

"My customers prefer dealin' with a woman, one with your special kind of talents. Heard tell you was lookin' for part-time work. Interested, Chessie?"

Hootie Barnes eye-balled me from across the Waffle House table. It wasn't the worst place I'd been interviewed for a job. Or propositioned for that matter. "What's it pay?" I asked.

"Reason I got a hold of you was I thought you'd fit right in the job. You been fishin' with your old man since you was what, eight?" Hootie didn't wait for an answer. "You ain't scared to get dirty and a little smelly. I know you work hard." The old boy licked his lips and looked sheepish. I wondered if he'd have guts enough to say it.

"Lot of women can do that." I prompted him, "Aren't you saying your customers are mostly male and they'd enjoy staring at my boobs and butt if the fishing gets slow?" He laughed. I expected that.

"You know me for what, twenty years?" he said.

"Twenty-five."

"You'd know I was lyin' if I said it weren't true. Look, Chessie, that body of yours is fine eye candy for any normal man, but you also know how to handle a situation if one should arise. You and your family are old Vero, not some snow birds turned sand fly. You ain't no violet. Hear tell you didn't waste the four years you spent in the Marines. I won't have to worry about you takin' care of yourself."

"What's it pay?" I ignored what I assumed was a reference to a bar incident a couple years back where I broke a drunk's arm for trying to tweak one of my nipples.

"It will fit in with what you were tellin' me. You'll have four full days a week to volunteer at that archeological dig. Make your professor happy as hell." He was stalling. Hootie hated parting with a dime. The birds around his house didn't say "cheep" they said "cheapest."

"What's it pay?"

"Aren't you goin' to ask what you have to do?"

"I know what a mate on a head boat does. I clean the boat, cut bait, bait hooks, take fish off, teach the idiots to use their rods." Hootie grinned, but I ignored it … my stupid choice of words deserved the jab, "repair the equipment, make up rigs, clean fish, and clean the boat some more." I leaned forward. "What *does* it pay?"

"It's ten dollars an hour on the books, but you can make a lot on the side."

I got up to leave. "Find someone else, you asshole." I couldn't get my words out fast enough. "Despite what everybody in this town thinks, I didn't screw the whole

Vero Beach basketball team my senior year. Find someone else to spread them for you."

Hootie grabbed my arm and said, "That's not what I was tellin' you at all. Cool off, damn it. Sit down. You've got everybody in the place starin' at us. Last thing I need is one of these folks tellin' my wife I was tryin' to hit on you."

I eased back into the booth, still furious, but everybody in the Waffle House *was* staring at me and the last thing I needed was another incident to fortify my image as the village Wild Child. It was fifteen years since I graduated from my free-wheeling high school career and my deeds, some imagined, some true, clung to me like the smell of dead fish on a mullet boat. Small towns don't forget.

Hootie shook his head at me. "I run a damn fine bottom fishin' service. They ain't no sign on my boat sayin' pussy on the side and I sure in hell ain't no pimp. You know me better'n that. If you can keep that hot head of yours from blowin,' I'll tell you what I meant."

I took a deep breath and shrugged my shoulders. "I'll listen."

"Mary Perez told me she made more on tips than what I paid her. And I know Mary wasn't spendin' any time on her back. She wore tee shirts with some funny stuff printed on them and no bra. She giggled a lot. *That's all.*"

"Mary has a face like a movie star, I don't."

"Mary is an exceptional looker, but you ain't no worse'an average. Your body sure makes up the difference." He held his hands out toward me, palms up. "Mary said she averaged $630 a week all told."

"Why did she quit?"

"I don't know. Her family says she run off with her no-count boyfriend to get married, but I ain't heard from her.

She just didn't show for work." Hootie looked uncomfortable, but managed a smile. "Her stupidity is your opportunity."

I sat quietly and considered what *did look* like a great opportunity. It would pay my college tuition and I figured I might even be able to pay some rent and expenses to my half-brother and roommate, Reading. His policeman's salary wasn't making him rich and he was currently suspended on half-pay. "What days would I work?"

"Friday, Saturday, and Sunday . . . I know it will cut into your love life. Sorry about that."

"I don't have a love life . . . right now." I extended my hand across the table. "You got yourself an employee. I'll cut bait with the best of them."

He beamed. "Good!" He grasped my hand and shook it. Hootie *was* old Vero and the hand shake meant something to him. "Can you start this weekend?"

"Sure."

"Good! You need to be at my dock Friday mornin', at six." Hootie pushed his head forward and put on a serious expression. He lowered his voice. "Now I don't want to be hittin' this real hard, but I got to say it. I have to depend on you showin' up. One day off where you don't tell me in advance, means you got all days off from then on."

I couldn't help but frown and look disgusted. I knew his concern was legitimate. I'd done enough to earn the reputation of only being dependable if it fit my whims at the moment. "Hootie, I'm turning a new leaf. I'll be there, on time, every day I'm supposed to be."

He looked relieved, but dubious. "Good to hear, good to hear." Hootie scrunched his face in a manner I'd seen many times. He was about to discuss something he wanted to avoid. "You'll be meetin' the bait man and helpin' unload the truck when you get there Friday. We get our bait fish and frozen blocks of chum from him. He sells us good stuff and it's inexpensive. You need to get those chum blocks into our freezer or in the boat cooler right away. If they melt, they are the worst smellin' things you can imagine. 'Gag maggots' as the sayin' goes. I think the bait man lets the chum rot some before he freezes it to get more fish to feed. You know you'd have to clean the mess." Hootie's face twisted more severely. "Anyway, I'll be there in time to pay him. The guy who delivers the bait is named Charlie Cocker, but don't call him Charlie. He goes by Rooster." He took a deep breath. "Rooster is different. He's a little rough around the edges, know what I mean?"

"No. That can cover a lot of things." I said.

Hootie wasn't a sand-blasted smooth character. He licked his lips as he formulated what he wanted to tell me about Rooster. "I guess he's like what you'd expect someone to be, doin' what he does. Rooster stinks. I don't know if the man ever bathes or washes his clothes. The old baseball cap he wears is what he uses to wipe his hands on. Fish slime, blood, don't matter. No tellin' what color it was when he got it. He has that cap on all the time. Willie Mitchell tried to take it off Rooster one day and Rooster pulled a knife on him." Hootie waited for me to react negatively. I didn't, so he went on. "He's aggressive and he'll argue about anything. Rooster just ain't fun to be around. And . . . well . . . he ain't *nice* to women."

"*Nice*? What does he do that isn't *nice*?" For the hundredth time I wished I could get a concealed carry permit. My record wouldn't let me.

"Truthfully, he gave Mary a bad time. Made a lot of nasty remarks to her. Tried to intimidate her all the time. She wouldn't come in to unload the truck by herself. Mary was scared of him. Until I found out about her runnin' off with her boyfriend, I figured that's why she quit."

"Did he ever get physical with her?" The job grew less inviting.

"No. I asked and she said not. He just kept after her, wantin' to get in her pants. I can't imagine any woman wantin' to get within a mile of a bed that man was in." Hootie managed a grim grin. "You won't be alone with him most times. I get in by six, mostly."

I put Hootie's last comment in the "fairy tales can come true" category. "What else do I do before you get there?"

He sighed, fished in his pocket, pulled out a ring with three keys on it and handed them to me. "After I show you what I want, you can get the rods out and check the rigs, get coffee made, do a final check on life vests, that kind of thing. Don't worry 'bout that. We'll get around to showin' you the routine after you start." He looked relieved.

I took the keys. "See you Friday *morning*." As I stuffed them in my purse, I wondered what Rooster was really like. I wasn't worried about being able to handle him. Mary Perez was a wus and Hootie was a typical fisherman, he exaggerated everything . . . still the smell . . . I'd find out in two days.

Two

The first blue-grays of dawn were showing above the Atlantic as I slowed my pickup to turn down the sand lane to Hootie Barnes' fish camp. The 250-foot strip of land that ran from Ocean Boulevard to the narrows of the Indian River was a time capsule inserted in the terrain which had evolved into the modern city of Vero Beach. Native oaks, sand pines, and cabbage palms fought for dominance over foreign intruders like Australian pines and Brazilian berry bushes. The road led to Hootie's fish camp and dock. Both dated back to the 1950's when Hootie's grandfather decided to use his knowledge of fishing the local waters to start making money off of the "Damn Yankees" rather than cussing them. Hootie did a good job of "keeping them up" partly because of family pride; mostly because of city code enforcement. Well-to-do property owners on either side seethed with suppressed anger at the barnacle that clung to the ground in the midst of their upscale homes with their tropically landscaped yards and fancy waterfront scenes. Hootie rejected the weekly offers to buy him out and was grandfathered in by so many ordinances, political maneuvers weren't practical.

I parked my truck as far away from the forty-foot square building that housed Hootie's store as I could. The store is nestled close to the water and the wooden seawall that Hootie's hundred-foot dock springs from. My father bought my first rod and reel there. Before Bass Pro Shops and the like, the Barnes Fish Camp sold lots of tackle. Now, its primary purpose is providing live bait, ice, sandwiches, snacks, cold drinks, and fishing odds and ends its customers forgot. Both edges of the property have thick screens of Areca palms planted to obscure the business from its residential neighbors. The rest of the area between the woods and water is sand. It's a, park-where-you-want, unrestricted lot.

It was 5:40. I purposely arrived extra early to quell any fears my new boss might have about punctuality. I didn't want the bait man giving Hootie a bad report about me on the first day. Besides, dawn was one of my favorite times of day. The golden grayness of first light added magic dust to my view of the Indian River and Intercostal Waterway. It soon became evident the bait man wouldn't be early.

Headlights bounced down the sand ruts providing access to Barnes' camp at five after six. They were too high and far apart to be Hootie's Jeep. I was about to meet Rooster, a man who piqued my curiosity since I'd accepted my new job. A cloud of sand fleas swarmed around my pick-up so I elected to stay in the cab as long as possible. The truck rolled onto the marl and sand parking lot and Rooster maneuvered the rear of the refrigerated box truck up to the shop's rear entrance. It was daylight enough to see there were no markings of any kind on the white body. There was no company name or contact information. Strange, the only indication of what was in the truck was a chemical warning diamond that is a legal requirement for vehicles that carry hazardous materials. Since when was fish-bait hazardous?

I had a clear view of the cab when Rooster opened his door and stepped down. The man was big. You didn't have to be anywhere close to realize that. He had to be at least 6'4" and weigh over 250 pounds. The baseball cap Hootie described looked to be four sizes too small for the head it perched on and though I was too far away to see his features in the dawn light, the string of curses coming out of his mouth were clearly audible. He wasn't happy . . . no one was waiting to meet him. I got out of the truck, walked toward "Mr. Crude" while swatting at the sand fleas descending on me. I asked, "You Rooster?"

"Who the fuck are you?" he growled. I got close enough to see he had a red beard and mustache that were both caked with grease or something worse. His eyes were yellow, deep set and clung to either side of his pointed nose. Rooster's ears were large and waved outwardly from a skull that showed no sign of hair. And . . . Hootie was right. The stench was over-powering ten feet away from him.

"I'm Mary's replacement."

The cursing stopped. I'd gotten close enough for him to see the curves under my camo shirt and pants. He examined me like a used car he was thinking of buying. I figured I'd find out what he was like in the next minute.

Rooster asked, "You are?"

"Chesapeake Partin. My friends call me Chessie."

"How'd you get a name like that?"

"My father likes railroads. I was named for the Chesapeake and Ohio. My brother's name is Reading."

"Are you as weird as your name?" I thought it was a strange question coming from its source.

"Most people think I'm even weirder."

He approached me, towering over my 5' 6" frame. "Not bad, I bet you wiggle your big ass real good in the sack."

As Hootie said, Rooster was into intimidation. I choked, partly from the sand fleas in my nose and mouth, but mostly from the sickening smell.

"Scared?" he asked.

"No. Repulsed? Yes." I didn't budge a centimeter. "I can't tell what's worse, the sand fleas or your odor."

Rooster smiled. "I see Hootie swapped a rabbit for a pit bull. You one of those feminist types that watches TV and thinks those women can really beat up men? You *think* you're a Kate Becket?"

"No. I *think* I can protect myself. Learned that in the Corps. I might not always win, but anyone who bothers me, wishes they hadn't." I stared up at him, maintaining eye contact. "Can we get past the tough guy stuff? Hey, you're a bad ass, okay? Now, let's unload the truck." I shoved past him and walked to the rear of the van.

"Know how to operate the lift?" he asked.

"Probably. Show me one time and you won't have to again."

Rooster stood by the side of the truck's rear door. He pointed to red and green buttons on a small panel. "This one unfolds the deck." His finger moved. "Red is down, green is up." He stepped away. "Do it."

I cycled the lift without saying a thing. When finished, I said, "Okay, let's get this done."

"Your load is in the front." Rooster grinned. He was missing a few teeth.

I lied, "Hootie told me it's your job to get the stuff loaded on the lift and my job to put it away. I'm not getting inside that truck."

"That's not how it's done. You help me move it to the lift, I help you get it on the boat and in the cooler. You get the best part of the deal." Rooster had turned friendly. That disturbed me a lot.

"It's not happening. Hootie told me how he wanted it done. That's what I'm going to do." After the conversation Hootie and I had when he hired me, I was sure he'd swear to my lies.

Rooster's eyes reverted to smoldering pools of disdain. "Have it your way, cunt."

Rooster opened the back door, rode the lift up, and wheeled a pallet load of cardboard boxes onto the lift gate. "It's all yours."

"What goes where?"

"Didn't your boss tell you that? Thought he gave you complete instructions?" His face said, 'choke on it.'

I nodded. I'd outsmarted myself. The whole load would go to the cooler . . . this time. As I took armloads of the boxes into the office and cooler, I heard Rooster sing a children's song over and over, but with changed words. "My dog is in your buns, my dog is in your buns, hi ho your dairio, my dog is in your buns." I could understand why Mary Perez quit.

Three

"Well?" Reading's long legs were elevated on his recliner, a bag of potato chips sat on his lap, and he clutched a beer in his right hand. As usual, he was stripped down to his boxers and a tee shirt.

"Well, what?" I asked.

"How did your first day go? Like working for old Hootie? Anything exciting happen?" He laughed. "Are you still employed?"

I walked over to the coffee table in front of him, picked up the remote, and turned off the TV. "I'm not going to yell over that thing."

"Having you live with me gives me all the problems of having a wife and none of the advantages." Reading's good nature even made things that might offend, palatable. He *was* grinning.

"Want to start over?"

"Like I said, you're a wife without sex. Okay. How did your first day of being Hootie's mate go?" Reading took a sip of beer.

"Surprisingly good. I didn't have to do anything I haven't done a hundred times before." I ignored Reading's wicked smile. "It will be a breeze when I know where Hootie stores all his gear. The fishermen liked me. And I got paid." I reached into my jeans pocket and pulled out a wad of bills.

Reading's eyes widened. "That's a healthy roll. How much?"

"All told, $229.50. Hootie is paying me cash . . . off his books. I worked from six until four-fifteen this afternoon. He shelled out a hundred before I reminded him of the extra fifteen minutes. He smiled and said he forgot. So, I got that straight with him from the beginning."

Reading chuckled, "Same old Hootie."

"The rest is tip money. I did a good job for the customers on my side of the boat. Willie Mitchell has the other side and he said I did great. I made more than he did. I hate to admit it. Hootie is right. Swishing my hips and flopping my boobs got me $35 more than Willie." I peeled off five twenty dollar bills and handed them to Reading. "First time you've seen that in a while."

Reading's smile broadened. "Wonders never cease. And . . . I'll take it." He put the bills next to the potato chips. "Thank you."

"Let's see. You asked about working for Hootie, if I was still employed, and if anything exciting happened. Okay, yes I'm gainfully employed." I curtsied and Reading laughed. "Exciting? Let's see. One lady caught a 110 pound Jewfish."

"Goliath Grouper, you have to learn to be politically correct," Reading interjected.

"I am around politically correct people. It's a Goliath Grouper when I'm with them. Around you and other rectal apertures it's still a Jewfish."

Reading smiled as he shook his head. "Go on."

"What was exciting was her husband. He had to take a dump right when she hooked up, got flustered, and stayed longer than he should have. He couldn't make it to the head so he dropped his shorts and did it over the side while his wife and I kept him from following his used breakfast. The whole boat was roaring. His wife laughed so hard she almost let loose of him."

"That's visual," Reading grinned and sampled his beer again.

"Working for Hootie, is exactly like I knew it would be. He's a good guy, just cheap. The only negative thing he had to say to me was to be sure I didn't cut up the bait fish in too big of pieces." Reading laughed again. "He couldn't say enough nice things to me right before I left. He told me that four of his regulars said to put them on my side next time out." I left out the portion of the men's suggestion that I "lose the bra."

"Sounds like you've found a land of wine and roses."

"Almost."

Reading looked at me questioningly. He held his hands out, palms up and bounced them up and down.

"And, then there is the bait man." I put my hands on my hips and wasn't aware of the severity of the frown on my face.

"A *bait* man? Does Hootie have someone passing out the bait? He's too cheap to hire a body for that, isn't he?"

"No . . . Yes . . . This is the guy that Hootie buys his bait from. The asshole delivers the frozen bait fish and chum blocks to the fish camp. Part of my job is to meet him and unload the truck. I store the stuff in the fish camp cooler and put what we'll use for the day in the ice box on the boat. Hootie tells me I'll probably only see him once a week, but that's enough."

"Asshole? Not rectal aperture? This guy really did rub you wrong." Reading fished for some chips. "What did he do to get you so bent?"

"Besides smelling like the Indian River landfill and trying his best to scare the shit out of me?" I took a deep breath and removed Reading's beer can from his hand, took a swig of Coors and returned the can to his hand. "He made it clear he'd like to screw me and probably would . . . whether I liked it or not."

This got an entirely different reaction from Reading. The police officer replaced my happy-go-lucky bro. "He threatened to rape you?" He tossed the potato chips on the coffee table as he dropped the recliner's leg support. "That's serious or are you just blowing air?"

I said, "I don't know." I really didn't.

"Tell me about it."

"I met him at Hootie's place before anyone else was around. You know I'm certainly not a prude, but he never put ten words together that didn't contain a cuss word or a lewd suggestion or something intended to intimidate me."

"Did he?"

"Did he what?"

"Intimidate you."

I snorted and said, "What do you think? I wouldn't let that SOB think he bothered me, even if he did." I shrugged my shoulders. "He's a big man. Maybe, bigger than you. He's six-five or six-six, probably 260 pounds. They're hard pounds, not soft ones. He's got narrow-set eyes and a sneaky look. The bastrd looks like a wanted poster waiting to happen."

Reading looked at me asking to tell him more.

"Okay. One of the things he did was sing, *Farmer in the Dell* to me, but with different words. Instead of saying "the farmer's in the dell," he sang "my dog is in your buns," over and over.

"He is trying to intimidate you. Don't get into a verbal pissing contest with him. Remember, you have a habit of letting your mouth overload your ass." Reading paused and looked at me with his fatherly look. He considers himself my parent though he is six years younger. "You want me to visit you at work wearing my uniform? That will probably solve the problem."

"No, Reading. Let me handle him. I'm pretty sure he's all thunder and smoke."

"What's this guy's name?" Reading searched for something to write with.

"His name is Charlie Cocker, but he goes by his nickname. That's Rooster." I handed him a page torn from the small notebook I always carry and a pen, both retrieved from my purse.

"Next time I go into the office, I'll see if there's anything on him in the files." He wrote the name down.

"Don't bother. He just wants everybody to think he's a bad ass and get them to shake."

Reading wrinkled his nose and rubbed his chin. "No problem. Remember you said smoke. Remember what goes with that."

Four

If Dr. Mark Card is selling it, I'm buying. The man is handsome, dashing. He does his best to present himself as the updated image of Indiana Jones. Even to the Fedora. His smile and silver-tongued line of bullshit, is designed to make all the co-eds palpitate at his approach, which they do. I should know better. I do, and I don't care. The man has so much sex appeal it pours out of him and inundates all females in the flash-flood. With the exception of Brad Pitt, I've never seen a man who qualifies more as a true jeans creamer than Dr. Mark.

Even at nine in the morning, sitting on the tailgate of his pickup, perspiring in the hot Florida sun, he is as regal as a prince out of one of Anderson's fairy tales. His court is made up of a dozen volunteers that are here to do his bidding as he supervises what he hopes will be an important archeological site. I'm one of his students; more correctly, one of his minions, and I'm hoping to learn a few things about 1700's Indian culture and spend a lot of time with Errol Flynn's reincarnation. I'd drive the sixty miles from my place in Vero to this trashy dirt road just east of Lake Okeechobee off Florida Route 714 just to look at him. I truly love archeology, but having Dr. Card as my mentor triples the pleasure.

As I walk up to join the nine girls and three guys lapping up his preparatory instructions, the assembly reminded me of a litter of pups admiring their father. Actually, there isn't much difference. At thirty-three, I'm at least ten years senior to the rest of the students and probably more than ten years junior to Mark . . . and I'm as spellbound as the rest. I'm a half-hour late and hope he won't notice me slithering up to join the group standing in a semi-circle at the back of his truck. No such luck.

"Ah, Miss Partin, I'm so glad you've graced us with your presence." Mark smiled and nodded to me. "I really miss you when you can't be here, Chessie."

"Sorry," I mumbled. Of course, all the other volunteers swiveled their heads to look at me and, of course, all the males viewed my showing up as neutral . . . all the females looked disappointed.

"Chessie, I'll fill you in on what we've been talking about…I have something I'd like you to do for me." The female feelings went from disappointment to disgust. I just felt wet. "Okay, let's summarize what we're doing today." He pointed to a large number of stakes driven into the ground with numbers and different colored ribbons attached. "If this is the site of the 1738 battle and massacre, it will become a highly important dig. Before we do any significant work, I want to be sure all twentieth century materials are removed and any nineteenth century artifacts are removed and isolated." He motioned toward three groupings of stakes in front of his truck. "The stakes with the green ribbons and numbers one through twelve are our target for today. Those show preliminary possibilities that they may also be sites of 1800's cow camps . . . one might have been a crude house. Unfortunately, our contemporary brothers and sisters have used this place as a trash dump. It will probably take most or all of today to clean the debris off the site."

"What kind of things are we looking for?" The tall blonde girl had been on several sites with us. She knew what we were trying to achieve. Her real intent was to announce, "Don't forget I'm here."

Mark placed his fists on his hips and struck a pose intended to reproduce Flynn's characterization of Robin Hood. It was pretty damned good. "Tin cans, cardboard, anything plastic, light bulbs, anything you know is something used today, put in the 55-gallon drums. If you're not sure, what's the rule?"

The group answered in elementary school unison. "Stay where you are, raise your hand, and wait for the man."

"What about these?" One smart-assed boy asked. He held up a badly abused condom.

Mark smirked. "Really, Terry. Really." He pointed to the wise-guy and added, "He's not sure what to do with that. Ladies you can cross him off your date list and warn your seventh-grade sisters about him." Everyone laughed.

"Just a couple reminders. If you see something like a pottery shard, a bone, teeth, an arrow head, or something that could have been a tool, don't touch it, don't disturb it, mark it with a stake," Mark pointed to a large pile of sharpened stakes with red ribbons stapled to the blunt end, "and get me. Second thing, remember the rules we're working under. This is a dig that is suspected of containing Native American remains. If we discover any human bones, Indian or not, remember they belong to the Seminole Nation until they're proven not to be. They have to give us permission before we can resume any activity here."

"Or until we discover it's some mobster from Miami that was dumped here, one with gold fillings in his teeth," the same smart-ass volunteered.

"So what's the rule, Terry?" Dr. Card asked.

Terry recited, in a sing-song voice, "Stay where you are, raise your hand, and wait for the man."

Mark slid off the tailgate, "Let's get at it. There's a box of garbage bags here. Take a couple to reduce the number of trips you have to make to the drums." He looked at me and smiled, "Miss Partin, will you come with me?"

Dr. Card walked around to the passenger side door of his pickup. He reached through the window and pulled out a Nikon camera with an expensive looking lens attached. "Chessie, I want you to be my wing-man. It's important that we are extremely careful in documenting everything we find here. We need a photographic record and written notes. If this *is* one of the battle sites...how cool is that? There were Mayaca, Bomto, and Jororo, tribes that had villages around here. We might possibly ID items from the raiders...that would be Calusas, Pojoys, and Amacapiras. The Mayacas are more closely associated with St. Johns culture, particularly pottery, so I brought along some identification manuals. You have a good eye and more dedication than the others. Let's face it, you're more mature and honestly I'd prefer working with you. Since you're here all the time, I want to train you to—"

"I need to tell you something." I bit my lip. "Dr. Card—"

"Mark, Chessie. Please call me Mark."

"I feel bad, but I just took a job and I'm not going to be able to be here on Fridays." The words were spoken by an alien that I'm sure had invaded my body.

"You'll be with us Monday through Thursday?"

"Yes. I only work Friday and the weekends."

"Fine. I'll train someone else to do what I need on the days you can't be here." He put his hand on my shoulder and moved his fingers over it slowly and gently. I wondered how thorough the training would be. "Can you hang around when we finish? I'd like to cover a few things with you."

* * *

Mark and I sat together on his tailgate and watched the last of the work detail pull away from the site in their vehicles. We'd filled half a legal pad with notes about our discoveries and had taken sixty photos. We sorted through the scribblings and viewed snapshots noting which had the most importance. There wasn't very much. It had been labor suited for a Waste Management crew. The consolation was it had to be done.

Dr. Card wasn't discouraged. He seemed just the opposite. Mark recognized I wasn't as happy with the day's results. "No Piltdown Man or Wooly Mammoth today, but we have things ready to start preliminary planning to do the dig."

"No Piltdown Man or Wooly Mammoth," I repeated. I considered that for a few seconds. "Wasn't the Piltdown Man a fake?"

"Yes." He smiled. "You have a legitimate interest in archeology. That's good. I have a legitimate interest in working with you. Those are both good things."

I didn't answer. The old saying, "Be careful what you wish for, because you might get it," buzzed around in my brain.

Mark smiled and the ethics problem began to lose its importance. Doing a few laps in a king-sized bed seemed like a good idea, but one I wasn't close enough to dive into, yet. "Let's see how things work out." I punted.

"Sounds good to me. Let's start professionally, and, like you say, we'll see where things lead."

I nodded, not quite sure what was next.

Mark eased me off the hook. "How did you get interested in archeology? Is your interest something new or has it been around a while?"

"I guess it depends on how you define interest."

Mark Card is a master at the art of attracting women. His smile could melt a glacier. He leaned toward me . . . slightly . . . and winked. "Define it anyway you want."

"Wanting to do it as a profession, in the last five years, but I've been fascinated with the subject since I was a kid. My dad used to take me fishing up by Sebastian Inlet, in the Indian River, and the creeks surrounding them. There were a couple of places father told me were Indian middens. He called them mounds. We'd spend hours there, nosing around, that was if the fishing stunk. We found arrowheads, and things dad said were tools and pottery. I'm sure he didn't think we were screwing up a site. I loved doing that and never lost interest."

I expected a mild lecture about the value of protecting antiquities. I didn't get one. "Wow, that's interesting. That's up near where Jece was located." Mark saw I didn't know what he was talking about. He grinned. "Bet you never knew how many peoples shared this land before us. Jece was the largest village of the Ais Indians. Their territory was from Cape Canaveral down to where Ft. Pierce is today. I'd like to take a look at the middens. Think you could find them and take me there?"

"I know how to find them. Getting on that property today is a different issue. It's all fenced and posted. It would take some kind of court order, or something, to get in there."

"I can arrange that." Mark leaned away, his smile making me think things that could complicate my life.

I looked for a negative. "Dr. Card," I avoided using his first name to make my point–things were moving too fast, "How are you going to get something like that? Isn't that going to take some legal or political power?"

"Yes. And there are ways to do it. I'll work on getting you some paper that will do the job."

"Really? On private land?" I wasn't sure if he was or wasn't blowing smoke.

"Chessie, my dear, I can get a legal document that will get you on any piece of private property that isn't sensitive to national defense."

Five

I smelled him. Rooster had to be behind me though I hadn't heard him or seen him since he off-loaded the pallet of boxes containing the frozen bait fish and chum blocks. The vulnerable position I was in, bent over with my butt in the air, forced me to stand up straight and spin around. Rooster stood four or five feet behind me. He held a broom in one hand and a huge Bowie knife in the other. The man was using the knife blade to flick out some type of refuse that was sticking in the broom bristles. He laughed at me. "Scared?"

"No. Why should I be? It's just you, Rooster." He laughed harder. I remembered Reading's lecture on avoiding confrontation with him. It was Reading's version of the "attracting more flies with honey" cliché. I remembered it too late.

"You're right. No need to be afraid of harmless old Rooster." He wiped the knife blade off using his pants as a rag. He held it up two feet in front of my nose. "I'd never slit your throat with it, or maybe cut off one of those tits of yours for a souvenir." His lips smiled, but hate and madness burned in his eyes, eyes that he used to bore into my psyche. "Wouldn't even think of something like that."

I knew better than to say anything. That would only provide more incentive for him to escalate. Hoping to send a message, I tried to make my features display as disdainful and disgusted look as I could. I sincerely wanted them to mask the fear he'd been able to generate.

"You don't have a thing to worry about, little cunt." Rooster slid his hand up the broom handle until it was about a foot from the end. He wiggled the knife at me. "Why would I use this on you," he dropped the knife to his side and thrust the end of the broom in my face, "when I have cock that's this long and hard, but twice as big around. It would do you and me both a lot of good. I'll take and spread—"

The headlights from Hootie's Jeep flashed their beams on us as he pulled around the store.

"See you in a week." Rooster stuck his knife in its scabbard. "Don't let *that tongue of yours wag* or I'll stick *that knife of mine in your mouth and fix it*." He laughed, turned, and stepped into his truck's cab, leaving me shaking.

I was carrying a couple of boxes onto the pier when Hootie caught up to me and asked, "You okay. Your face looks mad and scared at the same time."

I thought about relating the confrontation I'd just had with Rooster. I decided against it. Instead I said, "I understand why Mary Perez quit."

The next time I went to Hootie's fish camp to meet the bait truck, Hootie was already there, waiting. I suspected . . . hoped, my problems with Rooster were over.

Six

The stern line vibrated in my hands as Hootie revved up the twin diesels. Hootie said in an authoritative voice he only used when issuing commands as boat captain, "Free the lines." After only a month of being on the job, most of what I did was so automatic I didn't have to think about it. My arms, legs, hands, and feet just did what was needed. I untied the figure eight knot from the pier cleat with the robotic hand attached to me.

"Cast off … all on board."

My foot hopped onto the step on the seventy-two-foot charter boat's transom and I swung into the walkway as smoothly as if I had been doing it for thirty years, not days. I ignored the comments made by a few of the regulars about my "flopping." That should mean an extra good tip in the afternoon.

Willie Mitchel was grinning as I met him at the cooler. We each carried a few boxes of bait and chum to our cutting station as Hootie drove the boat to one of his GPS sweet spots. We'd be able to get our customer's lines in the water as quickly as we could. It made them happy and us richer.

"You've got your big three on board today." Willie was talking about three fishermen who made the trip from Lakeland to Vero every Saturday to fish with Hootie Barnes. They were the first to request they be assigned to my side of the boat. I'd become used to their adolescent comments and leers at my bod. We had an understanding. Things were look, but no touch after a test attempt early on. They'd qualify as jerks if they didn't pony up a twenty a piece at the day's end, which meant I averaged fifty dollars more in tips on the trips they took.

Tim, Stevie, and Fred are three forty-year-old teenagers who never outgrew their memories of the hormone attacks they'd suffered. Stevie and Fred are boob boys and Tim, well, he's just a horny, dirty, middle-aged man. Despite all their protestations of being misunderstood at home, not having sex but once a month, and individually bragging about once having been stallion of the year, they're harmless.

"Chessie, take a couple of extra boxes of bait with you today. It's gonna be a windy bitch out there." Willie pointed to the pennants that whipped and popped in the brisk breeze. "The fewer trips you make, the easier it will be." I nodded and picked up two more cartons.

The intercom sounded and Willie pushed the button. Hootie's voice came from the speaker. "Hey, you down there?"

Willie answered, "Yes, Hootie."

"It's too windy to go out Sebastian Inlet. I'm gonna take her south and we're staying close to shore. That's an angry west wind and it will get worse as the day goes on. Make sure you load your pockets up with Dramamine. Lots of folks gonna need it."

"Okay." Willie groaned and shook his head. "This ain't going to be a good one. We'll have them puking on us and we'll be replacing rigs all day. I know where he's going. There's lots of fish there, small ones, and there's a big bunch of shark that hang around. We'll be lucky to get one out of two hookups to the surface whole. Big shark will tangle a dozen lines at a time. You best just cut them and start over. Damn shark love the chum blocks so you better take a couple extra of them. We're going to earn our money today. One other thing; the way that wind's blowing you're going to get wet if you have to lean over the rail, so take off anything that will get hurt by salt water."

Willie left juggling six boxes as he exited the storage compartment, allowing the door to swing closed behind him.

I didn't hesitate. My bras are very expensive because of the extensive wire supports inside them. I had a heavy weight tee shirt on. I peeled my bra off and placed it in my locker. Maybe no one would notice or be too sea sick to give me a hard time.

* * *

My hope that no one would notice didn't last fifteen minutes. As I prepared to begin working, one of the three regulars said, "Hey boys, there's more sag in the bag today." Immediately, Tim, Stevie, and Fred hung around me like three vultures waiting for an animal to die.

"What kind of fish are those?" I stood at the cutting board preparing as much bait as I could before Hootie dropped anchor. Tim spoke and was practically leaning on my right arm. I barely had room to swing the knife I was using to cut the bait. I took a hard slice and exaggerated my hand outward. "Better give me a little more room or you might become part of the bait."

Tim moved back six inches and repeated, "What kind of fish are those?"

"They're Tilapia."

"I thought those are fresh water fish." Tim leaned forward.

I snorted, "The grouper and snapper don't care so I don't think you need to worry."

"Seems like you could catch mullet easier," Tim insisted.

"No. We buy them from a bait man. We catch them by moving the boxes from his truck to our boat. That's easy."

Fred snickered and Stevie remarked, "She's got you there, Tim."

"Attention, I'm dropping our anchor." Hootie announced we were about ready to fish. "It will take a few more minutes to maneuver the boat and get the other anchor down. Mates, you can put the chum blocks out. I want to warn all of you it will be rough out here. We'll bounce a lot. Stay away from the rail. If it gets too bad, I'm sorry, but I'll have to take us in."

I picked up two chum blocks and cut the top of the box off each with a cutter. The smell oozed out. Even still frozen it was disgusting. The chum was frozen in a nylon mesh bag with straps on the top. I securely attached the straps of each bag to a separate ten-foot cord we used suspend the chum under the boat. We tied the chum bags far enough away from the fishermen to avoid tangling when our guests hauled their fish up on the heavy rods they used.

I heard the chain rattle as Hootie released the second anchor. In less than a minute he had the boat positioned in seventy feet of water over a reef full of hungry, if not large, fish.

"Lines down." Hootie declared us ready to go.

All the customers on my side were baited and ready. Heavy weights and chunks of cut bait clunked in the water and raced to the bottom. Coinciding with the lines going down, the boat began its rhythmic rise and fall of two to three feet. Water rolled up the hull with some spray that occasionally blew into the boat. Within a minute an obese lady screamed and began cranking on the reel. I hurried to her and removed a pitiful little grunt that didn't weigh a pound.

"One for the pan," she yelled at her husband. "I got first blood." She was as proud as a Hollywood screen actor playing an Indian with a scalp.

Hootie was next to me and said, "I'll get that in the box. Go help someone else." The rods were bending; it was going to be a hectic day.

As I worked back and forth, helping the customers, Tim muttered, "We need to get that shirt wet." I knew he had something in mind. What I didn't know was that a simple prank would change my life.

Seven

The action was steady. Half the day was gone and I rarely had time between taking fish off the hook, rebaiting lines, replacing rigs that sharks cut off, and placing fish in the cooler to worry about what mischief the "three musketeers" were planning. When it came, I wasn't ready. I'd made a trip to the cooler to place a couple fish in it. I noticed Tim had worked his way to the stern of the boat and was positioned farther back than we allowed the customers to stand. I told him, "Hey, Tim, move forward. You'll get caught in the chum bag."

"Kill joy," he said good-naturedly.

I helped an elderly man wrestle a four-foot black tip shark to the surface. The mouth full of teeth still clenched the remains of a snapper that had been first to bite the bait. Leaning over the side I grabbed the leader with a gloved hand, held the steel, and clipped it with the wire cutter in my other hand. As the leader pinged and parted, a wave broke against the boat's side almost drenching me. I had just come close to winning the wet tee shirt contest for the day. Enough of the wave dampened my side to drip water in the boat.

"Hey, Chessie, I need some help back here," Tim shouted at me from the boat's stern. He was farther back than when I'd chased him forward before, in fact he was at the transom. "I got a fish on."

I started to weave my way through the fishermen lined up against the railing. His rod was bent severely. I yelled, "Keep him away from the chum."

He answered, "Too late."

When I reached Tim and looked over the side, I could see his line was wrapped around the line suspending the chum bag and a grouper in the ten-pound class was swimming next to the bag. What I couldn't tell was if the fish was hooked into the mesh or not.

Tim, Stevie, and Fred were huddled around me, I thought to help.

"Wear this," Hootie said. He walked up, stood next to me, and held out a yellow rain jacket. "Put it on and it will keep that tee shirt of yours nice and dry." He smiled. Tim, Stevie, and Fred deflated like punctured party balloons. Finally, I figured out what the "plan" was.

I grabbed the cord and started to raise the chum bag to the surface.

"Chessie, DON"T bring that shit on board! It will stink-up the boat and I'll have people heaving up their breakfasts." Hootie was adamant. "That fish is snagged in the bag. You'll have to cut it out."

I nodded. The best way to clear up the mess was to untie the chum-bag cord from the cleat and unwrap it from Tim's line. Then I'd have to lean over the transom and cut loose the fish since it was hooked to the mesh. The cord could cut my hands. After putting gloves on, I told Tim, "Tighten your drag down so the fish can't take off. I'll loosen the cord and unwind it from your line. When that's done, I'll cut the mesh and you pull the fish away from the bag so it doesn't re-tangle."

Unwrapping the cord from the fishing line was easier than I imagined. Cutting the fish loose from the bag wasn't. The boat's bouncing, the fish's movement, and the position I'd have to assume made just thinking about it challenging. I would have to lean over the transom as far as I could, grab the bag with one hand and cut the mesh with a knife held in the other.

Hootie saw my predicament and volunteered. "When you lean over to cut the hook out, I'll hold both your legs."

Fred and Stevie said in unison, "We'll help."

At least, I wouldn't go swimming. I removed my knife from its scabbard, got one hand on the cord as close to the bag as possible and said, "I'm ready," then leaned over the transom. Hands got firm grips on my legs and I pulled the mesh bag to the surface. It was a foot and a half from my face

As soon as the chum bag was out of water, the stench thrust into my nostrils. I gagged and said, "Oh, shit!" I knew why Rooster smelled so bad; the odor was the same … his was just tempered quite a bit. I blinked my eyes to clear the salt water that splashed into them. My thought was, *Get this done!* I focused on the hook that protruded from the Grouper's mouth and was stuck through three strands of nylon.

A wave thrust the sack and fish to within inches of my face and my eyes which I refused to close. What I saw behind the hook shocked me. Mixed in with chunks of rotten flesh were two human teeth attached to a small portion of a jaw bone. I quickly cut the grouper away, heard the fishermen cheer as Tim swung his fish on board, but my attention was riveted on those teeth. Another wave pushed the bag within six inches of my nose . . . I wasn't mistaken, they were human teeth. The smell was over-powering and I pulled my head away. I looked up at Hootie and yelled at him, "We need to bring this bag on board."

"Are you crazy? Don't you have a nose? Cut that thing loose!" Hootie was screaming.

"But, there's teeth in it. Human teeth."

"That shit isn't coming into this boat. Cut the damn bag loose," Hootie pointed at the shore two miles away, "or you can swim to the beach with it. Take your choice."

I let the mesh loose, watched the bag float down a foot, then sliced the nylon straps that were tied to the cord. As Hootie, Stevie and Fred helped me back inside the transom, I watched the chum bag drift downward into the clear blue water as dark shadows circled below.

Eight

Hootie didn't want to hear about it. No one else saw what I did. Was I even sure what I saw were human teeth? And what could I do about it if they were? The evidence, if it was real, probably rested in some fish's digestive track. There was every reason to put the incident out of my mind and go on with life. The problem was; I couldn't. My archeological training made me sure of myself . . . they were human teeth. That's what I was thinking about as I drove home.

There was a familiar car in the parking place where Reading normally parks his pickup. It was his sometime girlfriend Lisa Lister's Mercedes convertible. Reading's truck was gone. That meant my brother was off someplace, with Lisa, probably mussing bed sheets.

Lisa is a home-grown celebrity. She's an anchor on the local STB affiliate morning news. Reading dates her on and off, but says he isn't interested in any serious relationship at this point in his life. Lisa hauls Reading around like a trophy. My brother was the high school football hero and voted best looking. Lisa is attractive in an emaciated, over-dressed, up-tight way. Reading teases her saying he can't tell whether she's coming or going. She has bumps, not boobs. With the exception of having a highly inflated opinion of herself, she's not too miserable to be around. I guess we get along.

Reading's duplex is located on Banyan Rd. It's "old Vero." I can walk to the beach and shopping and the people who live around us I consider real. Living there makes me feel safe. For example, we seldom lock our part of the building. It's quiet and everyone looks after their neighbors. Opening the door and going inside is like entering a moated castle.

Walking to the beach usually helps me clear my head when I'm troubled. I need that right now . . . and to organize my thoughts. Figuring a way to convince Reading that my suspicions are correct, that Rooster Cocker is a murderer and that he needs to investigate won't be easy. I have no facts, just my intuition. Reading's a fact guy. Sometimes he's so analytical I could choke him. I haven't mentioned the second face-off I had with Rooster. That omission won't help.

I'm still stripping clothes off when I hear the door and Reading call, "Hey, Chessie, you decent?"

"No."

"You by yourself?"

"Yes."

"Good. I have Lisa with me. We're going to take a shower and catch dinner. You want to go?"

"I guess so." Reading always needs time to think . . . before he commits to thinking. I decided to try to start the process. "Could you come in for just a minute? By yourself?"

I sat on my bed in my bra and panties and tried to come up with a gimmick to get Reading to at least hear me out. The light lit.

"Knock. Knock." Reading stood out of sight in the hall outside my room.

"Come in."

Reading eased his huge frame through the door and grinned. He ambled to the bed and sat down. My brother winked at one of my breasts and suggested, "You should consider contributing ten percent of those to Lisa so she'd have something for her A cup." He waved his hand in front of his face, wrinkled his nose, and scooted a foot farther away from me. "You still smell like fish . . . or worse."

"I just got home and I've got to get in the shower." Faking innocence is sure way to get Reading's interest. I asked, "Look, if you and Lisa want to be alone, I'll understand." My eyes were wide and my mouth soft.

"We've been at her place and at the beach all day. Lisa and I had plenty of alone time." He nodded and produced a slight smile. "Any more and I might develop blisters."

"Reading!" I faked a frown so he'd know it was a fake.

He got up to leave. "We're going to shower the sand and salt off. I promise not to use much hot water."

"Reading, before you leave, I need to ask for some advice." Reading has a Good Samaritan or father complex. He can't resist a call for help.

He stopped and faced me. "Sure. Ask away."

"Say a friend of mine found something that might be evidence. Maybe in a murder. A part of a body. And say she thinks she may have an idea about who did it. But she doesn't have any hard proof. What should she do?"

"Who's the friend?" Reading looked interested, in fact, consumed.

"No. Don't talk about it now. We have to get ready to go out. Think about it. When we come back from dinner you can tell me what to do."

"Okay." He started to leave, hesitated as though he had something to ask, shook his head and continued out the door.

I smiled and said, "Yes!" I knew I had him roped, tossed, and close to hog tied.

Nine

My first confirmation that Reading's interest was burning came before we reached the restaurant. The showers in our rooms are back-to-back. The immediate rapid thumping and the fact Lisa's moans were over quickly told me Reading was rushing to get to dinner. Casey's Place was a great spot to eat if you wanted to get good food and get out. When Reading selected that restaurant, I was sure I'd been able to plant a seed in his brain. Observing his actions at dinner, all of which were designed to speed the evening, convinced me I had him.

Those actions also confirmed that Reading saw through my fable . . . that the problem revolved around a friend. When you grow up and live with someone, it's difficult *not* to see what's working in your roommate's mind. Reading isn't assertive, but that doesn't mean he isn't really, really smart.

Lisa was disappointed and probably shocked that she wasn't invited back inside our place when we returned home. I'm sure she was looking for "dessert." Lisa isn't bashful about beating up the bed's headboard with me in the next room.

The headlights on Lisa's Mercedes were still easing out of our drive when Reading opened his interrogation. He never attempted to turn on the TV when we both flopped down on our couch. Reading *was* serious.

"What you talked about before dinner, tell me about the body parts."

I decided it might be strategically wise to fake the charade a bit longer. "I don't know if my friend would want me to spe—"

"Cut the crap, Chessie. We both know this is you we're talking about."

I stared at him for a few seconds hoping to put his mind in neutral. I pinched my lips together before I said, "I need you to give me a fair hearing on this. Forget you're my brother. Listen to all I tell you before you come to conclusions."

"I can do that."

"Good. I need you to be Sherlock Holmes, not Inspector Lestrade." Reading nodded, so I continued. "I'll start by telling you what I saw then tell you what I think."

He nodded seriously, "Go ahead."

"I saw two human teeth and part of jaw bone." I waited for the info to register.

"Where? When you were on the dig with Dr. Card?"

"No. In a bag of fish chum on Hootie's boat this afternoon."

Reading looked at me quizzically, but seriously. "Really? Was it on top when you opened the box?"

"No. One of our customers got his line and a fish tangled up in the chum line. I had to pull up the chum to get it loose. When I cut the fish free, I saw the teeth and bone in the bag."

Reading was giving what I said a thoughtful evaluation. "Let me see them," he said.

"I wasn't able to get them in my hands." I saw the flicker in Reading's eyes. "I was bent over the transom two thirds of the way out the boat and it was bouncing around like a cork. There was no way to cut into the bag and get it out."

"Why didn't you pull the bag out?" he asked.

"I asked Hootie to let me. He wouldn't because of the smell. It was horrible. Hootie made me cut it loose." I saw the shadow of doubt. "Reading, you said you'd hear me out."

He returned to trying to be objective. "Go ahead."

"The smell. Reading, the bag smelled just like that guy Rooster I told you about."

"That would make sense. He's the one who's selling them to you." Reading hadn't gotten my point.

"Yes, and *he's the one who is filling the bags!*"

Reading straightened up. He remained quiet for several seconds. "Do we know that for a fact?" Because they smell the same . . . you see where I'm going."

"All I know is he is the one that delivers. There are no markings on the box like if it was from a big company. No markings on the truck. As far as I know, Rooster is a one-man band."

Reading asked, "Have you seen any paperwork. They must have delivery tickets . . . something."

"I've never seen any. Hootie always has handled that. Hell, Reading, you know Hootie. He might do it all cash."

Reading shook his head. "I doubt that. It's an expense. Maybe, if he's getting it super cheap." He thought for a second. "Nope, Hootie would still get something he could deduct from his taxes. If, he's your one-man-band . . . Hmm, do you know where he docks his boat?"

"No. But I know it's not around here. Or, at least, it's not on the river."

"Why is that?" Reading asked.

"Because the fish he's furnishing for bait are Tilapia. That's fresh water."

"Ever notice his license plate? Like what county it's from?"

"No."

Reading leaned back into the couch cushions. I could see he wasn't sure what to think. I decided it was time to update him on my run-in with Rooster. "Reading, Rooster is bad, *bad* news. The bastard threatened me."

Reading shot up and sat erect on the couch. "Threatened you? When and how?"

"It was a few weeks ago. I was unloading one morning and he snuck up behind me and scared me shitless. Basically, Rooster told me sooner or later he'd screw me whether I said yes or not. He also told me if I said anything, he'd cut my tongue out."

"Damned, Chessie! Why in hell didn't you tell me about that?" Reading was agitated . . . his face was reddening and voice raised a half octave.

"Because I think my problem with Rooster is done." I could see the upset and hurt in his eyes. "Hey, you have enough problems to solve for yourself. My problems? They're my problems. I have to try to solve the ones I can for myself. You always tell me I have to face things head-on. The thing has worked out. Hootie noticed I was upset, asked if it was because of the bait man, I let him know it was. Now, Hootie is there every time Rooster delivers. The asshole delivers the bait and leaves, so no problem."

Reading stayed quiet for a few seconds. "You said murder. Why?" It appeared he was satisfied with my explanation.

"Mary Perez. As far as I know, not Hootie, nobody has heard from her since she supposedly ran off. If he got her alone and raped her, I don't believe he'd think twice of killing her and getting rid of her body . . . that way."

"How sure are you that what you saw were human teeth?" I knew Reading was confirming facts and deciding what he'd do next.

"The bag was within six inches of my face. I know what I saw were human and still in a part of the jaw bone."

"Did anybody else, Hootie or the fishermen, see what you saw?" Reading was looking for some way to verify, sister or not. That is my brother.

"No. And I asked. The best I got was they said they could see something white. Nobody could say they knew what it was." I shrugged my shoulders. "I know there isn't anything solid, but I also know I'm right about this." After a couple of seconds, I asked, "Now what?"

Reading never blurts out things. He thinks about what will come out of his mouth, once, twice, and then again, when he's discussing something important.

"I'll look into it the best I can. My hands are tied until I'm reinstated. I'm not supposed to be carrying on *any* department business. I can wander into the office and check records, look to see if there is anything on the Perez girl. I did a quick and dirty on Rooster. *If* his name is Charlie Cocker, *if* the description you gave me is close, *if* it's spelled correct, you know the drill. There isn't anything alarming about him. No warrants. No priors. Biggest thing wrong is I can't find *anything* on him. He sounds military. I'll look there. Give me a few days." He reached out and put his hand on my shoulder. "Sis, you know what you can do?"

"What? I have some ideas—"

"Then forget them. I want you to do absolutely nothing. Nada. Zip. Zero. The worst thing that can happen is for you to go charging in and, if there is something here, alerting Rooster that we suspect him. I want your promise on that."

I nodded, but I didn't say anything.

"Chessie, say the words." Like I said, when you live together you know each other too well, at certain times.

"Okay."

"Okay what?"

He pissed me off. "I won't do shit until you bless it." I told him what he wanted to hear. My tendency is to lie a lot.

"Remember you promised. There is one thing you *do* need to do. Be very, very careful until we find out about this guy. Avoid being near him. Don't talk more than you have to if he is around. Be on the lookout for him everywhere you go." Reading thrust his head forward to emphasize what he'd say next. "Consider this, if he killed Mary Perez, it's more likely that this Rooster guy followed the girl to a mall, or her house, or a MacDonald's and abducted her. You're not going to know you're safe until this guy is cleared or we get his ass off the street."

Ten

Every time I had to handle one of the chum blocks, I felt chills race through my body. I couldn't help wondering if I was carrying a part of a human being that would end up as dinner for a fish. The feeling of guilt mounted during the next weekend. I found my hands trembling each time I stripped off the cardboard. I hoped my four days at the archeological site would take my mind away from murder and body parts. This wasn't to be. Some of our volunteers unearthed human remains on Tuesday. The very first thing found . . . a jaw bone, with a skull with one side of the cranium crushed immediately under it.

Dr. Card called in a representative of the Seminole Nation. The lady brought ground penetrating radar. We spent the next two days working with her, exploring the site with the fascinating equipment. She found several sites where humans were buried—some Native American, some definitely not. Images on the screen brought surprises. One wore a business suit with an automatic handgun clutched in its skeletal hand. What looked like a lap top registered on the radar's screen next to the remains. Our dig was halted on Thursday and Mark said he'd find an alternate site to explore for next week. The Martin County Sheriff's department had yellow tape strung completely around the acre-plus area we had hoped to excavate. It was designated a crime scene, probably murder.

Hootie called me during the week and told me we'd be receiving a load of bait Friday. This added pressure. Knowing I'd have to have contact with Rooster pushed my emotions to a slow boil. When Friday morning arrived, I was very happy to see Hootie turn down the road to the fish camp in front of me. Rooster wouldn't have a chance to agitate me more and I wouldn't be alone with him. I relaxed a little.

Hootie and I were talking when Rooster drove his truck into the parking lot at a high rate of speed, slammed on the brakes, jumped from the cab, and yelled to us, "Is the store door open? I have to take a shit." He ran up the porch stairs.

"Yes, but I'll need to get you some toilet paper." Hootie grinned at me and said, "Well, at least we'll know he ain't full of crap this mornin'." He stopped for a second and asked me, "Chessie, there will be an invoice on a clip board hangin' on the truck's dash. Go sign it and remove the yellow copy for me."

"Sure." I'd just been handed a gift. The two of us walked together as far as the truck. Reading had asked if I had seen any paperwork. I'd be able to do better, I'd furnish him a copy. After I jerked the cab door open, I wished I hadn't; the same oppressive smell Rooster exuded, floated out. I gagged, held my nose and removed the clip board from the dash. HM Bait Company was printed on the top of the invoice. I signed it Hootie Barnes, removed the yellow copy, there were only two, and started to return the clip board to the dash when I noticed a number of additional invoices. If I did it fast enough, I could safely sneak a peek.

The first two invoices were for other charter services. The third was an invoice, but from another company, *Special Medical Solutions*. The billing was to a hospital in Ft. Lauderdale. The next invoice was from another company, *Circle X Ranch*. This paperwork was more elaborate. There were international shipping papers addressed to an import/export firm located at Port Everglades. The description said, "Refrigerated animal products." I grabbed a pen from the truck's seat and scribbled the other two firms' names on the copy of Hootie's invoice.

Hootie was coming through the camp's office door. I'd run out of time, so I folded the invoice and stuck it in my pocket. "You get that signed for me?" he yelled as I closed the cab door.

"Yes, I have the copy, but can I give it to you later? I want to run unlock the boat so we can get the truck unloaded and get Rooster out of here as quick as possible."

Hootie smiled, "I'm all for that. Go ahead."

When I returned from unlocking the boat cabin and cooler, Rooster already had the loaded pallet on the ground behind his box truck. His contemptuous look told me he discounted me as any type of a threat to him. It might be an opportunity to weasel a piece or two of information from him. I volunteered, "Rooster, just help me get the boxes to the pier that I need for today, I'll load the boat myself. And if you'll take what's left and put them on the porch, I'll tote them inside and load the cooler."

"That's not much of an offer. What do you really want?" Rooster leered at me as he approached, bringing his stench with him. I gagged and he laughed.

"I have to rotate the stock that's inside the office cooler. It will double my work if you put it in there." My lie sounded convincing. It wasn't.

"Come on, what do you really want? It's something else." He came close and hovered over me. His odor gave me an opening.

"Rooster, what makes you smell so damned bad? Do you fill those chum boxes?"

"Sure do. I like filling boxes. Need yours filled?"

"Damn, is that all you think of? A woman's vagina?"

Rooster leaned forward and down so his face was a foot from mine. "Oh, no. I like soft lips, a warm mouth and lots of suction or a tight smelly asshole just as well. Which would you prefer?" He eased his face a little closer to mine.

My control snapped. "You pervert!" I shrieked and I swung my hand to slap him. He ducked so my hand knocked his hat off rather than hit his face. When the hat came off I stared at a huge scar in the shape of the letter R.

Rooster cursed, "Fucking bitch," snatched his cap from the ground and put it on his head in a continuous motion, then pulled his fist back. He suddenly stopped and smiled. Rooster said in a low voice, "Not now, later."

"What's going on?" Hootie sprinted to us and ended the confrontation. It was the confrontation Reading had told me to avoid and one that doubled my fear.

Eleven

I couldn't wait to get home after the boat docked. The fear my dust-up with the bait man had produced, had transformed to a boiler full of anger. I had what I saw as items that would incriminate him. My steam was supercharged and I wanted to blow all over Rooster Cocker. That loathsome man didn't deserve the normal protections of the Constitution. I dwelled on ways to waive the cruel and unusual punishment clause. Suitable methods of execution? I was undecided between seeing him burned at the stake, fed to sharks, or having him fully submerged in sulfuric acid. None of those were severe enough. Was I a little ahead of myself? I didn't think so.

My enthusiasm quickly turned to disappointment when I aimed my Ford 150 into our duplex's drive. Reading's truck was missing. Maybe he had a date with Lisa; it was Friday night. Patient, be patient, I told myself. After I parked, I slumped over the steering wheel. I'd have to wait. But, I didn't want to wait! I fumbled in my purse for my cell phone. He'd be some place in Vero. Hunting him down wouldn't be that hard. I auto-dialed his cell number. After one ring, his voice mail cut in.

I dropped the phone on the seat and beat my fists on the steering wheel. "Damn you, Reading!" I shouted. The thing I should do was to go in our duplex, turn on the TV, and wait patiently. Reading would have. I knew that. But I wouldn't. It was DNA. We both inherited the same high levels of stubbornness and intensity from the father we had in common. Reading's mother imbued him with the ability to remain calm and patient. My mother's gift to me was the fire to attack anything without hesitation. Those traits rewarded and costed us about equally.

Repeating the phone call produced the same results. I repeated my tantrum, thumping my fists on the steering wheel until I hurt one of them. Frustration doesn't produce my finer moments. The copy of the invoice I'd "borrowed" sat on the seat next to me. I rested my elbows on the steering column and buried my face in my hands. The horn tooted. That propelled me back in my seat, my hands still covering my face. After a couple of minutes of wasted time, something tapped on my windshield. Reading stared through it, looking at me like I'd lost my last marbles.

He shouted. "What are you sitting out here for?"

* * *

We sat across the kitchen table from each other. Reading's beer can left a ring of moisture each time it traveled to his mouth. I noticed that he'd cut himself shaving and still had some dried blood on his chin. There were seven fractured potato chips sitting in the basket a few inches to the left of the invoice I'd swiped and brought home. A wadded up paper towel rested on the left hand edge of the table. Noticing things like that is something you do when you are either bored silly or impatiently forced to wait on something, anything to happen. I was suffering from both. Reading listened to my story. With the exception of chewing me out for being stupid enough to have tried to slap Rooster, he wasn't as harsh in his criticism as I expected. He also wasn't as excited about the invoice or the little info tidbits about Rooster admitting he filled the chum bags and the fact Rooster was delivering to a lot of places besides fishing guide services. He did show some interest in Rooster's scar that was shaped like the letter R on the top of his head. Reading asked, "Do you think it might have been caused by an accident?"

"No. It was too uniform and perfectly formed to be an accident. It looked like a brand. Maybe he had it done to stand for Rooster. The man's crazy enough to do something like that."

"That is something we can ID him with," Reading said.

Reading examined the sheet like it was the plan for a nuclear device. Twenty minutes had passed and I was coming unglued. He must have read everything on the sheet ten times; no twenty or more. There weren't 350 characters printed on the sheet and that included the boiler-plate that always is on invoices. Finally, I needed noise even if it was my voice making it. "What are you looking for, Reading?"

"I'm about done," he said. It was his way of telling me to keep my mouth shut. After another ninety seconds of eternity, he said, "It doesn't tell me as much as I hoped. But . . . It does give us a little to consider even if some of it is confusing."

"What does it tell you?" I asked.

Reading pushed the invoice in front of me. "You tell me."

"Come on. You've kept me sitting on my hands for a half hour. Does this invoice or anything I told you help us go after Rooster?"

"I'm serious. I want to see if can find something I missed."

I sighed, spun the invoice around, and looked at it. The lack of information was startling. "There's practically nothing on it. Quantity. An item description. Total per item. There isn't even a unit cost. There's a sales tax line and another line for the total." I looked at the document's header. "Beyond the name, HM Bait Company and a PO Box address in Orlando, there's no business info. No email, no website, and no phone numbers. It's like they don't want you to know much about them or even contact them."

"It is like HM Bait Company wants to stay invisible." Reading spoke while thinking. "That's good Chessie. They don't appear to be concerned about expanding their sales."

"I can see why. Did you notice what they're charging Hootie for his bait and the chum? It's unbelievably cheap. No wonder Hootie buys it from him. I don't see how Rooster can keep in business. At those prices, the more he sells the more money he loses."

"You're right." Reading stared at the ceiling for a few seconds. "Smells like it's a cover for something." Finally, he looked at me and asked, "Can you find out how long Hootie's been buying from him?"

"Sure."

Reading rubbed his chin. "Do you know if Hootie keeps a directory or a card file with phone numbers and addresses for the people he does business with?"

"If he does, I haven't seen it." I thought for a few seconds. "I could probably get the truck's license plate number. Hootie keeps a list of the vehicles that park in his lot on a regular basis. I had to give him mine. Something to do with insurance."

"That's real good, Chessie. When can you find out about those two things?"

"Tomorrow, when I go to work."

"Good" Reading's interest returned to the paper. He pointed at the invoice. "See anything else?"

I shook my head.

Reading took the yellow paper back. "Okay, here's what I noticed. This goes with the invisibility thing. The heading is printed on the computer; usually that means the name is expected to change and they don't want to print up many forms. Or, they may not want to leave a commercial paper trail." Reading pointed to the invoice. "Usually there's a place for the customer to acknowledge receipt. That's there. There's also usually a place for the delivery person to indicate the material has been received by the customer. There isn't one on this form. Why? I don't know." Reading pointed to the boiler-plate terms and conditions in the fine print listed on the bottom of the page. "Notice it's in only two languages, English and German. You'd think it would be Spanish instead of German in this area if you are only going to show two languages." Reading turned the paper over and lowered his head almost to the level of the table. "Last, and kind of disappointing, I'd hoped we might get something to help find out who this Rooster character really is. Fingerprints on the paperwork would do it. DNA testing is too expensive. Unfortunately, I don't think your buddy Rooster has any fingerprints. There's plenty of places he's handled the paper. You told me this copy was the bottom one, right?"

"Yes."

"Okay. If you look at where you handled the invoice on the other side you can see prints, ridges, certainly you'd need to do a regular print job to learn anything or ID them. If you look at where your buddy touched the back of the sheet, there's nothing but a flat smear."

I shook my head. "I'll take your word for it. I think you're telling me he's probably a career criminal if he's had his prints removed."

"I think we can be sure he doesn't want people to be able to identify him." Reading looked at me. "Look Chessie, I know you aren't going to like this. You're scared and you have a right to be. This guy could be very dangerous. But . . . do we have enough information to make a good guess that Rooster is into something illegal, smuggling something, drugs maybe, he could even be a killer? Yes. Do we have enough to take this to my boss or anyone else in law enforcement? No. What can we say the man's crime is? He hasn't committed one we can *prove*. The paperwork isn't evidence. The only thing we can assert that has to do with a *possible* crime is what you *said* you saw. We don't have those teeth or anyone else who can say they saw them. We don't have a witness to any of the threats he's made against you. There's nothing."

"Rooster is a killer. I know it. We're going to do nothing?"

"I didn't say that. We'll do something. Let me sleep on it over-night."

I glared at my brother. "You sleep on it, eat it, screw it . . . do any damn thing you want to, but that bastard needs to get in jail or get dead." My fist slammed the table. "Damn it, it's me that could end up in bags of fish chum. If you don't come up with something, I will!"

"Chessie, don't do anything stupid. Don't you even think of going after this Rooster bastard. He'll chew you up and *he will spit you out in pieces.*"

My blood boiled and forced reason out of my head. "You don't have to hold a .45 to a man's head and blow his brains out. There are other ways I can pluck the feathers out of Rooster." All kinds of ludicrous thoughts circled my forehead so I blurted out one. "Your boss is always nice to me. I bet he'll help. Yes, I'll just pack my ass up and visit good old Chief Benson McGill. I'll tell him what a shit he has—"

"That's as stupid as going gunning for Rooster. You won't do anything except look foolish and probably get me fired." Reading stayed remarkably calm.

"You don't want that? Then make something else happen."

Reading left the room, leaving me seething. To my surprise, he returned in a few moments with a .25 caliber Colt automatic that was so small it fit in my hand with hardly being able to be seen. He said, "Give me two days. And I have no idea where you found that thing in your hand. You need to keep it with you all the time." He paused. "Don't get a damned traffic ticket."

Twelve

"I'm glad you called, Chessie." Dr. Mark Card's perfectly modulated voice caressed my ear. I could hear him doing voice-overs for science documentaries. "I couldn't reach you at your house," he said.

"I'm on my cell because I'm still at work." I was walking from the boat to the office to lock up the fish camp. Hootie and Willie had left an hour ago. "Are we going to the dig on Monday?"

"I'm saving your cell number now." He cleared his throat. "You and the rest of the dig-site volunteers will have at least two weeks off. The Martin County Sheriff's office tells me the site off Okeechobee is likely to be unavailable to us for a minimum of three weeks. I don't have another place for us to dig without kissing some asses and going through bureaucratic bull shit."

"I can use the rest," I said. Working seven days a week was a grind. Hootie extended my work hours by having me close up for him most of the time. I liked the money, but not the long, long days.

"I'll miss your smiling face," Mark said. The message was clear.

"Same here."

"If you get bored, come up to campus. You can help me catalog some items from the Hontoon dig." I didn't respond because I didn't want to sound too eager, so he added, "Or you can get me the location of those mounds your dad and you used to visit. I'll get you some egress papers. You can check them out and if they're still there, the two of us can do some investigating."

"Okay." I tried not to sound enthusiastic. "I'll call you next week."

Getting time away was good. I needed the rest and I'd have free time to do a little sleuthing on my own, if Reading didn't come through with his promise to help.

I put my cell phone in my pocket. There was one thing more I wanted to do before I left. I already learned that Hootie had been buying bait from Rooster for slightly less than three years. A quick peek in Hootie's file cabinet would provide me with the license plate number for the bait man's truck.

Thirteen

"Here's what I found out about Rooster's truck. It's mounted on a Mercedes diesel chassis. The plate number is KRTS 990." I read the information to Reading who was somewhere, riding in Lisa's convertible. He asked me to repeat it and said he'd see me later before ending the call.

Usually, I spend Sunday evening relaxing in front of the TV, watching reruns of *Castle* or *Bones*. I tried, but couldn't get interested in the programs. Even Nathan Fillion couldn't spark any interest. The bait man ruled my thoughts. His hulking form hid in the shadows of my mind. I fancied I could smell the stench that accompanied his presence, hear his filthy comments, and feared that he lurked in the corners of the next room. Our home was my refuge; my thoughts of Rooster turned our duplex into a torture chamber. The bait man was making my life unbearable. Something had to be done. If Reading didn't come up with that something, it was up to me. Doing nothing wasn't an option.

The phone rang. Hootie's familiar voice answered my hello, "Hey there."

"Did I forget to lock up something? I thought sure I got everything—"

"Everything's fine. I'm sure everything is just like it's supposed to be." Hootie hesitated.

"So what's up?" I asked.

"I know you ain't goin' to work at that archeology thing you do tomorrow. I was wonderin' if you could do something for me? I'll pay you for it. Three hours and it won't take but half that." Hootie was in beg mode. "My wife's makin' me drive up to Daytona early or I wouldn't ask."

"What do you want me to do?"

"Art Gibbons ran out of bait and wants to borrow some of mine. He's done me some favors and I owe him big time. I said yes before I knew I'd have honey-do duty tomorrow. Can you deliver six boxes of bait and six chum blocks to him before 7:00 AM? He gets a delivery from Rooster tomorrow, but it won't be 'til after 10:00AM. He keeps his boat at the Municipal Pier." Hootie pleaded, "I'd owe *you* big-time."

"Okay. I'll do it."

"Thanks, Chessie."

I felt like thanking Hootie. He presented me with a wonderful opportunity. To take advantage, I'd have to swap pickup trucks with Reading for the day and come up with a convincing lie for the reason I needed different wheels. One of my strong points is my imagination and one of Reading's weak points is being trusting beyond belief with people he knows. I judged my chances as excellent.

Fourteen

I couldn't risk missing the opportunity. Following Rooster and his truck would provide me lots of answers . . . I hoped. My insurance against missing his delivery to Art Gibbon's slip and storage building was to get back there an hour and a half prior to the bait man's scheduled arrival. Swapping trucks with Reading was disappointing. He didn't even ask for a reason. The parking place I chose was in the shade of stately old oaks that formed a canopy over most of the parking area. I wore a broad-brimmed, floppy straw hat, sun glasses, and a long-sleeved shirt so if the bait man happened to glance my way I'd be hard to recognize. Reading's truck is black. Mine is white. Rooster knows that, which might have prompted a second glance.

It turned out sitting in the parking lot in front of the Vero Beach Municipal Pier was more of the problem. I'd been parked for about thirty minutes when someone said, "Hello."

The lady standing outside my open window was sixtyish, short, plump, and looked at me suspiciously. I tried to look friendly, smiled, and said, "Hi, how are you?"

The lady ignored my attempt at congeniality. "Why are you sitting here?" She scowled at me.

"Just killing some time. I have an appointment later today and this is a good place to do that. It's cool and I can watch the boats." My smile remained.

"Where's your appointment?" The woman was humorless.

"Sexton Plaza." It was a very public place.

"What for?" She was persistent.

I stared at her for several seconds, allowing some of my steam to dissipate. I answered coldly, "This is a public parking lot. I'm not doing anything wrong. This is the place I've chosen to wait. Which, I'm going to do. And . . . I'm not answering any more of your questions." I decided to bluff a bit. "If you choose to call the police, ask for officer Partin. That's my brother."

The woman was pleasingly shocked by my half-truth. She took a step back and looked as though someone slapped her with a dead fish. "Well, we'll be watching you."

"Go ahead and watch," I recommended. Before I could add anything, the woman was in full waddle, retreating to her residence.

The next hour was hot, uneventful and boring. I started to worry when my watch told me Rooster was ten minutes late. Maybe I'd missed him or maybe he wouldn't show at all.

The distinctive sound of a diesel turning into the marina lot from Indian River Drive caused my senses to charge to full alert. I looked into my rearview mirror and waited. The sound of the diesel's injectors chattering as it idled down the asphalt behind me, came closer. The familiar van showed up in my rearview mirrors. To be sure, I checked the license. KRTS 990—Rooster's truck.

Rooster parked in the middle of the roadway in front of the pier. His back was visible as he stepped down from his cab. He would have to walk in my direction to get the load from the truck's rear. I slumped down low in my seat so he couldn't see me. I listened as I heard the rear door unlock and open. The ensuing silence was eerie. With the exception of birds chirping, I couldn't hear anything. Time passed slowly. I became apprehensive. Ten minutes passed, then fifteen. I expected to look out my windows and see Rooster's face in one of them.

The diesel engine started. I sat bolt upright in my seat and started Reading's pickup.

The parking lot road created a circle that returned to Indian River Drive. I backed Reading's truck up and quickly maneuvered so I caught up with, and was close to, the bait man's rear bumper. I was successful in hooking up, but the thing I realized for the first time was I hoped my vengeful feelings and imagination hadn't overloaded my ass.

Fifteen

When you've never done something before, doubt and insecurity infects you at the beginning. At least, that happens to me. Those two emotions clutched at me trying to get me to change my mind. Reading would have told me how stupid I'd be to attempt such a thing. Trying to follow Rooster through traffic would be difficult, but manageable. Following without eventually being discovered might prove impossible. The bait man's white van turned right on to Indian River Drive and I followed. There wasn't any traffic so my first effort was simple, but what would it be like if a string of vehicles blocked my attempt to turn?

The van's signal blinked and Rooster turned right onto Beachland Boulevard. There were no vehicles between us as I followed. As I crossed the Indian River bridge, I realized I was committed and what the consequences of that commitment meant. To date, Rooster and my relationship was a heated one, but it hadn't gone past the equivalent of a barroom confrontation. My actions were escalating the possible ramifications, making it the same as taking a bar fight outside. My decision confirmed my dedication to causing Rooster serious problems. If he discovered me trailing him, his inescapable deduction would be my intent was to do him harm. If he became convinced I was planning his destruction, no doubt he'd reciprocate. If his intent hadn't been to do me serious harm before, it would be now. If, if, if. I had to trust my gut and that told me he had made his decision to harm me. Yes, I was committed.

Finding evidence that the man was a vile pervert and engaged in some types of illegal activities, wouldn't be difficult. At least, that's what my gut said. The binoculars and camera that rested beside me on the front seat would help me do that. The .25 automatic in my pocket would protect me, if needed.

Surprisingly, the bait man scrupulously observed traffic laws. He never exceeded the speed limit and traveled at a few miles an hour less than allowable. There were no rolling stops at stop signs. He yielded the right of way for no apparent reason, and slowed his pace when he approached a stop light, so he never risked running one.

This was so contrary to the behavior pattern I'd observed, it shocked me. I'd expected the man to drive like a maniac. At first, I wondered if Rooster's obscene behavior toward me was part of a vendetta toward women rather than the profile of a pathological. I struggled with this for a while, but rationalized my doubts away by explaining to myself that his behavior was rational . . . if his intent was to *not* have law enforcement stop him with some nefarious cargo in his van.

In any case, it made tailing Rooster easier than I anticipated. It occurred to me that it would also make it easier for him to become suspicious of the same vehicle remaining right behind him and matching his every turn. I allowed a few cars to get between us. Rooster never missed using his turn signals well in advance so that wouldn't be a problem.

Rooster guided his truck, following State Route 60, into the older section of Vero. When he made his first turn, he traveled one block before he pulled into a thrift shop parking lot. That was entirely unexpected. By the time I circled around and parked on the street, Rooster had left his truck and I could only guess that he entered the thrift store. I decided I should disguise my appearance as much as possible in case Rooster looked my way. I tucked every strand of my long curly auburn hair into the farmer's hat. The sun glasses I wore covered my dark green eyes and help camouflage my slightly pug nose. The oval shape of my face wasn't distinctive enough to worry about.

I focused my binoculars on the store windows, but most were covered by signs. There was a vacant building adjacent to the parking lot that Rooster might have disappeared into, but unless he'd gone into a back room, he wasn't in the deserted space. I sighed, checked to be sure the camera in my hands was ready, and waited. The fourth person to exit the thrift store was the bait man. I put my camera down when I saw what he carried. He used one arm to hold a stack of clothes on hangers over one shoulder and carried a shopping bag in his other hand. When his body turned to the point where I got a better view of the clothes, my surprise increased. They were women's dresses. He placed them in the cab, not in the van. One good thing occurred. Rooster paid *no attention* to his surroundings, my truck, or me as he wheeled his truck back on the road and to Route 60.

Next he stopped at a farm supply store. I parked in a strip mall across the street. He never entered. A forklift appeared with a pallet full of sacks. Rooster dropped the tailgate and loaded that pallet and three more into the van. Through the binoculars I could see the bags were labeled for cattle feed and fish food. The last pallet had a number of unmarked cardboard boxes that sat on top of the sacks. I snapped a few pictures, though I saw no particular value in taking them. So far the excursion was a bust.

After a long ride up the interstate to Melbourne, the day turned more discouraging. Rooster drove his truck to one of the poorer sections of the town and stopped in front of an old store. A hand printed sign in the window proclaimed: St. John's Helping Hand House.

Below those large words were phrases. Let God help you and we will too. When you are at your lowest you can only go up. We provide food, shelter, and clothes for those in dire need.

I parked on the street several spaces behind the van. When Rooster left the truck, the clothes he picked up at the thrift store were draped over one arm. He carried the large bag with the other. After disappearing inside the store for several minutes, he reappeared. An elderly lady walked next to him and gave him a hug before he hopped into his truck and continued on his way. Was Rooster doing good deeds instead of criminal activities?

He returned to I-95 and traveled south until he reached the exit for State Road 514. Maybe he was delivering the load he'd picked up at the farm store. With the exception of a small town called Feldsmere, there was little on the road except cattle ranches, swamp, and raw land. This area was familiar to me. My father had hunted and fished in this area when Reading and I were children. I followed Rooster and guessed where he headed. My bets were misplaced—he followed the two-lane road to its dead-end at a four lane super highway, Florida 60. He turned right into an area populated by cattle, gators and snakes, not humans.

Rooster drove the van farther and farther into the boonies. He passed the turn-off to Blue Cypress Lake and left the area I knew. Several miles down Route 60 he abruptly turned down a graded sand road. No sign identified it, but power transmission lines that paralleled the road told me what its original purpose had been. I slowed to a crawl as I passed the road. Rooster was proceeding down its string-straight length. I turned around at the first opportunity, returned to the road where Rooster and the van had disappeared. Dust from his passing, hung over the lane. I turned onto the sand road, though I was concerned about being spotted, and getting into a situation that might create problems for me. Concerned hell, I was fearful.

As soon as I got onto the road, the only fresh tracks had to be Rooster's. They led me down the road for over a mile, when the tracks abruptly turned into a side road. A large gate blocked the entrance, one much more substantial than the normal cattle barrier. I noticed the fence around the property for the first time. It was deer fencing; high, sturdily constructed, and in this case a triple strand of barbed wire crowned its top. One hundred yards into the property the road disappeared into an oak forest. The van vanished. A wooden framework above the iron bar gate contained a circle with an "X" inside followed by the word ranch, identifying the property. I couldn't park near the gate, it would be impossible not to be discovered. Besides, I was scared shitless that Rooster would suddenly come face to face with me.

I drove down the road for another couple tenths of a mile. The high deer fence on one side and a small canal on the other made it impossible to turn around. The terrain on both sides of the road became cypress swamp. I crossed two small, one lane bridges over streams flowing through the thick tangle. Past the second bridge, the road widened and created a pull off space.

The pull-off would allow me to watch for Rooster's exit from the property. I parked there, picked up my binoculars and waited. It was three PM … he'd have to leave soon to go home, wherever that was. I waited and waited and waited. Gators appeared and disappeared in the swamp, a hog and her two piglets, and some squirrels whose chatter told me they objected to my being there, all helped pass the time.

My cell rang. "Where are you?" Reading asked.

"Out looking for places to hunt," I quipped. Reading knew my fear of snakes kept me out of the woods if I was by myself.

"Okay, so you don't want me to know. When will you be home, or should I eat without you?"

I looked at my watch. "Four-thirty. Damn, I didn't realize it was so late. I'll be home by 5:30. Want me to pick up a pizza?"

"Pepperoni, sausage, mushroom and onion."

As I started the pickup truck, I realized I had learned one important thing. We knew where Rooster lived. I thought that was all … but it was something.

Sixteen

"Where did you get this?" Reading studied the pizza on his paper plate like it was a clue to a murder.

"Antonio's." That's Reading's favorite pizza place.

"You can't beat their stuff. Best pizza in three counties." He bit the tip off of a slice. "What were you doing out by I-95? Don't tell me you drove out there just to get this for me." He smiled. "I figured you wanted my truck so you wouldn't stink yours up if the bait melted. I didn't realize you were going by way of Paris to deliver it."

I hadn't mentioned anything about delivering bait and chum to Captain Gibbons. It caught me unprepared to answer.

"Don't be so surprised. I'm clairvoyant, you know." Reading wasn't upset; he showed no emotion.

"No, you're not." I was miffed, but didn't have a reason to be.

Reading chuckled. "Hootie tried to reach you by calling my cell phone, he said by mistake. He told me what he wanted you to do for him."

"He said by mistake? What do you mean by that?"

"Come on. You know Hootie. He was afraid to leave a message on our machine. If you didn't want to do the delivery, he figured you could have simply not returned his call." Reading took another bite and spoke around the wad of dough, cheese, and pepperoni. "Art Gibbon's boat slip isn't anywhere near where you ended up. You filled my gas tank. Thanks. You put almost a hundred more miles on old Blackie than you would have going to Barnes Fish Camp to the Municipal pier and back." He swallowed the pizza and chased it with a couple gulps of beer. "You going to let me in on your secret? Or are you not going to tell me if you learned anything by following the bait man around today?"

"Did you know what I was going to do before I asked to borrow your car?"

"Yes and no. You know I knew you were going to do Hootie's delivery for him. I didn't know you were going to do the Mata Hari thing or I wouldn't have loaned you my truck." He took a swig of beer. "But, you're alive. At least, for this evening. So . . . was it worth the risk? Did old Rooster rob a bank? Pick up a truck load of cocaine? Fly an ISIS flag on the truck? Tell me what you learned and I'll tell you what I found out. I went into the office today."

It wasn't like Reading to be a smart ass. Starting a spat over that wasn't worth the effort. Besides, I was happy he had checked up on Rooster. I ignored his jab and answered, "Truthfully, it surprised and disappointed me. I might be wrong about him. Rooster didn't do anything even remotely suspicious."

"You spent the day trailing him. He must have done something."

"Okay, blow by blow. He delivered to Gibbons, he went to a thrift store and picked up a bunch of clothes, stopped at farm supply place and picked up four pallet loads of stuff, and then went up to Melbourne and delivered the clothes he'd picked up. He took them to some sort of homeless shelter. After that he drove out into the boonies. I followed him out 60, past Blue Cypress Lake, I don't know, maybe six or seven miles to a powerline access road. He drove down it and turned into a ranch. Locked gate, posted. Nothing visible from where I could get to. I waited for him to come out for almost two hours. That's where I was when you called. I'd guess he lives there." I shook my head. "That is a surprise. Rooster isn't the type you picture as being a cattleman. And I sure as hell can't imagine Rooster as the Good Samaritan. Maybe I was wrong."

"Maybe you weren't." Reading's *I know something you don't know look* was smeared across his face. "The license plate number you gave me, KRTS 990, provided some interesting information. Picking on it was like pulling a thread on a knitted sweater. Any guesses?"

"None."

"The registration says the truck belongs to the HM Bait Company. The address on the paperwork is a PO Box in Orlando. It's right at the International Airport. But it is not the same box number that's on the invoice. Whoever signed the paperwork gave the name Joe Smith. The truck is registered in Martin County. I checked the method of payment. It was a check from the Circle X Ranch's bank account. Trying to find out who signed the check will take a bigger effort than I could handle off-the-record. However, the PO Box for it is the same as HM Bait. I called the post office and asked a few questions. They told me what they could with only our department name showing for them to verify who I was. There are five PO Boxes, one for each of the following companies:" Reading removed a slip of paper from his pocket. "HM Bait, Circle X Ranch, Special Medical Services, and one we hadn't heard about before called Poof. The fifth one receives mail for all of them. The only other things I got out of them were a description of the man that picks up the mail for all the boxes and a fact about much of their mail. The man doesn't sound like Rooster. The woman I talked to described him as very well-spoken, genteel, handsome, and well dressed with a full head of salt and pepper hair. She volunteered that the majority of their mail came from and went to foreign destinations. Most of the out-going are packages, the incoming fifty-fifty."

"What does that tell you?"

"Somebody's going to a lot of trouble to make it difficult to learn about those companies. With all the foreign traffic, it sounds like smuggling." Reading nodded once. "There's plenty of smoke to believe there's fire somewhere. I decided to ask someone to help me. My buddy says she'd check if there are any service records on Charlie Cocker. This bird sounds like ex-military."

"Who did you ask to help you?" I asked.

"Caralene Wills."

Caralene and I were enemies since high school. Our differences covered everything from athletic competition to classroom dustups. "Shit, Reading, you know the history the two of us have. If you told her I have any—"

Reading grinned and held his hand. "I know you get along as well as two pit bulls fighting for the same bone. No, I didn't tell her anything about you. I just asked a personal favor and she agreed."

I shook my head and changed subjects. "Did anything I told you do any good?"

"Yes. I wonder why the farm supply store didn't deliver. I know they deliver large orders like what you described. Could you tell what was on the pallets?"

"Three of them were sacks of livestock feed and fish food. The fourth one had all kinds of bags and boxes on it. I don't have a clue what the shit was."

"It sounds to me like Rooster and whoever else is involved doesn't want anybody on that property." Reading rubbed his chin. It meant he was thinking of doing something.

"They had an extra high deer fence with barbed wire on top. Maybe it isn't to keep deer in . . . Maybe it's supposed to keep humans out." I couldn't help but believe that the location, barriers to entry, and clandestine way business was done all reeked of secrets, possibly evil ones.

"There's another thing," Reading added.

"Something about the clothes pickup and delivery?" I asked.

"No. I think we can assume Rooster is spending the night at that ranch. Finding out where the bastard is living or staying gives us a place to find his truck tomorrow when we follow him."

I never gave my younger brother a bigger hug.

Seventeen

The sun was at least an hour from pulling itself over the horizon when Reading and I turned down the sand power line access road. We bumped along the rough surface, glad that our coffee was contained in covered sip cups. Reading turned the radio off. The apprehension I had yesterday when I drove the same vehicle on the same road had evaporated. I knew I was completely safe when I was with Reading.

He asked, "You bring the camera and the binoculars?"

"Yes. They're behind my seat."

"Did you bring the .25?"

"It's in my pocket."

"Let's not take a chance on a State Trooper or a deputy stopping us and you having a gun on your person. Put it in the glove compartment." He must have known what I was thinking. He added, "Sorry about that."

"Some . . . frigging . . . day." I put the gun in the glove box.

"How far to the ranch road turn-off?" Reading hunched forward over the steering wheel, peering into the thin ground fog brought to life by the pickup's headlights.

"We're probably half-way. It's the first road to the left. It's not something you'll miss seeing."

Reading nodded, not willing to break his concentration.

"There's an old style entrance. You know, two big poles on either side of the road and one over the top with the name on it."

He nodded again.

"The sign has a big circle with an X in the middle with Ranch spelled out behind it."

Reading nodded and added, "That's what their cattle brand probably looks like." He whistled as he glanced at the property. "You weren't lying when you said there was one hell of a fence built around the property. That thing has to be close to nine feet tall with what, two strands of barbed wire on top?"

"Three if I remember correctly."

"If that's for deer they must weigh 400 pounds and stand twice as tall as the rest of the white-tails in this state."

The gate became visible when we were about two hundred feet away. "There's a place to turn around and park down about two-tenths of a mile," I said.

We crossed the two small bridges, turned around, and parked where I had the day before. Reading turned off the headlights and we were surrounded by the pitch-black night. He asked, "The only places I saw any breaks in the fence were where we crossed those two little creeks. Did I miss any?"

"No. I didn't go any farther back than this. Maybe there is a break down the road."

"I doubt that. Whoever owns this place is damned careful and obsessed with security. It's surprising whoever runs this ranch neglected those little creeks."

I shivered. "If you'd seen the number of snakes and gators swimming around in them I saw yesterday you wouldn't say that."

"If you got caught inside there, which would you rather face, the snakes and gators or Rooster?" I couldn't see Reading's face in the dark, but I knew he'd be smiling.

"I wouldn't get caught inside." I knew Reading wouldn't let it pass, but I tried.

"You don't have a choice, you're in there."

"Okay, I'd prefer—"

Reading reached over and grabbed my arm and said, "Whoa, baby! I see light on the fence and road. I think someone is approaching the gate from inside."

We watched as headlights approached the gate and rolled to a stop. Red lights on the body identified the vehicle as a truck. Someone opened the gate. Reading said, "Damn, we didn't get here any too early. That's got to be him. I'll try leaving my lights off and follow very slowly. We'll see which way he turns and catch up with him on 60. There's no place for him to turn either way for some distance."

Eighteen

"That the right truck, Chessie?" We caught up with the vehicle after a couple miles as it traveled east on Florida 60.

"I'm sure it is," I said.

"Let's be positive. Get the binoculars out and check the license plate number," Reading said.

I pulled the binoculars from behind the seat, lifted them to my eyes, adjusted them and read, "The license is KRTS 990. That's him."

"Okay, it's the truck." Reading lives in a world where nothing is obvious without 100% proof. "Does he always drive under the speed limit?"

"Yes. Never runs lights. No rolling stops at stop signs. Always uses his turn signals. He drives like a poster child for the National Safety Council."

"He's driving that way for a reason. We have to figure why he doesn't want to be stopped." Reading took a deep breath. "That van is refrigerated. Is it always on?"

"Yes. At least, the cooling unit's been on every time I've been around the truck.

"You don't need to refrigerate drugs. That's the first possibility you think of in a situation like this. That's strange."

"There isn't anything about Rooster that's normal," I added.

We rode in silence. The truck's tail lights were the only thing to see on the traffic-less highway. Other vehicles didn't appear until we approached Interstate 95. Following Rooster consisted of simply holding Reading's black pickup on the road. When we reached the I-95 intersection, Rooster turned south toward Miami. We followed. Staying with him wasn't a challenge. He left the Interstate at the Ft. Pierce exit.

The first stop the van made confirmed Rooster as its driver. He guided the truck to a dock with a large sign painted on an arch over the pier's entrance that read, Shady Lady III, Half and full day trips, Bait and tackle furnished, No fish – no pay.

Reading said, "You're right, he is a big son-of-a-bitch. He's in top physical condition."

Rooster and Reading's body size and build were close to identical. Any similarity stopped there. Reading's hazel eyes, olive skin, and brown hair were a contrast to Rooster's bald head, ruddy complexion and unique, evil-looking yellow eyes. The bait man had a red beard and mustache, Reading . . . clean shaven. And Rooster had a face that drove women away from bed. Reading's looks caused women to throw open the sheets.

I was surprised how efficient Rooster was during his delivery. He moved swiftly, didn't dally with the dock workers, and was back on his way in minutes.

Following the bait man proved very unenlightening—at first. He stopped at many of the offshore fishing marinas, head boat docks, and bait store locations from Ft. Pierce through Stuart, eleven in all. He delivered a pallet load at most stops. Rooster was doing exactly what a man selling bait would be expected to do.

At nine-thirty, Rooster steered into a House of Pastries restaurant. We parked on the opposite side of the lot. His movements were the opposite we observed during his deliveries. He was in no hurry, took his time eating, and spent time on his cell phone after he finished. When Reading saw the cell phone, he wrote a note to himself. I craned my neck to read what he'd written. *Check for phones listed as belonging to Cocker, or the companies he delivers for*. We also observed several restaurant customers move away from the vicinity where Rooster chose to sit. The man showed total contempt for others. When Rooster finally climbed back into the van's cab, it was close to eleven. He looked comfortable—my bladder wasn't.

"Reading, when you're staking out someone and you need to pee, what do you do?" I asked.

"Hold it."

"I don't know how long that will be an option."

"Awww, shit, Chessie!"

Reading scowled, so I tried some humor. "No shit, just pee."

"Let's see where he goes. Maybe it will give you a chance."

I squirmed in the seat and hoped Reading was right.

* * *

Rooster stopped at a small bait and tackle store on US 1, north of Stuart. We pulled into a real estate office parking lot next door. As we watched, Rooster prepared to make a delivery.

I restated my problem. "Reading, I have to go."

Reading swiveled his head around. The only place close with a toilet was the real estate office and I'd be visible from Rooster's truck if I got out and went inside.

Reading said, "I've got an idea. Scooch down in the seat as low as you're able. I'll be back as quick as I can." He opened his door, slid from the front seat and ran to the bait store, slamming the door behind him. I slid down below the level of the windows.

When you're unable to watch what's going on in stressful and potentially dangerous situations, two things occur. First, each second that you spend unable to watch what may affect your safety, defies the laws of physics and first doubles then quadruples in length. A minute becomes a day. Second, with time stretching to eternal borders the tentacles of panic silently slide around you, gripping you with increasing force until your breath comes in gasps and your hands refuse to stop shaking. I reached that point when I heard the thuds of running footsteps approach our truck.

The pickup truck door jerked open. Reading hopped into the driver's seat repeating, "7-7-2-5-5-5-8-9-6-2, 7-7-2-5-5-5-8-9-6-2, 7-7-2-5-5-5-8-9-6-2," continually. He threw a bag containing something on top of me. Reading started the pickup's motor and said, "Write down the number." Then he continued with his chant.

I found a pen and scribbled the number on the paper bag. "Is that a telephone number?" I asked.

"Yes." Reading backed the pickup around and pulled onto the street following Rooster's van as he spoke. He explained, "We caught a break. I went in to buy you something to pee in and get a close-up look at your buddy. He was talking to the store owner. Long story. Anyway, the store owner asked for Rooster's cell and Rooster gave the man his number . . . that's it."

"That is good luck!" I said. My bladder continued to remind me forcefully that I had a problem. The bag was supposed to hold a solution. Being careful not to destroy the phone number I'd just written on it, I opened the bag. Inside was a small plastic bait bucket. I know my face looked as if I'd just emerged from a pity party.

Reading glanced at me and said, "Sorry, Chessie, it was the best I could do."

"You expect me to drop my pants and pee in that?" I was between anger and tears.

"Hey, you asked for this party. And . . . don't get any on the seat."

Nineteen

To both Reading's and my surprise, Rooster didn't head toward Vero Beach and home. Instead he turned south on US 1. Even the heavier traffic didn't cause a problem following the truck because of the driver's dedication to obeying traffic laws. Times when a separation occurred were always remedied at the next traffic light or two. He stayed on US-1 until he was able to get on I-95 south.

After a twenty-minute drive, Rooster exited the interstate at the Palm Beach International Airport. He didn't go to the passenger terminal. Instead, he drove down a road fronted by rows of warehouse type buildings. Reading slowed, which gave us reaction time if the bait man stopped at one of the garage-door fronts. Since there was a lot of activity in front of most buildings, finding a point to observe from wouldn't be easy. Rooster slowed and turned into a business called World Wide Special Freight. Reading drove at a crawl. We watched Rooster leave his truck and enter the building. Reading turned the truck around and parked in a vacant lot on the opposite side of the road and cattycornered to where Rooster had stopped. Our vantage point was partially obstructed by other trucks and cars, but we could see the area immediately behind the truck.

We didn't see Rooster until he wheeled a cart loaded with odd looking shipping containers behind his van. Reading described them as he spied through the binoculars. "They're white, three feet long and about two feet square. Each has straps wrapped around them. I think there are two separate lids on top. The lids aren't level. Looks like the straps fasten with airline seatbelt latches. There's some type of mechanism on the container's end. I've never seen anything like it before." He paused for a second. "Two of them have an X or a cross on them."

Reading remained silent for several minutes. "They're heavy. Rooster isn't tossing them around like bean bags. Either the containers or what's in them must weigh a lot. Oops, they're empty. One turned on its side, it came open, and nothing fell out."

"Let me see." I grabbed the binoculars and handed them back immediately. "Reading, the tops and seat belt latches look strange because they're all held open by wedges. He's venting them." Even from our distance his rage was evident. He reached in the truck, removed a spray bottle of some sort, and sprayed the inside of the one that opened.

"I'd bet he's disinfecting or deodorizing the compartment," Reading guessed.

After loading five of the unusual containers in the van's rear, Rooster disappeared with the cart. The next we saw of him was when he climbed into the truck cab, started the diesel, and headed for the interstate. I read aloud the printing on the door that the van blocked from our vision, World Wide Special Freight – We specialize in high value, time sensitive, exotic agricultural, and perishable shipping. Reading shook his head and his countenance looked as though he was puzzled. I said, "What could a loser like Rooster possibly be shipping with these people?"

"I was thinking the same thing." Reading allowed the van to get a block ahead of us then started after it.

The next two stops were as mystifying. We wound through Palm Beach until the van turned into a modern opulent looking building. Gold letters identified Roosters stop as Southeast Medical & Surgical Supply. Rooster never left the cab. A man emerged from the building dressed in a white shirt and tie. He carried a large box and disappeared behind the passenger's side of the truck. When he became visible again, he walked to Rooster's open window and handed him some papers to sign.

I said, "That's not hard to figure. The people that run that place don't want that smelly bastard in their building. I bet that guy stuck the box in the passenger side."

"I don't blame them. I got a good whiff of Rooster when I went into the bait store. He is repulsive." Reading waved his hand in front of his face.

Rooster resumed his travels. We followed him through increasing traffic where staying on his tail grew more difficult. Then, he went to a place we couldn't follow. The van entered a part of Palm Beach that doesn't make the post cards or travel brochures. Reading followed Rooster as he went deeper into a severely blighted part of town. Rooster's turn signal flashed and the truck disappeared in a narrow alley.

Reading eased past. "We'll have to wait out here and catch him as he leaves." The place where Rooster's van disappeared, had a sign that read Down – Not – Out – Safe – Place. We parked on the street 200 feet past the alley. Fifteen minutes then a half hour went by. No Rooster.

I asked Reading, "What do you think? Is he still in there or has he given us the slip?"

"You said he went into a place like this yesterday, right?"

"Yes, but he didn't stay near this long."

Reading rubbed his chin. After a few more seconds, he said, "Lets ride around the block and maybe we'll learn something."

The first right turn and a few hundred feet brought us to another alley and a vacant lot. We had a clear view of the rear of the Down – Not – Out – Safe – Place. Rooster's truck was gone.

"What now?" I asked.

"We try to find out if he has the same home tonight. We're going to drive back to Route 60 and the road to the Circle X Ranch. If we find him on the way back, we'll follow him. If not, we'll wait and see if he shows up at the ranch."

Reading drove at eighty most of the way north on I-95. We never saw the van. Nor on Route 60 when we reached that part of our trip. It was still full daylight when we parked on the powerline road pull-off. Time passed. The sun went behind the horizon and everything was turning shades of gray. Reading said, "We struck out. Let's head home."

"I'm ready." I tapped Reading's forearm as he steered his Ford 150 on to the sand road. "We did learn a lot today, right?"

"Yes, but I don't have a clue what it means. There's always tomorrow."

Good! Reading is all in, I thought. I closed my eyes and let my head drop to my chest. Reading pushed a CD in his player and George Jones was reincarnated. It finalized the message, *today is done*. We reached the intersection with Route 60 when only the faintest hint of daylight remained. Reading blurted, "Look at this!" Slowing, with its turn signal on, the white van we'd trailed all day was about to turn down the road and pass by us. I looked at the driver's side and thought I could see Rooster's bearded face.

"That's him! We know he comes back here." I felt triumphant.

"Yes," Reading said, "But I wonder who is sitting next to him." Then his cell phone jingle sounded.

Twenty

"I'm driving. Give me a few seconds to pull off the road." It was too dark to see Reading's face clearly which meant I couldn't decipher his expression.

"Who is it?" I asked.

"Chief McGill," Reading answered in a low voice. The truck decelerated until it eased onto the grass shoulder. Reading sighed, picked the cell up, and slowly placed it at his ear. He said, "Yes, sir. What can I do for you?"

I couldn't tell anything about the conversation or how it was impacting Reading. Reading's part of the conversation was the occasional, "Yes, sir" or "No, sir." That's what you would expect anytime you had a discussion with Benson McGill. With the possible exception of me, he was the most talkative person in Indian River County and Reading was the last person who'd interrupt anyone. He only spoke when he had a question or supported someone else's opinion. That was particularly true of individuals he respected and who were in authority.

Reading said, "I appreciate it very much." Pause. "Yes, sir. I'll be there tomorrow at 9:00 AM."

"That was good news, Reading?" I asked.

"Very good. He said he's decided to cut my suspension short. Old Benson said all kinds of nice things about me. Even said the department missed me a lot. He said there is one thing he needed to discuss with me, but it wasn't a big problem. To quote him, 'it's an ant sized thing'."

"Congratulations, bro. That's great news."

"Yes. I always believed there wouldn't be a problem for me going back, but it's a relief to have things settled." I knew Reading was smiling though I couldn't see his face clearly.

"Can I borrow your truck again tomorrow?" I asked.

"Are you planning on following the bait man?" He didn't sound happy.

"Yes … I'll be very careful."

"That's not a good idea." Even in the dark I could see Reading reach up and rub his chin.

"I'll stay far away. Just see where he goes rather than try to see what's going on up close. I promise I won't take a single chance. Hey, I'm the one that thinks this guy is really dangerous."

"Shit." Reading shook his head. "You can have the truck." He faced me and I knew what his expression would look like even though I couldn't see it in the dark. "Keep your promise this time."

"I promise."

Twenty One

"We've missed you." Benson McGill ushered Reading into his office and waved him to a seat. "I'm glad you understand the reason I had to do what I had to do. You're one of my best young officers, Reading, but rules are rules. However, it's to your credit you accepted the suspension with a positive attitude. That's one of the reasons I've decided to end your suspension early."

"I did break rules, sir." Reading sat like a contrite child in the seat opposite his boss.

Benson held up his hand and began counting off the offenses on his fingers. "Too many instances when you should have issued traffic citations, and didn't. You let off those kids who damaged that barn." Reading had let off a couple of youngsters whose pranks damaged a county representative's property. "You intimidated a child molester with seven arrests on his sheet to 'look for another city' without legal grounds."

Benson spread all five fingers out. "But, the worst was when you arrested Vero Beach's most powerful influence peddler. I don't like the man, but that doesn't mean we can change the world from round to flat. Don't matter the man was speeding, ran a red light, side-swiped another car, and left the scene of the accident. Your offense was when you wrote up the ticket with the details about finding him in a secluded parking lot where his mistress was in the final moments of finishing a blow job. Your detailed police report did not help the guilty man in either court—traffic or divorce."

Reading remained quiet, watching the hand as Benson counted off his offenses, trying his best not to show his disdain for the politics.

Benson looked at Reading. He considered the boy an important member of his force. Reading was smart, hard-working, college educated, had a flare for understated verbal communication, provided a dashing departmental image in uniform, was *the* local high school football hero, and had a girl friend who was the local TV anchor. For a man like McGill with higher political ambitions, the last factor certainly wasn't the least important. "I'm cutting your suspension by ninety days. That means you only have three more weeks of killing time." McGill didn't mention that he'd be announcing his candidacy for county sheriff during that time. That race was sure to be a bitter one with the incumbent possessing strong special interest support. "I'm going to increase the portion of time we devote to your detective training. I'd like to bring you along pretty darn fast on that. Cyrus is talking about retiring." McGill winked at Reading. "Be nice if you're ready."

Reading remained serious, "I appreciate your confidence in me. I'll do my best."

"I know you will. I know you will. I wouldn't be setting you up to be detective if I didn't. You play those cards right, keep on doing the outstanding job you've been doing and you'll be one of my right-hand men." Benson leaned back in his over-sized chair. The upholstery swallowed his 5' 8", 160 pound frame. "There is one thing ... well, maybe the one thing is two things, but it's really one thing. You need to be real sure you don't make any waves between now and when your suspension would have been up." The sheriff tilted his head to the side and fixed his eyes on Reading's. "Let's be real honest here. Politics, Reading, politics are a fact of life. I know someone like you don't like them, but that's the way it is. You're getting preferential treatment here because you earned it, but there are folks in this department that aren't going to be happy with you coming back early and you going on the short-cut to being promoted. Old Willard Wilson isn't going to like it either. His soon to be ex-wife will kiss you if she has a chance, but I'm sure you understand all that. You do know what I'm saying?"

"I believe so," Reading said.

"Just so there's no questions here, you have to keep your nose *real, real, real* clean. If you're going to drink a six-pack, you do it at home, hear?"

"I understand."

"For future reference, you call me if you have a situation arise before you dig a grave that's big enough for both of us. If you find a senator or congressman or minister porking some little gal or driving a hundred miles an hour in a school zone, we'll discuss it, right?"

"We'll discuss it."

"Good. Now that last little thing. Caralene was in the records room for a long time the other day. When I asked her what she was doing, she told me she was checking someone out for you. You *are not* supposed to be doing any work for the department and I don't want anybody in this department thinking *you are using department resources* for personal use. You aren't, are you?" The chief shook his head as a prompt.

"No sir, I'm not using the department for personal gain."

"Good. Now you can ask Carlene if she found out anything, but after that, nothing until you are back on the job. Let me restate that—no police business until you are an *active* official member of this force." McGill tried to sound stern, but was sure he came across more like a concerned parent.

Twenty Two

I wondered how Reading's meeting with Chief McGill would go as I sat in the dark, peering down the power line road. Reading was still in bed when I left the duplex. Sitting and waiting for Rooster's truck to come through the Circle X Ranch gate was terribly boring. Since Reading wasn't with me, I decided to wait for the van on 60. The thought of being trapped on the narrow, sand road with my only escape route being on foot through the swamps or rattlesnake infested pine and palmetto pastures, wasn't appealing. Our arrival at 5:00AM the day before had barely been in time to catch Roosters departure. I had Reading's truck parked in a pasture entrance gate, a few hundred yards from the power line access road at 4:15 AM. I'd promised Reading to be extra cautious and I was trying to keep my word.

Inconsistency was to prove the only thing consistent about Rooster's comings and goings. I spent a monotonous two-and-a-half hours waiting for the truck to show. The last portion of my wait found me dropping off to sleep for seconds then awakening wildly, wondering if I'd missed Rooster. Finally, the white van emerged from the thick oaks, pulled through the gate, and bounced to the highway. To my surprise, Rooster steered the van *west*, not east. This meant I had to make a U turn for I'd anticipated he'd head toward Vero Beach. Rooster's adherence to the speed limit made it easy to catch up and follow him. The four-lane highway had little traffic on it and there were few roads crossing it. All I had to do was keep steady pressure on the accelerator. By 8:10 we'd reached US 27 in the town of Lake Wales. Rooster turned north, heading, I thought, toward Orlando. As soon as Rooster drove onto US 27, following him became a nightmare. He didn't change his driving style, but the time of day coupled with heavy stop and go traffic changed everything. The heavy traffic made it easy to get trapped in a lane and either fall far behind or pass him. I tried to stay far enough in front or get behind him so he wouldn't recognize me. My disguise wouldn't fool Rooster if he got a prolonged look at me.

When I passed his truck, I got a shock. Rooster was sitting in the front seat, however, he was dressed in a gleaming, clean white shirt, sported a tie, wore a white baseball cap, and his face and beard looked clean.

The traffic created a game of tag, with me alternately chasing or being chased by Rooster's van. One of the times when I was in front, I saw Rooster get into a left turn lane with blinker on. I frantically looked for a place to make a U turn. After I succeeded, there was only one place I saw the van could have gone. That turn led to a large modern hospital. I steered the pickup into its parking lot, expecting to see Rooster's truck. It wasn't visible. Panic set in. Had he turned around and gone the other way? Had I missed a place he could have driven to? Had he caught me following him? What should I do? I did what I *could* do. Nothing. I parked. I waited. I hoped.

Five minutes passed, then ten, then fifteen. There was no sign of the van. A road led to the rear of the hospital, but if I chose to use it, I was asking to be exposed … if I hadn't been already. After twenty minutes, I thought of returning home and was becoming resigned to the fact I'd made a very long trip and learned very little, when Rooster's truck appeared from behind the hospital. Within a minute, I was in pursuit, again. I glanced at my watch; it was a few minutes after nine. Reading's meeting had started and I hoped things were going well. At least, I hoped better than things were going for me.

* * *

Following Rooster the rest of day left me totally confused. The first place he went after he left the hospital was a ranch on US 92 between Haines City and Kissimmee. I watched him drive down a long farm road to a cluster of buildings and disappear behind them. I parked in an abandoned gas station and waited. In twenty minutes, he reappeared pulling a livestock trailer filled with bellowing beef cattle. I also noticed he had changed clothes and was back to his soiled khaki shirt, filthy hat, and, I presumed, stinking jeans. Following him would be easy. I thought he'd head straight back to the ranch.

Instead of returning to the Circle X, Rooster drove in a different direction. I followed him to the St. John's Helping Hand House, in Melbourne, the same shelter I'd seen him visit the first time I trailed him. He sat in the cab and talked on his cell phone. Within minutes an elderly gentleman, carrying a suitcase, climbed into the passenger side of the van, assisted by a man and woman who came from inside the shelter. Rooster was off again much to the displeasure of the raucous moans of the cows.

It didn't take long to reach the next stop. Rooster drove to the Melbourne bus station and parked on the street a block away. I took a chance, circled around, and parked in the bus station lot. I guessed right, Rooster carried the old man's suitcase and accompanied him into the building. When they emerged, the elderly gentleman boarded a bus after shaking hands with Rooster. The bait man returned to his truck, this time driving back to the ranch. This didn't fit my scenario of the man being a vile killer. There didn't seem to be any rhyme or reason connecting what I'd observed during the day.

I called Reading and asked, "I'm near Antonio's. Want me to pick up a pizza?"

"Yes. I'll open a bottle of wine so we can celebrate."

"You must have had a good day."

"I did. Tell you about it when you get home." There was a *but* in Reading's tone. "How about you?"

"Okay, I guess. I'm more confused now than when I left the house this morning. I followed Rooster all the—"

Reading interrupted me. "Hold those thoughts until you get here. We'll discuss it then."

"Hopefully, we'll have better luck trailing him tomorrow. It'll be a lot easier with you in—"

"Chessie," He stopped me again, "We need to talk about that, too."

My only thought and comment was, "Shit!"

Twenty Three

"That's the way it is, Chessie. Until the first of next month, I've got to stay out of it. Look, if you don't stir the pot, things should be fine until then. Stay clear of the bastard. When I'm officially reinstated, we can really get after the guy."

"What if he smuggles a load of dope or kills someone in those three weeks? That sucks, Reading." I couldn't believe that Reading wouldn't budge a little. "Can't you at least ride with me, maybe check out something away from the office? Benson won't have a clue you've done a damn thing."

Reading starred at me silently. He took a deep breath and said, "What part of *NO* don't you understand? I am not taking a chance on losing my job."

"Big whoop! What part of me getting killed don't *you* understand?" I picked up my glass of chianti and raised it like I was making a toast. "To my funeral."

"Don't be such a drama queen. Look, Chessie, if I thought you were in serious danger I wouldn't put this on hold. But, unless you have proof that Rooster's some kind of maniac, like a bone or body part in your hot little hand, or Mary Perez's parents file a missing person's report, or Rooster threatens you in front of somebody, we're going to have to wait. We have as much evidence that he's some kind of unrecognized saint as we do that he's a monster."

"Well, maybe I'll just have to find one of those things." I was mad and in blurt-out, don't-think, speech mode.

"Chessie, you have a fine looking ass, but don't show it right now." Reading was getting sarcastic and that meant he was getting exasperated. I was far past exasperated. I prepared to throw the wine from my glass into Reading's face. I've done that type of thing before. He looked at me disapprovingly and said, "You don't want to do it."

I put the glass down and tried a few tears. They always worked better on Reading.

His face softened. "Okay, how about this. You promise to stay as far away from Rooster as you can until the first of the month, and I'll promise I'll jump in and help *if* he goes out of his normal way and bothers you."

I thought about ways I could get around what Reading wanted me to do as I answered, "Okay."

"That includes following him around or checking on him."

I nodded.

"Chessie?" Reading held his palms out toward me, tilted his head, and had a stern questioning look in his eyes. "You keep clear of him and postpone checking him out until after the first."

"Yes," I lied.

Reading starred at me for several seconds, hoping that I'd told him the truth, but suspecting that I wasn't going to keep my word. He decided pursuing my commitment any further was fruitless. "Fine. Let's eat the pizza before it gets stone cold and that will give us each a little time to cool off. Then I'll tell you what I did find out today and we'll match that up with what you saw."

* * *

Most of the pizza had disappeared and the wine bottle was empty when Reading decided it was time to discuss what he'd learned from Caralene. I'd already told him what I'd observed following Rooster.

"Before Chef McGill found out that Caralene was snooping for me, she found out a few things." Reading rubbed his chin. "Caralene is good people. I don't understand why you two women don't get along. You're a lot alike."

"Maybe we're too much alike." Caralene and I are both super competitive and have been on opposite sides too many times.

Reading shrugged his shoulders. "When I looked up Cocker, I started assuming he had a record. Caralene started looking at drivers' licenses. She found a Charles Lorenzo Cocker. When she checked the address listed for where he lives, the tax records show that it belongs to a Joseph R. Smith. It's not the ranch. Then she checked licenses for Joe Smiths. There are plenty of them, but none listed at that address. She checked who paid the taxes on the property. It was a corporation, Circle X Ranch, LLC. It was handled by an agent, paid by a check from an offshore account, and issued through a legal firm out of Washington, DC. She pulled the property tax records for the ranch and noticed that there was a note in the assessors file that an aviation permit had been issued to that corporation. They have an airstrip back there. The taxes for the ranch were paid by Special Medical Solutions using the same agent and legal firm. That was as far as she got before McGill told her to stop."

"Reading, I'm sorry. I lost what is going on. I don't know who owns what," I said.

"That's the point. Whoever is masterminding whatever is going on doesn't want anyone to know who controls things." Reading took a deep breath. "I don't understand it either. But I do think we can make a good guess. Whatever is going on at that ranch is something illegal. Why else would the owners take such pains to keep people out of there and try to hide the ownership?"

"It sounds like something big." I tried skirting the problem. "Maybe I should go to the chief directly and keep you out of it. I'd be making waves, not you."

"You think McGill would believe I didn't have anything to do with that? That's a pipe dream, Chessie." Reading waved his finger at me. "We still don't have evidence of a crime. There's another thing. Whatever's happening behind that gate at the Circle X Ranch is big. And you can bet somebody a lot bigger and more powerful than Rooster is in control. Rooster is just one feather on the bird."

"So we're going to do nothing?"

"Until I'm reinstated, yes." Reading eye-balled me. "Remember what you promised. No following Rooster or sticking your neck out so your head is likely to get cut off."

All I could remember was I lied. And, there were several ways to skin cats.

Twenty Four

"What are you doin' here today?" Hootie sat on the front porch of his fish camp store, grinning at me like I'd lost my mind. Even though he worked six or seven days a week, Hootie considered himself semi-retired since he only captained fishing excursions on three days. Willie Mitchell did most of the work, selling bait, tackle, snacks, and the other odds and ends fishermen needed. Hootie was in charge of dispensing bull shit and he is the best at that. "You do know it's only Thursday."

"It's Thursday from now until midnight. Actually, I'm just early for work tomorrow." I climbed the steps and parked my rear in the chair next to him.

"Chessie, I thought hirin' you would be a good thing." He slapped his thigh and laughed. "Now I'm beginnin' to believe it might could be the best thing I ever done."

"I'm glad you think that way. I've come to ask a favor."

Hootie's smile faded and he looked at me with an Uh-oh expression on his face. I could see his mind racing. He said, "I don't give no pay advances."

"I don't want or need one. I want to buy a couple of chum blocks."

The smile returned along with surprise and shock. "Lord-a-mercy girl, what in the world do you want with one of those?"

"I've been wanting some good, fresh, blue crab. I figure those chum blocks tied on the end of some roast beef twine ought to do the job."

"You could get a couple boxes of bait fish. I expect they'd work darn near as well."

I tilted my head and squinted my eyes. "They'd cost me more. You can appreciate that."

"Ha-haaa!" Hootie looked like the Cheshire Cat. "You'll never say a truer word. Why don't you go down and visit Ward Baxley. I'm sure he'd give you enough for a meal. He and your pa have always been friends. Hell, he gave Mary Perez some; I know he will give you enough for a meal or two."

"Now, Hootie, I said I'd pay for the chum. Besides, I don't want a few crabs. I want a bunch of them. I'll invite Reading and his girlfriend and a couple more people from the sheriff's office. Crabbing is fun and I enjoy it. You know you can take a redneck out of the swamp, but you can't take the swamp out of the redneck." I pointed to my bare feet.

Hootie said, "I heard that." He yelled into the store. "Hey, Willie, bring four of the chum blocks out here and stick them in the back of Chessie's pickup."

"How much do I owe you?" I asked.

"Awww. Nothing. You did me a big favor by takin' the stuff over to Gibbons. I might need another one sometime." Hootie smile was magnanimous. "I gave you four because those bags the chum is in, are made to fall apart into little pieces after they're in the water for a long time. They're made that way for the environment. And, you might not catch enough at the first spot you go and you don't want to haul those stinkin' things around. They'll ruin anything they're gonna touch." Hootie leaned forward. "You have crab nets?"

"Sure do. My brother has three."

"Is Reading going back to being a cop soon?"

"First of next month."

Hootie's smile broadened. "I'm sure glad of that. Reading is a fine man. Yes, sir! He's the best defensive end we've ever had play for the high school." Hootie nodded a couple of times as he thought. "It's a bit late to go crabbin' today. Tides won't be right. You got a place to go?"

"I'll probably go Monday. I'm going to go to the old Borden place on Mullet Creek. There are usually plenty of big blues along that old wooden seawall." I leaned out of Willie's way as he struggled with taking all four boxes of chum to my truck in one trip.

Willie spoke as he passed, "That's where I go to get crabs. I told Mary Perez about it and she said her and her boyfriend got a five-gallon pail of them out there. Hey, Hootie, you told me to remind you about that box of Mary's stuff, remember?"

"Oh, yeah. When Mary left, I cleaned her locker out on the boat. I put her stuff in a box for her to claim if and when. I ain't heard from her, so you'd be doin' me a favor if you'd go through it, take anything you can use on the boat and take the rest to her parents. Their address is in there. That'll make us even for the chum." He got up and went into the store.

I said, "Sure," loud enough for him to hear and smiled broadly. I'd just been given a great excuse to poke my nose into Mary Perez's departure. If I was lucky I might find some type of a clue in the box. Digging through Mary's belongings wouldn't be the terrible task I'd have looking to find a bone or some trace of human remains in the chum blocks.

"Don't forget you have those damn stinkers in your pickup. Those things leave an odor you can't get out. That's even if they melt just a little." Willie blinked and shook his head as he brushed by me when he returned to the store. "Get them back in a freezer quick, unless you're gonna use them right now."

Hootie waited for Willie to reenter. The box he held, then handed me, was a large one. He said, "She left lots of things. I'd have thrown it out, but I thought her parents would want some of the stuff. There's tools for handlin' fish that I'm sure she won't mind if you keep." He shook his head. "I hope she does okay with that boy. From what I hear tell that young'un is sorry-ness itself."

"I'll go through the box and take the fishing tools. If she comes home and wants them, I'll either give them back or replace them." I smiled to reassure Hootie. "I'll be sure to get the rest of the stuff to her parents."

Twenty Five

"What have you got there?" Reading asked as he opened the refrigerator door to retrieve a beer.

The material from the box of Mary Perez's personal effects Hootie had given me was scattered over the kitchen table. I'd just started the process of determining how to organize them. I expected a negative reaction from Reading since he might think I had initiated the event to find something on Rooster. I hesitated. That's what I wanted, but I honestly could say I hadn't asked for the duty. "Hootie gave me this to go through. They're things that belong to Mary Perez. I'm supposed to take out anything I can use on the boat and take the rest to Mr. and Mrs. Perez." I waited for the dog to bark. There wasn't even a whimper.

Reading scanned the box's contents carefully. He whistled then said, "That's an awful lot of items to leave behind ... unless you don't know you're not coming back."

"Yes. A lot of the things are items I wouldn't leave. See that pushup bra? That's Victoria's Secret. Very expensive. Three pair of panties and two are the type you'd wear on a date, not working on the boat." I began sorting through items, putting apparel, fishing paraphernalia, feminine items and keepsakes in separate piles.

Reading watched for a while then pointed to three framed pictures of Mary with her family, with her boyfriend, and with Hootie. "Those definitely aren't the kind of thing ..." He stopped talking, walked to one of the cabinets and returned with several large zip-lock bags. "Mind if I put a few of these things aside?" Reading took the picture of Hootie and Mary, a compact, and a comb from the stacks on the table and placed each in a separate plastic baggie.

I looked at him and waited for an explanation, but he didn't volunteer one. I snorted and removed specialized gloves used to handle fish and another that were cut resistant for chopping bait, picked up two fish dehookers, and took a combination tool that served as a pliers/screw driver/wire cutters and more.

I couldn't resist any longer. "So why did you take the picture, compact and comb?"

"The Highway Patrol sent out a notice a few days ago that Sean Boyd's car was found abandoned at Palm Beach International in Long Term Parking." Reading was being evasive.

"So how does that affect the cost of tea in China?" I thought a smart-assed comment was called for.

"Sean Boyd was Mary Perez's boyfriend."

Twenty Six

Friday, Saturday, and Sunday. Friday, Saturday, and Sunday. That's just three days. The next three days. Those three days consisted of hours that were each 240 minutes long. The trips on Hootie's boat made it worse. The fishing was off, meaning I had less to do and Hootie stayed out longer hoping to corral a few more fish for his customers. The customers were not regulars. That meant stupid. They were doing stupid things, asking stupid questions, stupid, stupid, stupid. All three days were the same. Hootie and Willie said I was just having a bad hair weekend. I overheard Willie ask Hootie if he thought it was my rag time. I blew up and they both avoided me the rest of Saturday. I brought a dozen donuts as a peace offering on Sunday and I was forgiven. Both of them told me Friday, Saturday, and Sunday were like every other one we worked. They lied. I thought the three days would never end.

Monday came and I felt like a penned-up wild horse released into the fields. If I needed any reinforcement for my decision to do an "autopsy" on the chum blocks Hootie gave me, the news that Mary Perez's boyfriend's car was found abandoned in an airport parking lot had provided it. The unending three days' wait intensified my eagerness to get started. My faint, gut-guess suspicion was elevated to being a real possibility. Reading's selection of items that would harbor Mary's fingerprints and DNA were obvious reflections of his thought that there may be a connection. Combined with the fact that the type items Perez left behind weren't likely to be discarded voluntarily, foul play seemed more likely than possible.

The place I chose for my inspection of the chum blocks was the best spot available to me. Abandoned, the Borden property on Mullet Creek was an isolated location. There was a good reason for that. Modern human values decreed the slice of sand barely elevated above the surrounding mangroves was valueless even though it was minutes from Vero. Mullet Creek wasn't a creek at all. It was a series of saltwater ponds that were connected by swallow breaks in the surrounding mangroves. The lack of continuous navigable water prohibited anything larger than a kayak access to the Indian River. The three acres that was the Borden home-site struggled to stay above high tides that flooded the surrounding 150 acres. Seldom used ruts that led to Borden's place and its 1840's salt making business often were covered by exceptionally high tides. Only young couples wanting a private place to park and those who cared little for their vehicles used the road. Its nick name, Rubber Road had factual significance.

The mangroves providing isolation guaranteed the land's failure to stimulate any interest. Environmental rules barred the 1950's practice of dredging canals to create retirement dreams for refugees from northern winters. Even nature lovers avoided the deserted land. The sands and mangroves around it were ideal breeding areas for mosquitoes, sand flies, and vicious biting yellow deer flies. The only life that prospered in the deep holes in the so-called creek were blue crabs, mullet, and oysters. Even wading birds and raccoons weren't overly fond of the land.

I eased my pickup over the ruts at five miles-per-hour, swerving to avoid puddles of salt water. My father took me crabbing and cast netting at the Borden place when I was in elementary school. I knew to wear long pants, a long sleeve shirt, a hat with mosquito netting to protect my face, and to carry two cans of insect repellent as insurance. When my truck approached the place I wanted to park, I remembered my father telling me how timeless nature was and how it reclaimed what humans spoiled. What I saw in front of me proved his words.

When I'd made my visits with my father, the Borden house, pole barns, and outbuildings were collapsing and on their way to complete disappearance. Now, all that remained were pilings that grave-marked their locations. Several huge cast-iron kettles the Borden's used to boil water down to salt, had long disappeared, taken to a museum. What was left of a decaying wooden seawall protected the sand bar where the house was built. It was the spot I'd chosen to melt and look for human remains in the chum blocks. Deep pot holes, dredged by the Bordens to elevate their land, provided me the opportunity to dispose of the block's contents, and, if I decided to, catch the crabs that infested Mullet Creek.

I was surprised to find that people had parked where I was in the not too distant past. There were faded tire tracks from a sizeable vehicle and passenger cars. Most out of place were three licenses plates. None were badly rusted and were still easily visible through the weeds growing around them. They were all Florida plates. It occurred to me they might be from stolen cars. I made a mental note to tell Reading about them.

I'd come prepared. I purchased a cheap plastic rain suit to keep the disgusting contents off my clothes, brought rubber gloves, three paper masks to reduce the stench my nostrils would endure, and cheap but strong cologne to douse the masks. My work surface was a four-foot square piece of plywood and two battered sawhorses I could discard when finished. An assortment of old knives, a hatchet, and a saw would let me "operate" on the still frozen blocks that I hoped to be able to finish exploring before they melted and became too vile to work with. I had plenty of bottled water to keep hydrated. I made a table from the plywood and sawhorses at the seawall's edge, placed my tools on it, and removed the battered cooler I'd placed the chum blocks in after removing them from our freezer. There were empty glass jars and plastic bags in my truck bed to store any evidence I might find. I was ready to start.

My first act was to open one of the boxes. Though I'd handled the blocks on every fishing trip, I examined the mesh bags carefully for the first time. Embossed on the draw straps was the manufacture's logo. It was an oval with "Bio-D" formed in it and repeated every couple of inches. I cut a section of the strap and stuck it in my jeans pocket. A tag sewn to the mesh proclaimed that, "This is an environmentally friendly product, Keep absolutely dry until disposal." I removed the box by cutting it away, loosened the draw straps, and peeled the bag off. The string material was embedded in the chum telling me the material was poured into bags while they were in the box then flash frozen. That was hardly a mom and pop, back yard, business technique. I tossed the mesh bag in the water to see what would happen.

The surface of the cube was a jigsaw puzzle of definable and mystery items. Dr. Card cautioned us to observe closely before we made any attempts to begin our digs. It was advice that was difficult for me to practice, but I'd learned the wisdom that rushing in and then regretting brings. I focused on each of the cube's six surfaces. The largest identifiable pieces were two inches square. I identified two species of fish, tilapia and catfish, both fresh water varieties. Chunks of tissue that resembled cuts of beef and pork were mixed with the pieces of fish. On two of the surfaces, I observed hard off-white items I had to conclude were bones. But of what? Everything was mixed together in a random manner. It told me nothing.

I used the knives to extricate the items that I believed were bone. The good news was that it was possible to pry the objects from the block. Once they were removed they told me very little because, like everything else in the block, they had been shredded to a two inch by two inch piece approximately an inch thick. The bones had a serrated pattern where they'd been cut. There wasn't enough material for me to have an idea if they were animal or human. The flesh told me less. DNA would give me a correct answer, but that was out of the question. I put several of the bone pieces in a jar and put a lid on it.

My next effort was to saw the block into one inch thick slabs. It worked far better than I thought it would. But, as soon as I started to examine the cut surfaces, I realized I would have to be dumb-lucky to find any kind of evidence. What I was attempting required a sophisticated lab staffed by knowledgeable scientists and technicians. I sighed, resigned myself to the effort, and prayed for dumb-luck. I pried out pieces of bone and separated tissue I thought might be identifiable. As the material softened, I was able to identify white objects frozen in with flesh. Maggots. Forty-five minutes after I started working with the first block, the stench began to penetrate the precautions I'd made. When I took off the mask to drink water to replenish what I lost working in the raincoat sauna, the odor attacked my nose and I immediately gagged uncontrollably. Even after I replaced my mask and administered more cologne, the vile odor clung to my nostrils. The slabs had melted and the stench was horrific.

I mumbled, "I can't do this." The sawed slabs were now piles of red, gray, purple, green and black mush. Grabbing the plywood, I tried to lift it and its piles of vile, decaying flesh, and dump everything in the water without spilling fluids back on me. It didn't work. The piles of flesh and the board made it into the pothole next to the seawall. The horrible smelling juices went everywhere including on me. I vomited in my mask.

It took two miserable hours of cleaning myself and my tools to get to the point where I felt I could get back into my pickup without ruining its interior forever. The results of my attempt to find a smoking gun were stored in seven jars. I had no idea if they had value.

I *had learned* a couple of things. Attempting to do something I didn't have the qualifications for, was a huge waste of time. When I tried to lift the mesh bag from the water, it disintegrated in my fingers, so I knew it worked as claimed. I knew who the bag's manufacturer was. I knew there were several types of fish and animal flesh contained in the chum, but that was all.

I removed the remaining three chum blocks from my cooler and stripped off the cardboard. The boxes and sawhorses formed a funeral pyre for the raincoat, gloves and my hat, all of which were so vile smelling they were unusable. The last things I did before leaving was to puke again and throw the remaining three chum blocks out as far as I could into Mullet Creek.

Hootie would never have to tell me to keep the chum blocks from melting again. I never wanted to smell that putrid odor again and I wondered how difficult it would be for me to handle the damn things on my next day out on the boat.

Sure that I'd wasted the day, I cussed myself out when I finally slipped into my pickup and drove over the soggy ruts to paved roads.

Twenty Seven

"How much?" Reading looked up from his Sudoku puzzle and put down his beer.

"In quantities of ten, Bio-D's website says they cost $3.17. I'm sure that the company Rooster owns buys in much larger quantities, but still, they won't be that much less." I spun my laptop around so Reading could see the website. "I can tell you this, they really do disintegrate. There's nothing left but dust."

"How much did you say Hootie pays for the chum blocks?" Reading asked.

"He pays $3.79 for a block."

"Damn, if you assume the crap they fill bags with is free, you have the cost of the bags, the cardboard box, labor to fill it, flash freezing, and the cost to deliver, Rooster and whoever aren't selling those things to make money." Reading rubbed his chin. "What does he sell a box of bait for?"

"Each box is $14.00. There's thirty-five to forty fish in each box. But, they don't use the mesh bags to ship them in. There's a cheap plastic bag in the box. That's it." I thought for a second. Hootie mentioned why he bought bait from Rooster's company. I said, "The chum blocks are why Hootie buys his bait from Rooster. I can remember him saying how good the blocks worked attracting fish, that it saved several hours labor every trip, and that amounted to a lot of money. Maybe that's what Rooster does. He sells chum very cheap to sell more bait. My marketing professor would call it a loss leader."

Reading looked at me for several seconds before shaking his head. "That seems like an awful complicated strategy to sell an item like bait." He turned my laptop back around to face me. "So Chessie, what else did you find out today?"

I opened my eyes wide and fumbled around for my best *I don't know what you're talking about* tone. "What do you mean?"

"Chessie, you may think you're a good liar. Maybe you are around other folks, but I've heard your shit too long. Besides, I walked by your truck. It smells like a freshly Cloroxed dumpster. Did you find out anything interesting in those chum blocks beside who made the bags?" Reading leaned back in the kitchen chair and placed his hands behind his head.

"You can be a smart ass without trying to show it." He was good at putting pieces together. I frowned. "What did I learn? There are still lots of blue crabs in Mullet Creek. Folks still drive down there to park and dump trash. I learned I don't want to screw around with another box of that chum again. I took one of the blocks, cut it up, and scrounged through it. I found some little pieces of bone and some stuff that is flesh and maybe organs, but I have no way to know what it's from. I'm going to try to get Dr. Card to look at them and see if he can help. I doubt it, but...." I leaned toward him and asked, "I guess there's no way to check DNA on the samples I kept."

Reading laughed and shook his head.

"You asked what I learned. The most important thing is that anyone who mucks around with those things is an idiot. After they melted, the stench was so bad I couldn't stand it. I had a perfumed mask on and it didn't do much. I gagged, I puked, I gagged, I puked, and I promised myself never to be around another one of them if it melted. It took me hours to clean myself and the stuff I used. Nobody that has anything to do with that gross shit would ever get near it again. You can get rid of anything in them and not worry about anyone looking for it."

Reading leaned forward, rubbed his chin, tilted his head to the side and said, "No one is looking for it?" He paused. "No one is looking in it! Chessie, you may have the answer right there. Think about what you just said. No one in their right mind would go looking in those things a second time. If you wanted to smuggle something, putting it in the middle of those chum blocks would be a very good place to do it."

What Reading said made sense, but that didn't explain what I'd seen. "That's well and good, but why would they use part of a human body in something like that? They'd want to discourage, not encourage, people to snoop."

Reading tapped his fingers on the table and stared at me for thirty seconds. He took a breath then said, "I know you saw teeth, but can you be absolutely sure they were human? How long did you actually see them? Can you even be sure they were teeth?"

"I know what I saw. My eyes were a foot from them. I had more than a minute to look. They were teeth and they were human!" I was pissed. "I'd expect one of the assholes around town to doubt me because of my past reputation. But not you, Reading."

"If you say you saw human teeth, you saw human teeth. I'm looking for motive. Ask yourself, does what I'm saying make sense? You use a really cheap item that no one wants to tamper with to disguise a really valuable item you want to hide. Like drugs. Like gems. Like a lot of things. Which makes more sense to you?"

"What you said." I shrugged my shoulders. He was right, but I sure wasn't going to elaborate on it.

"There are two weeks and a day before I get reinstated. I can't afford to make waves. Particularly, if the waves have anything to do with questionable evidence or false charges. I know better than to believe you're going to do what you should ... keep your nose out until I'm back where I can do something. Just be sure you don't get my name tied into this. If Benson believes I'm involved I'm in trouble." He let that sink in. "Look, you think Rooster is a killer, maybe even a serial killer, I know that. That's serious. That seriousness is why we can't go around accusing a person without hard proof. If we do, and Rooster's guilty, and we don't have enough to put him under the jail, we've warned the bastard we're after him. That's a get out of jail free card."

"Don't you worry that the possibility exists he could kill someone now?" I couldn't understand his lack of urgency.

"If I were 100% sure he was a killer, yes. I think it's possible he *is* a killer. I also *don't* have enough evidence to think it's probable."

"But shouldn't we, the police, everybody, be looking for evidence?"

Reading shook his head. "I'm not getting through. Look, two weeks isn't long. I know better than to think you'll sit on your hands and do nothing. Take Mary's stuff to her parents. Ask some questions. Take the items you took from the chum and let Dr. Card look at them. Hell, you can see if you can find out anything about those other two companies Rooster delivers for." Reading put his elbows on the kitchen table, interlocked his fingers, and pointed his index fingers at me. He tilted his head forward and eyeballed me while he warned, "There are some things you can't do. You can't go nosing around the Circle X

Ranch, you can't follow Rooster any more, and you can't do anything that lets Rooster and whoever else know you're checking them out. If they're warned, they're armed. And, if you're right about Rooster, you don't want to end up in one of those chum blocks."

Twenty Eight

I packed the box of Mary Perez's personal items in my pickup early the next morning and crossed the bridge to the mainland. The Perez family's home was located in a modest residential neighborhood near Vero Beach Regional Airport. The streets I passed all had a Spanish flavor to their names: Cordova, Bonita, Cortez, Buena Vista, and the street I looked for Verde Mar. I was familiar with the area. High school friends had lived on adjoining streets.

Verde Mar was close enough to the airport to see portions of it. Some of the houses on the street might have been old enough to have been there when Navy fighter pilots trained at Vero during WWII. Today's airport was an infrastructure seed that sprouted in the 40's and only grew modestly since its planting.

The Perez home sported gray siding, a car port, a low roof covering what looked like 1400 square feet of house. A few palm trees, bougainvillea bushes, crotons, and a lonely oak dotted a lawn that tried, but failed. The heron statue that stood guard at the front door, replaced the flamingo replica that had been a south Florida household requisite fifty years before.

I pulled into the drive, trapping a rusting late ninety's vintage Impala. Arriving unannounced because I didn't want to be denied the visit, I didn't know what kind of reception I'd receive. After a last deep breath, I exited my truck, removed the box of Mary's belongings, and headed to the front door. Before I reached it, the door opened and a short, plump, matronly woman stepped outside. Her blonde hair and pale skin told me she wasn't Hispanic. She might have had Swedish DNA.

"Hello. Can I help you?" There was a shred of caution behind her smile.

"Are you Mary Perez's mother?" I asked.

"Yes. Don't tell me, I know you." She looked at me for several seconds. Mrs. Perez gave up. "I know your face, I am sorry, but I don't remember your name."

"I'm Chessie Partin."

"Ohhh. You're Reading's sister! Mary had a little girl crush on your brother. I remember you from the high school's football games." She smiled, "How is your brother? Is he still single?"

"He's doing fine." I wasn't going to volunteer Reading for anything. "Can we—"

"Yes. Please come in." Mrs. Perez ushered me inside her immaculate living room that contained more knick-knacks than many local gift shops. She led us to a sofa that sucked me down into its soft cushions. I placed the box on the cushion between us. "Mrs. Perez—"

"No, no. Please call me Colleen."

"Colleen, I took Mary's place working for Hootie. She left some clothes and other items in her locker on the boat. I thought you might want to send them to her or keep them until she returns. A lot of these things are something I think she'd want. Victoria's Secret bras and panties, a Timex watch. There's several nice pieces of jewelry, good clothes … not the stuff she'd wear working the boat. L'Oreal and Chanel makeup. That's all pretty expensive stuff. They're in this box."

The smile left Colleen's face. "I appreciate you going to the trouble, but I don't know where she is. She left to marry that … that … *Boyd* boy. Mary sent us an email to tell us she was eloping. We haven't heard one word from her since she left." She peeked into the box. "If there is anything you can use, you should keep it."

"There were a couple tools I could use on the boat. I have them. If she wants them when—"

"When she comes back? She'll be back with a baby or two and no husband. I tried to warn her about that Sean Boyd. She is so pretty and could do so much better. You keep what's in there."

"Mrs. Perez—"

"Colleen, dearie."

"Okay. Colleen, what's in there, the lingerie and clothes are not my size." I wouldn't tell her that I'd never wear someone else's underthings. I waved a hand over the box. "… and the personal items like makeup and pictures. I appreciate the offer, but there's really nothing that I could use." I tried to sound grateful for the offer.

She looked at my chest. "I definitely can see why." She hesitated then said, "Pictures?"

I reached into the box and handed Colleen the pictures of Mary with her boyfriend and of Mary and her family. Mrs. Perez's face became a storm cloud. She dropped the picture of Sean and Mary to the floor and crashed her heel on it. Her face softened as she placed the family picture reverently on a coffee table. "I'm sorry. That's just the way I feel."

"You haven't got an address to send her things to?" I asked.

"No. I don't know anything past her email saying they were going to Oregon."

I thought for several seconds. "You have her email address, don't you? Have you tried to—"

"Yes, of course. She doesn't answer." Colleen took a deep breath. "I'm sure she doesn't want my husband to know where she is. He would go and get her. Heaven forbid if he saw that Sean." She leaned close to me. "Jorge would kill him!"

"Colleen, would you give me her email address? I have questions about how she handled some things on the boat. She might answer me and I might be able to get her to contact you."

"Would you?" Colleen's smile returned. "Here it is and her phone number, too." She picked up a slip of paper and a pencil from the coffee table and wrote Mary's information. As she handed me the paper she asked, "Would you like something that helped Mary make a little extra money?"

"Sure."

Colleen left the room. She came back after a few minutes. "These should fit. She ordered them extra-large because she didn't want them tight." She handed me three tee shirts. The words "Tips 4 Tits" were printed on the front of each shirt. "Mary told us the men got the message and she averaged 20% more after she started to wear them." Colleen shook her head. "It surprised me she didn't even tell Hootie she was leaving. She liked him and he was nice to her. Mary liked all the customers and Willie. The only person she didn't like was the man that delivered bait. She said he was a creep. At the end, though, she said she never had to deal with him." Collen leaned toward me. "He tried to get her to go to a motel with him." She sighed deeply. "Men can be so bad."

"If Mary contacts you would you let me know?"

"Most surely, dearie." Colleen scratched her temple. "You should tell Hootie to let you know if she emails or talks to him. She did that you know."

I nodded and asked, "Anything else I can tell her or you want to know if she contacts me?"

"No. Just ask her to call her momma."

Twenty Nine

It's amazing how distracted your mind can get when you do two things at once. I weaved through the residential streets that surrounded Mary Perez's parent's home after I left. Thoughts about what Mary's mother and I discussed interfered with my focus on returning home. My pickup crossed the canal that fronted the airport before I realized I was heading the wrong direction.

The Vero Beach Municipal Airport is an antique that was originally built in the late 1920's and came of age as a WWII naval training base. The navy used the facility first for basic flight training, later for training F6F fighter pilots in the art of night fighting. After the war, the airport settled back into civilian use. Barracks built by the Navy served as an incentive to attract the Brooklyn Dodgers to Vero as their spring training center. Now the airfield's primary use is as a private aviation center.

Why? There was no reason for me to point my pickup toward the airport. Any path I selected to return to Route 60 and the bridge I'd have to travel to get home was absurdly out-of-the-way. The only person I knew at the airport was Clauson Stiner. He was a high school classmate, one that *had* been more than a casual boyfriend, and who opened an aerial photography business after serving a couple of hitches as a helicopter pilot in the army. We saw each other occasionally, but since his wife was the jealous type, our current relationship was best described as at "arm's length". I seldom even thought about him.

I told myself to dismiss my detour as a brain fart and turned east on Aviation Boulevard. Telling and doing are different. Instructions to dismiss those thoughts failed, something inside me would not allow it. My mind kept trying to relate connections between the airport, Mary's disappearance, Rooster, and the nefarious deeds I was sure the bait man performed. When Aviation Boulevard ended at US 1, I couldn't help thinking I'd made the turn toward the airport for some subconscious reason. Why? My focus returned to driving when the panicked screaming of a gasoline tank truck's horn kept me from pulling directly into its path. I shook, cursed myself, and looked several times at the vacant highway before turning right and south toward the bridge.

Reading's 150 was in the driveway when I reached our duplex. I slowed, but didn't stop. If I went inside, I'd get an interrogation from Reading and I really didn't want that.

The problem, I wasn't sure what I wanted. Colleen Perez's description of her last communication with her daughter left many more questions in my mind than answers. I wanted to think about what she said, draw conclusions, and, if I did, I knew I'd probably end up doing the exact things Reading warned me might get him fired and make me fish bait. At thirty-three, I had to concede my maturity level wasn't to the point where I could always say no to *want to*. *Could do* turns into *will do* if *want to* is involved. My standard approach was to avoid placing myself in a position to answer the *want to* question. I couldn't do that this time.

Conn Beach is my contemplation place. It had been since my junior year in high school. There, I'd made my decision to have sex with my first love boyfriend. It was a good and bad one. Good that I protected myself from pregnancy. Bad ... the boy was more interested in bragging than performing. I'd made bad decisions about which friends to associate with there, chose a used car that may have once been lemon-of-the-year, and decided that dancing in a strip bar would be exciting. Good ones including joining the Marine Corp., deciding not to marry a loser who was now being hunted for fraud, and quitting the job as a stripper.

I simply let my Ford roll its wheels down Date Palm Road until the street dead ended into Ocean Drive. The steering wheel turned left on its own, and in a few blocks my pickup found a parking place fronting the boardwalk that overlooked the Atlantic.

The warm afternoon sun toasted my shoulders under a lime green tee, as I sat on a bench and watched the sea breeze chase aquamarine waves to the white sand beach. Trying to avoid thinking is often more difficult than succumbing to the process. I attempted diverting my brain to escape. I needed a few drinks ... that was it. Nellie and Loretta were always ready for bar hopping. Did Nellie tell me she was going to Miami for a couple weeks? Or, I could make up an excuse to visit Mark Card. Let's see ... it was three months since my last time. I chuckled to myself, I could find out if the archeologist's bone was good, large, and hard or just an old fossil. The thought and potential visions bounced around my cranium and I laughed loud and long.

"That must be a good one, little lady." I hadn't noticed the *fossil* sitting two benches away from me. The man was old, I guessed in his seventies. He'd been a big man, still was attractive in an over-the-hill manner, and still fancied he had it. A big smile and his imitation of the John Wayne line was an opener I'm sure he'd used for a few decades. "Want to share the joke? I could use a good laugh."

"Having a bad day, old timer?" I smiled and hoped I hadn't been harsh.

"Honey, any day I wake up is a *good* one at this point in my life." He persisted, "Tell me what you were laughing about. A good laugh makes me feel better than ten ounces of arthritis medicine."

"Sorry to disappoint you. It wasn't a joke. I was trying to make a decision."

He threw his hands up and said, "Great, I'm one of the premier purveyors of advice you'll find. I'm never wrong because I'm never specific. My advice is advice about advice."

I laughed. The old boy was sharp. "So, my muse, tell me your first piece of advice?"

"My first advice is not to take or give advice. Think for yourself and don't try to think for others. Neither of those two work."

"Okay, what do you do when you don't know whether you should make a decision or not?"

"That would be advice and I don't give that." He grinned. He wasn't that easy to trick.

"Okay, for laughs, oh great muse, let's say you have to choose bet—"

"Okay, for laughs. I don't need specifics. You always make a decision even if it is not to make a decision. The only decisions in life I've regretted are the ones I didn't make."

I thought for a few seconds then I made mine. How could I risk becoming part of a chum block while being sure Reading didn't suffer for my actions?

Thirty

MacDonald's is my out-of-the-house office. I slid into a booth with my Big Mac meal and took a sip of Coke. There was too much ice in it. By the time I finished, the drink would be lightly colored water. Snooping into Rooster's business without him or Reading catching on would take time to think out.

I considered being honest with Reading and concluded, in this case, honesty would not be the best policy. If I told Reading about my plans, all kinds of things would happen, most of them bad. He'd try to stop me. He wouldn't succeed, but he'd make a hell of an effort. Reading was the type who'd single out each thing I planned, find a way to blow-up each element I wanted to explore, and make it near impossible for me to proceed. Would he go as far as telling Hootie? Get me fired, figuring I'd be better unemployed than deceased? Maybe. Reading is a relentless character who goes to extremes to prove, or disprove a point. He's smart and good at it.

I decided not to tell Reading anything so he could squelch my plans. Problem. There were no plans, I had to make some. Flying by the seat of my pants wasn't an option any longer. For the first time, I went through the process of determining what I did, and didn't, know. It forced me to look at Rooster and what facts we knew from a vantage point other than one that centered on my dislike for him. My simplistic view—Rooster was a killer, maybe a serial killer, and he was at the center of the crime. But was he? When I began to think with the logical portion of my brain instead of the portion labeled lame, all manner of questions popped up.

Rooster was the physical type. I could see him as a loan shark, an enforcer for the mob, a nightclub bouncer, or a professional wrestler. Leg breakers don't very often make business masterminds. He wasn't stupid, I knew that. Rooster had the raw cunning you'd better respect or end up screwed. Still, I couldn't see him as a participant in the medical business; even visioning him as a cattle baron was pushing his talents. Rooster sold his bait and blocks to Hootie priced at so low a level, it was difficult to see how he stayed in business. That seemed to attest to the bait man's lack of financial savvy. But Hootie had been buying from Rooster for a long enough time for the man to have gone bankrupt. Rooster was on the road all day and he delivered many things beside bait. All that indicated Rooster was just a strand of spaghetti in the big bowl.

That was a bitter pill for me. Reading's instinct saw something much more complicated than Rooster using his rod then killing and disposing of his rape victims as fish food. Every bit of my female intuition, instinct, sixth, seventh, and eighth senses told me that was exactly what Rooster was, a cold-blooded rapist-murderer. Could I have misjudged that badly? Here we had a fiend who appeared to buy and deliver clothes to charity shelters, give indigent old men rides to bus terminals, and buy them tickets. Really? This did not compute. And, what happened when Rooster disappeared behind the Circle X Ranch gate? What was back there? More than a little thought had been given to keeping trespassers out. Was the ranch just a house and some outbuildings? Or, was it much more? What was going on in there? Did Rooster live there as it seemed? Were there days that Rooster never left the ranch, making bait and chum or did he rely on someone inside to do the work.

If he didn't handle the materials, why did he smell so horrible, just like the melted blocks?

Was Rooster the person who made Mary disappear? Every gray cell in my skull revolted at the possibility that it wasn't Rooster. I was so sure he'd found a way to capture, rape and kill her, nothing else seemed a possibility. What woman would leave all the items she left on the boat? I knew I wouldn't. Maybe the teeth I'd seen were hers. That gave me the shivers. My run-ins with the jerky-creep underlined that probability.

Where did that leave me? My starting points were to find out what was on the property behind the mysterious Circle X Ranch gate, what was Rooster's day after day schedule, and I had to determine if Mary Perez was as dead as I thought she was, or simply mussing sheets with her boyfriend, shacked up in Oregon. After learning those three things, I'd be able to ask more questions. What enterprises, legal or possibly illegal, were going on in the ranch? Was it conceivable that drug smuggling was at the center? That would fit with Rooster's medical pickups and deliveries. Did Rooster own and run the ranch or was a mystery entity in control? What did happen to Mary if she wasn't in Oregon?

I had places to search for Mary, her phone number and email address. If she was alive, I was sure I'd eventually get in touch with her. She wouldn't want to change both. It was the only way for people she knew to contact her and it was hard to imagine she wanted to be isolated from *all* her friends. If her phone was discontinued and she changed her email, that told me something, too. Not conclusively, but it moved me closer to verifying my theory.

Following Rooster was going to be dangerous. He knew my truck. Using Reading's was obviously out. Borrowing friends' cars wouldn't work. I couldn't borrow Nellie's car, it was a Mustang. It was built low to the ground and wouldn't do well on the sandy ruts I knew I'd be forced to travel. Loretta's Buick was an antique. The clunker only operated occasionally and had a habit of dumping her on lonely roads. Besides, it was so rusted and afflicted with road rash that it was unique and easy to remember seeing. That was the last thing I wanted. But following Rooster was definitely something I needed to do. I wrote a note to myself. *Price the cost of renting a car for a week.*

That left mission impossible. How in the hell would I be able to get onto the Circle X property? The gate was kept locked. Even if I were lucky enough to find it open, I'd be riding into who knew what. It would be like playing Russian Roulette with five revolver chambers loaded instead of one. Trying to sneak over the fence or wade in through the creek was even riskier. The gators and snakes I'd seen made it the last thing I wanted to do. I wondered if Caralene Wills had discovered anything about the property she'd neglected to tell Reading. Asking her would be like asking Reading so that was out.

If I had some idea of what the land's topography was like I might be able to use Dr. Card's antiquities egress power to snoop around, but I couldn't do that without at least describing some feature to evaluate. A hump that could be an Indian mound, an old abandoned building that could have been a pioneer relic, anything like that might provide an excuse to use his investigation power. It might put him ... me, in position to do some snooping.

"Can I take those?" The MacDonald's clerk asked me if he could throw my Big Mac wrapper and empty Coke cup in the thrash. I clutched the remains of my meal's French fries in my fist. I nodded as I looked way up. The boy was tall, at least 6' 8".

"I'm still working on the fries," I said.

"I know." He smiled. "That's one advantage of being real tall. I can look down on stuff and see what's going on."

I looked at him for several seconds, not comprehending the relevance of his comment to my problem. Finally, I did. I'd been struggling trying to find an answer to a problem I didn't have. I smiled and said, "You're right. You don't have to be down on the table to know what's happening on it." I pushed the $2.17 change to him and said, "Here's a tip for your tip." He looked at me like I was crazy, but scooped up the change.

Thirty One

Lisa Lister's Mercedes was parked in front of our duplex when I pulled into the drive. I breathed a sigh of relief. The first thing I had expected was for Reading to cross-examine me about my delivery of Mary's things to her mother. Now, he'd be otherwise employed. Getting to my room without breaking up a porn show was my primary concern.

I knocked on the door forcefully with three hard raps, three quick raps, and three more hard ones, to let Reading know I was coming in. If Reading was in his bedroom, it wasn't needed, but I'd walked in on him and Lisa several times. When the mood struck, neither were mindful of surroundings, so a coffee table, the back of a chair, or a wall served them as ready substitutes for a bed.

There was no response. I cracked the front door a couple inches and listened. It was quiet. When I pushed the door, I could feel it dragging over something. It was one of Lisa's skirts. Reading's shorts were discarded a step toward the couch. All three cushions from the sofa were arranged in a unique pattern on the floor. Her blouse, panties, and what served her as a bra were tossed on the floor next to Reading's tee shirt and an overflowing box of condoms. Tiptoeing into my room, I closed the door behind me. Safe!

My room is always a disaster. It seems I never have time to put up all my clean clothes or hang up the ones I take off. The bed simply won't make itself and my nightstand always displays aspirin, makeup remover, used Kleenex, and anything else I might have used in the last week. The table my laptop and printer sit on doesn't need a cloth. It's covered with notes, bills, magazines, and lots of things that I have no idea why I left there. I waded through the stream of undergarments, jeans, and tees to my desk.

It was a good time to try to reach Mary Perez. Reading was occupied so I doubted I would have an interruption. Plopping down in my chair, I put my purse on the table and removed the slip of paper on which Colleen had written her daughter's phone number and email address. I picked up the antique that sat on my desk; the handset for our land line, entered the number, and listened to the beeps, before I thought about what I'd say to her if she did answer. Telling her I was surprised she was still alive wouldn't be cool. To my surprise it rang. Once. Twice. I supposed the best thing was to ...three times ... make up some story about ... four times ... working on the boat. Five. Six. Seven. Eight. Then, "Hi, it's Mary, leave a message and your number. I'll call back when I can." Her voice was light and sounded upbeat.

"Hi Mary." I cleared my throat while I searched for a few words. "This is Chessie Partin. I hope you remember me. Your mom mentioned you liked my brother Reading. Hey, I took your job working on Hootie's boat. I wanted you to know I took the stuff in your locker to your mom's house. She'd like you to call her. Also, please call me at 772-555-5421. I have a couple questions about how you did some things on the boat. Call soon, please. Bye."

The noise started as I lifted the lid on my lap top. Lisa's moans and grunts were loud enough to penetrate the thin walls between Reading's and my room. By the time I turned the unit on, booted up windows, and brought my email up, she'd built up some real pressure in her boiler. Her "Aaaahh.......aaaahhs," love call grew progressively louder and quicker paced. The bed wasn't banging against the wall much so I knew she was astride for the ride as she called her favorite position. Lisa muttered some unintelligible words urging Reading to a supreme effort. There was a mighty groan and things quieted down.

My fingers twitched on the keyboard. What was I doing? Oh, sending an email to Mary. I typed the same message I'd left on her voice mail, put the address on that Mrs. Perez gave me, and clicked the send button. Now, I had to wait ... and change panties.

I pulled up Dr. Card's email address on the message screen. The bone fragments and putrid flesh I extracted from the chum blocks were in the freezer on our carport. Those were a good excuse to visit him. He could tell me what I had in those jars, though I didn't think it would help. There was something I was sure he could do for me without much urging.

My message started with, *Hi Doc, I have some unusual samples of bone I've found. Can I come up to visit you on campus? I'd like help identifying them. I'd love to chat for a while. Have some time for me?"*

Thirty Two

Mark smiled at me. "It was almost like we had a Vulcan mind meld moment. I was thinking about you right before I opened your email. I was surprised that you asked if I'd have time to see you."

We sat in his Spartan office that was sparsely furnished, functional, but comfortable. A small round table positioned between us was our only chaperone. The fish-bowl effect the glass panels that formed his office walls produced made a chaperone superfluous.

"Chessie, I always have *time* for you." His smile had a smug twist I could have done without.

I had an urge to retort, "Good, we'll find out if you're worth mine," but I didn't want my mouth to louse up either reason I had driven the sixty miles. Instead, I purred, "That's so very kind of you, Doctor."

He pointed to the cardboard box I'd placed on the table. "Are the bones you want me to look at in there?"

"Yes. I have each sample in a separate jar." I opened the box flaps.

"In jars?" He stood up and peered into the box. "Are they small bones or pieces?"

"I think they're all pieces." I removed a jar and started to twist off the cap when Mark stopped me.

"Let's do this right." He went to his desk, removed a tray, a roll of paper, a magnifying glass, a toothbrush, a dental pick, a scalpel, a brush and several envelopes. He slipped a pair of surgical gloves on and tossed a pair to me. He wrote, *Archeological sample contributed by Miss Chessie Partin* on the envelope.

I sheepishly attempted to correct him, "Dr. Card, they aren—"

"Please, use Mark," he corrected me.

"Fine." I smiled and signed the contract his eyes offered. "Mark, these aren't archeological items I've found."

Dr. Card stood silently, waiting for me to explain. The time gave me an opportunity to make up a lie. "These are something a friend of mine—no, these are something *I* found on a side street in Vero. I'm really curious. There was no fur. Everything was cut or mashed into small pieces. I was wondering if they could be human."

Mark held his hand out and I placed the Vlasic Pickle jar in his palm. I warned him, "The bones are as cleaned up as I could make them, but they still smell really bad."

"Okay," Mark said. He held the jar and peered at the bone fragment. "Hard to tell, but I think …," he didn't complete his sentence. He tore off a piece of lab paper, placed that on the tray, then opened the jar and dumped the bone fragment on the paper. The smell exploded into our nostrils. "Lord that's bad!" He gagged, but continued. The odor abated after several seconds.

"Sorry, if you don—"

"No. That's nothing. You should smell human bodies rotting. I did some forensics in Kosovo. Smells like that, only worse." He thought for several seconds. "Where did you find these?"

"On a street a few blocks over from my place. I was just going to shovel it up to get rid of the mess, but I was curious as to what was killed."

Mark went to his desk and brought two paper masks to the table. He handed one to me and said, "Put this on." He looked like Dr. Card after he donned his mask. "No use taking chances. Tell me you protected yourself when you handled all this stuff."

"Yes. I had heavy rubber gloves, a mask, and a disposable rain-suit on," I shook my head. "It took a half bottle of Clorox to clean the tools I used."

"Good girl." Mark flipped the fragment over and looked at it from several different angles. He whistled. "This is one of the craziest things I've seen. I need to look at some of the other bones." He reached in the box and removed another jar. That one contained a flesh sample. He looked at me questioningly.

"That's the meat that created the pile. Mark, don't open that in here. It smells worse and it will ruin your office. There's that one and one more in the box that looked strange. I have seven more jars with bone pieces. No complete bones were in that mash so I took several pieces. That was what made me curious."

"What did you do with the rest?" he asked.

"It's feeding crabs in the Indian River."

"Good place for it if it smells worse than the bones do." Mark picked up the magnifying glass and examined the bone very carefully. He removed a jar that contained another piece of bone, released the stink, and poured the bone on the tray. The magnifying glass covered every millimeter as he scoured the fragment for identifying factors.

When Mark looked up he smiled. "I don't believe someone did a hit-and-run on Granny. It's a mammal; I'm guessing these are from a hog or cow." He motioned for me to come to his side of the table. "Look," he pointed to a feature on the bone with his scalpel after he removed a tiny bit of material, "The bones have a Haversian system, but," he was very specific in pointing to the pore in the bone, "These aren't the concentric circles I'd expect to find in a human bone. Judging from what I'm seeing, these are chips from a large beef cattle's femur." He shook his head. Mark took all the jars from the box, looked at them, and put them down without opening any more. "You say you found this on a street in your neighborhood?"

"Yes, but the pile was more the size that would be made by a small to medium sized dog. Not a cow." I hoped to eliminate more questions. I thought I'd learned all that I could from the chum block material.

"I'm curious," Mark asked, "Why were you fooling with this?"

I lied. "Originally, I thought it might be somebody's dog and I was looking for a tag."

"That doesn't surprise me. You are civic minded." Mark slid the point of his scalpel along every edge of the bone. "Look at this. See the serrated surface on every edge?" He tapped both bone fragments with the scalpel. "See how uniform they are in size? Chessie, these bones weren't hit by a vehicle or destroyed by hand. Some kind of a specialized, huge and powerful machine was used to do this. Somebody decided to make hamburger the hard way. My guess is that we'd find the flesh and," he pointed to the other sample of meat in the remaining jar, "that piece of what looks like kidney are all bovine. You'd have to do DNA on it. The samples are too deteriorated to be sure any other way."

"DNA?" I asked.

"Yes. You aren't considering doing that, are you?" He laughed. "That's an expensive way to prove you stumbled on somebody's discarded rare Big Mac. That is unless you have an uncle who owns a dozen oil wells. Even then you wouldn't have an answer to how it got there."

Patronizing comments aren't my favorites. I frowned and Dr. Card got the message. "I think I'll pass," I said coldly.

"I didn't mean anything neg—" Mark stammered before I cut him off by placing my finger over his lips.

"How good is your memory, Mark," I asked.

"Pretty damned good."

I stood right behind him, put my hands on the back of his chair, and bent over slightly. "Remember when we were at the Okeechobee site you told me I had a legitimate interest in archeology?"

"Yes."

"And remember you told me you'd like to work with me?"

"Yes."

I leaned over so that my breasts rested on his shoulders and against each side of his neck. I whispered, "So do you think we can find a private place where you can pick a part to start work on?"

Thirty Three

The hour-plus trip returning from Mark's apartment near the East Florida Sciences campus to Vero, was a pleasant one. Any trip that is successful tends to go by quickly and mine had satisfied my objectives. My objective to learn something about the chum blocks was fulfilled. They weren't human remains: that was disappointing. But, in addition to the info about Haversian systems, I learned several important points in identifying human bones. The *most important thing I learned* was that Rooster wasn't hacking up whatever he placed in the blocks by hand. He, or whoever, was utilizing a machine to do the work. That told me Reading was right; Rooster *was* just a feather on a bigger bird. It was discouraging news for my theory, but not defeating. He could still be the villain I thought him to be and was simply using his employers to his advantage in covering his crimes.

My second objective was satisfied by being satisfied … at least two out of three times. I reflected on the danger of idolizing anyone or thing to the point where reality could not match concocted fantasies. However, Mark was worth my time, definitely.

An unexpected bonus was Mark's asking about the middens we discussed getting access to near what he believed to be the work of Ais Indians. It gave me a golden opportunity to see if I might piggy-back on his authority to gain access to the Circle X Ranch. I responded to his question and asked one of my own. "I've only driven past the land to confirm what I remembered. It is entirely fenced and posted. What I thought I'd do is go to the court house, check the deeds, see who owns it and get permission. If that doesn't work, what kind of information do you need to get onto that property or any other for that matter?"

Mark pulled the sheets up over the two of us. "I have to adjust the damned AC vent." He ran his fingers through his hair. "Let's see, getting onto property." He adjusted his persona from lover back to professor. "What I'd require is a valid suspicion that an archeological site is on the property in question, that it could be at risk ... that's either being destroyed or disturbed ... proof an artifact has been previously discovered on that land, and some form of documentation showing reason to believe it is a site. An affidavit by someone that's been on the property and observed a site, a map or survey showing something that has been identified or looks like a spot having the potential to be a dig."

"So if I swear in an affidavit that I saw the mounds and have seen the artifacts there you could get us on?"

"Absolutely."

"Let's say," I hesitated to be sure I had his attention. "Say that I know where I believe there are mounds, but I've only heard about the spot. If I could get a map or, say, an aerial photo, would that do?"

"I'd say so. I'd have to be convinced before I'd sign the paperwork."

The smile would not stay off my face; I'd guessed right. "Would an aerial photo be enough?" I asked.

"Actually, a photo is better than a map for a number of reasons." Mark looked interested and asked. "You have a spot that you think might be a potential dig?"

"I think I do. I'll work on getting us on both places."

"Fine." Mark's persona reverted to lover. He sprouted a wicked grin along with another thing. "I like exploring."

There was no doubt in my mind I had at least a fifty-fifty chance I could convince him to sign whatever papers were needed to make a couple visits. I had my way to gain access to the Circle X.

Thirty Four

The sound of Reading's grinding coffee beans probably was my alarm clock, Thursday. The aroma of the fresh brewed coffee finished waking me. My legs swung out of bed and my feet hit the floor without effort. I stretched my arms over my head and arched my back. The tenseness and stiff feeling that plagued me the last few weeks was gone. I really felt good. A dose of medicine Mark proved to be a much needed elixir.

The thought of doing my once weekly room cleanup didn't even draw a frown. I began the chore by picking up the towels from last night's shower. By the time I finished the smelly pile of clothes was overflowing the huge plastic basket. I had three loads of wash and whatever Reading accumulated. It was my month to do laundry. We alternate tasks that way. Honestly, Reading is a great roomie. He does all of his house-work and some of mine. And he does most of the cooking, though his extra effort is partly self-preservation. I've been known to burn water.

"You up, Sis?" Reading yelled loud enough to wake me if I wasn't.

"I'm up." I went to my dresser and removed a bra, panties, and one of Reading's old shirts that fit me like a housecoat.

"Scrambled, bacon, and toast. I got some mango jam for the toast." Adding mango anything was sure to get me to the table quickly. Reading knew that.

"Any guests with us this morning that I should know about?" Reading frequently invited members of the department for breakfast.

"No. You wouldn't have to worry if you wore clothes. Not every human in the world wants to see your tits and ass."

"Just the males." I felt confident about that.

"No. There are a few women I know would." He tapped on the door before he stuck his head inside my room. "Good, you have the sty cleaned. Bring the basket out to the utility room and I'll do the laundry today."

I peered at him, tossed my head, and said, "Mango in the morning, get-out-of-laundry-free card? What do you want, Bro?"

"Do you think I want a favor, just because I volunteered to do laundry?"

I found my flip-flops, scooted my size sevens into them, and walked to the laundry basket. "Doing my laundry … no. Putting mango jam on my toast … no. Both of them together … yes, you want something." My nose was right over yesterday's underwear when I picked up the basket and carried it past Reading to the utility room.

By the time I got to the kitchen, my coffee was poured and a plate of eggs, bacon and toast were sitting at my place at the table. I sat down across from Reading who was making his breakfast disappear. He remained quiet, he never is a chatter-box, but choosing to stare at his eggs to see if they were really disappearing from his plate at the rate his fork dislodged them was making a point. Reading definitely wanted something, but I couldn't guess what.

"Okay … so I'll ask. What do you want?" I dropped my head down and tried to make eye contact, but he refused.

"Come on, Reading, I was just busting your chops … just a little. What do you want? You know I'll do it. Catch this." I blew him a kiss.

Reading looked up at me sheepishly. "Chessie, I know you would. I don't like doing this kind of thing. Look, if you don't like the idea, I'll tell old Benson to go fuck himself."

"Ohhhh. An F bomb from little brother this early in the morning? Must be big or bad or both." I smiled at him. "It's not like you're asking me to go to bed with someone."

Reading looked uncomfortable. Really uncomfortable.

I exploded, "You wouldn't. You wouldn't! Tell me that you wouldn't."

"No, Chessie, I wouldn't do that."

"Then what in the hell do you want?"

"Benson wants to have campaign events ... sorry fund raisers. He wants me to host one ... here ... and ... this is hard." Reading looked like a five-year-old that had soiled his pants.

"There's more than that. Where do I fit in?"

"He wants you to co-host this series of fund raisers, and ..." Reading looked wretched.

"Spit it out, Reading."

"He wants you to co-host them with Caralene Wills."

"Caralene? Why Caralene? Why me? That doesn't make sense. If you want to fund raise you go recruit a doctor's wife... someone like that." Why did Benson want two unlikely candidates to take leadership roles in a campaign that would be decided by just a few votes? Neither of us were president of anything, influential in any circles, nor had any friends or relatives that were. If we did, I had no idea who. In addition to that, why enlist two individuals who would feel more comfortable facing each other in a knife fight than working as bosom buddies in a political campaign?

Reading shook his head. "That's why I'm concerned about asking you. What bothers me more is I know Benson, he's smart, and I know he has some type of angle. I just have no idea what his scheme is."

"I'll say yes, but tell Benson I reserve the right to quit if there is something I can't or won't do." I motioned for Reading to pass the jam, and forced him to lock stares with me. "You owe me, Bro, how much depends on how messy this gets." After he nodded, I added, "And you let old Benson know he owes me. And that means more than dropping a future traffic ticket."

"Uh-huh." Reading returned to stuffing his mouth with scrambled eggs.

Having the Police Chief or possibly the Sheriff owe me wasn't a bad thing, particularly if my pursuit of Rooster and whoever he was partners with turned ugly. It might keep me from residing in dumpster city.

Thirty Five

"How long has it been?" Clauson Stiner leaned back in an office chair that should have been retired two decades ago.

"Probably ten years," I said.

"Probably. You'd just gotten out of the Marines, and it was before you had your problem with Bradden." Clauson sounded embarrassed about bringing up something that wasn't a highpoint in my life. It doesn't bother me anymore. Well ... not much.

"I made a mistake. If I knew I'd end up in jail over it, I'd have broken both his arms."

Clauson grinned. "If the asshole's name wasn't Jim Bradden, they'd have given you a medal." He shook his head. "Just another time the law got it wrong. You'd think a broken arm would have taught the little shit to keep his hands to himself."

"What can I say? To either one of the things you said."

"Your timing was off, another year and Bradden would be off to Taipei and out of reach of the law." Clauson referred to the fact Jimmy raped a woman a year after my sentence for assault. His wealthy parents sent him out of the country to escape prosecution. Clauson's eyes started at my hair and worked down to my shoes. "You *are* looking fine, Chessie."

"Thanks, you haven't changed a bit. I bet you weigh the same as when graduated."

"Five more."

I hunched my shoulders. "Eleven for me. So how is Janine?"

"Don't know. I haven't seen her in three years or so."

"Oh?" That surprised me I thought Clauson wasn't the type to spend time outside the fence. "Found someone else?"

"Not at that time. She did. Remember Harry Williamson?"

"Yes."

"I came home one night and found Janine with his dick halfway down her throat. I'm not into sharing." Clauson didn't appear to have lost anything. "Found a great lady I'm living with. We're going to get hitched if we make it for another year like this past one. It is better the second time around." He rubbed his palms together and observed, "The past is the past and isn't that a good thing? So, to what do I owe the pleasure?"

"Business, actually. I need to see if you have any aerial photos of an area open by Blue Cypress."

"Blue Cypress? The lake? There isn't much else out that way." Clauson got out of his chair, went to a drawing file and pulled out a drawer.

"I'm looking for some shots of the area where Highway 60 turns northwest. Say from the Blue Cypress Road west maybe ten miles and north of the highway the same distance."

He looked at me like I was crazy. "There's less than nothing out there. If you like examining pine and oak woods, pastures, and cypress swamps I'm sure I have lots of old, old aerials that were made by Zeke, the guy I bought this business from. Some of those are thirty years or older and I doubt anything has changed in most areas." He pushed the file door closed and leaned against the cabinet. "Can you tell me what you're looking for?"

"Sure. I'm studying archeology and I'm looking for possible sites to explore. Someplace where nothing much has been disturbed is exactly what *I am* looking for."

"I heard something about you going to East Florida and becoming some kind of scientist." My ex-boyfriend sounded as though he was having trouble with that. He patted the file cabinet with his hand. "Most everything I shoot now is for development and the bulk of that is close to the coast. I say there's no change out there, but I can't swear that's true. I rarely get anyplace close to Blue Cypress." He pulled open the drawer then closed it again. "You have some time?"

"Time I got."

"Let me find Linda. She's getting office supplies. I'll get her back here and then we'll take a little ride. Flying doesn't bother, you does it?" Clauson pointed to a Cessna 170 sitting on the tarmac fifty yards from his office.

"Hell, no. I love it." I'm sure I sounded like a prom queen at her coronation.

"Let me load up a couple cameras. We'll take her up and make some photos. I might be able to sell some shots in the future."

* * *

"I've never been up in a plane like this," I said.

"A first, huh?" Clauson was methodically reviewing a check list he held in front of him.

"Yes."

"You'll love it."

"I know I will. I'm excited. Should I be scared?" I asked.

"No. I do this all the time." Clauson put the laminated list in an alcove at his side. He laughed, "You worried about the list? That preflight check list is what makes sure you'll be able to fly another day. Safety first."

He finished taxiing his Cessna onto the runway, gunned the engine, and within a few seconds the plane was headed toward non-existent clouds. The feeling was exhilarating and I couldn't help shouting, "Look out you eagles, I have wings!"

Clauson maneuvered the aircraft so smoothly and effortlessly I felt like a bird riding the air currents. He said, "We're practically over 60. I have to stay out of the airports traffic pattern, but I'll get over the highway and follow the road out to Blue Cypress. Think you can direct me if I get you there? Things do look different from up here."

"That won't be a problem."

"Okay. I'll take us over the I-95, Florida 60 interchange and head west. When you see what you want to take a look at, tell me where you want to go." He circled the plane over the Atlantic then inland over the southern portions of Vero Beach.

It only took a few minutes to translate what I spent most of my life looking at on the ground to the "map view" passing under the plane. Off to my right I could see the 17th Street Bridge and farther north the Barber Bridge spanning the Indian River. I knew our duplex was somewhere fading behind us to the northeast.

The houses, streets, buildings, baseball fields, football stadiums all looked like features on a child's model train layout. I recognized intersections, the airport as we past it, Mullet Creek to the south, and ahead of us the traffic on I-95 and the Florida Turnpike sped on the roads like supercharged ants. Clauson flew the plane to I-95 and we paralleled the interstate until we reached the Florida 60 interchange. We made a graceful turn to our left. It changed the shadow we cast onto the newish four lanes that headed toward 60's destination in Tampa. Far on the horizons, I could see such features as Lake Kissimmee, Lake Okeechobee, and metro Orlando. Much closer, I knew the large lake I saw was Blue Cypress. It was shaped just as you'd see it on a road map. We were approaching it quickly.

I asked, "How fast are we going and how high are we?"

"We're running at 100 knots, that's about 110 miles per hour. As far as altitude, I have us at," he looked at his altimeter, "3200 feet."

"That's Blue Cypress isn't it?" I pointed to the lake we were nearing.

"Yes." Clauson adjusted something that I didn't understand. He saw the curiosity in my face. "I have a remote camera I'm getting ready. You would like some photos if we see something that interests you, right?"

"I certainly would. How close can we get to the ground?"

"VFR rules say 500 feet, but you don't need to be anywhere near that low to get the features you're looking for. The optics on my cameras will take care of that. I'll end up dropping down to 2000 when we start snapping." He made a circle dropping altitude as the plane did a three-sixty. "Where do you want to start looking?"

"Let's start at the road that goes back to Blue Cypress. The area I'm most interested in is west of the power lines. They run north. Someone told my professor that there are mounds and old Indian villages on those properties. I need to have something to take to whoever gets permits to get on private lands to hunt for artifacts. My prof will take care of doing that."

"So what you're telling me is we're looking for a little needle in a big haystack. Okay, what I plan to do is fly back and forth on parallel tracks and cover that area. You said roughly ten miles by ten miles?"

"Yes," I answered, feeling guilty that I was asking a lot and not planning to pay.

"If this is okay, here's what I'm going to do. I'll get up to where I can get photos that are a square mile and snap them so when we get done you have the area carpeted. You pay for my film and the processing. I'll donate my skills and flying time in memory of our ... let's just call it history. Tell me when and where to start."

I looked at the terrain flitting beneath the Cessna. I found the intersection of the power line road and 60. "Let's start where the power lines cross 60 and work our way north. Let's only cover by say six miles. That's thirty-six square miles. It should cover the area I want."

"No problem." Clauson positioned the Cessna on a line parallel to Highway 60. As we approached the power line road, I followed the transmission wires path. The gate to the Circle X Ranch was clearly visible. The ranch road meandered across a quarter mile of improved pasture until it played hide and seek in oaks and pines. I followed it as well as I could.

The land below was covered by patches of dense woods, some oak and pine, some cypress. Open areas with scattered pines dotting several acres of palmetto flats were interspersed. To our right, north, large blocks of improved pastures replaced the raw land we were flying over. I found where the ranch road exited the woods and headed through a pasture. When I started to trace the ranch road to its terminus, Clauson said, "Chessie, keep your eyes in the area in front of us and what we're passing over. If you see something, yell out. I'll get a GPS reading and come back to take more detail shots."

I redirected my focus. The camera snapped shots every few seconds as I concentrated on the land under us. Creeks snaked their way through the dense areas of cypress, small sections of their waters visible in areas where the flow widened enough elude the cypress canopy. Cattle grazed in both improved pastures and on rough palmetto encrusted land.

"Coming around," Clauson said. He circled and approached to make another pass over the property. The ground we were covering was identical to that we'd just flown over. Until my friend yelled, "Damn, would you look at that. Look over to your left, Chessie. There's a fish farm. Look at those cattle pens and loading ramps. Wow, look at that landing strip further north. It's surfaced! There's a couple of small hangers and I think ... yes ... that craft you see is one serious airplane, a Beechcraft Baron. That's a twin and one hell of a bunch more aircraft than this grasshopper." He remained quiet as he stared hard at something. He whistled. "Damn, that's a huge compound. If you weren't doing what we are now you might not notice it. See how it's painted. Earth tones and in irregular shapes. It's camo. That thing is big. And it's built like a prison. No windows ... the building is half the size of a football field. Look at the fencing around it. Ten feet at least. And there's razor wire on top."

My jaw dropped. I was shocked by what was on the ground beneath me. I followed the road back to where it emerged from the woods. Another much more formidable gate kept anyone who got past the gate on the power line road from going up to the complex. After the gate, the road progressed to an office complex that was built only yards from the prison like building to its rear. I swiveled my head around. The whole complex was entirely shrouded by thick woods. No one would have any idea that the installation even existed. A wind sock flew over one of several smaller outbuildings scattered about. Fences were everywhere, some circling and recircling the buildings, others penned large numbers of cattle, and some the several acres of ponds that Clauson said was a fish farm.

He asked, "Want me to turn off the camera? This won't do you any good. I thought I saw something that might be middens on our next go round. We can—"

"Just keep taking pictures. We might miss something up close if we don't. I'll sort through them later."

"No problem." He duplicated his turn and aimed the aircraft back on a parallel path in the opposite direction. I could see the pull-off I'd used to ambush Rooster. The creek that flowed under the power line road meandered through a large swamp that came close to the complex. I estimated that the buildings were a mile-and-a-half from the road where I'd parked and triple that distance from any other access point. It looked more like a military installation than a ranch.

"There! See those mounds past that cypress swamp? There's a good chance that is what you're looking for." He altered his course slightly. "I'll get you some good shots of those." Clauson made a few lazy circles over a large number of mounds that certainly could have been Indian made. He asked, "What do you think?"

"Let's take one more parallel pass as we go and that should do it."

Clauson lined the Cessna up for the last pass. As he cruised over the complex, snapping photos, I marveled at the size and intimidating construction. It did look like a prison or a highly secured industrial site. As we flew close, I saw a half dozen cars and pickup trucks parked by the office. Near the razor wire topped fence, around the major building, was a white van. It was Rooster's or one identical to it.

Thirty Six

Thirty-two photographs sat on my kitchen table. The more I studied them, the more I was astonished by what lay before me. Whatever portion of the business I was looking at didn't involve Rooster. If it did, I couldn't see a possibility that he was any more important to it than a drop of water was in one of thirty-eight long narrow lakes that were plainly an aquaculture venture. I counted several hundred head of cattle in what I guessed to be a small portion of the ranch that we photographed. It was huge. This was a multi, multi-million dollar operation. Unless Rooster was a magnificent actor, one who could play the part of a witless, obscene buffoon while actually being a shrewd wall-street type, Reading had pegged the operation correctly. Rooster was a pimple on the organization's ass. Was Reading correct about his supposition concerning drugs? It appeared so.

Besides being impressed, I was also depressed. Trying to get back to the complex seemed an impossible task. Deer fence I'd seen when I rode past the gate days ago, circled the property. The trapezoidal tract of land was immense, its narrowest dimension being over six miles. Swamps and forest surrounded the complex which made hiding any approach possible ... and access to get there a nightmare. There was an inner fence surrounding all the buildings that looked as formidable as the one at the ranch's borders. A guard shack was stationed at the only entrance gate and though the picture didn't disclose anyone manning it, why would a shack be constructed if it wasn't used? Armed guard protection was a surety—dogs a probability. The only reasonable entry point was the creek that flowed under the twin bridges next to the pull-off where I'd waited to follow the white van. Snake and gator-filled waters of the creek crept back to a place that came within 150 yards of the inner fence … if my guess was correct. There were another forty yards between the razor wire barrier and building itself.

The one hope I had was the pictures Clauson had taken of the mounds, probably two plus miles from the buildings. These certainly had the potential to be legitimate sites. I'd have to show Mark. It would be easier than even thinking about sneaking onto the property.

Now what? It was too soon to fill Reading in on what I'd found. He still had eleven days left on his suspension. I didn't see how this broke the intent of my promise, but by the letter, I had. It would probably take time for Mark to get approvals and paperwork to get on the property. The eleven days would be up long before Mark was successful, or as I presumed, was turned down. I decided to set up another meeting with Mark at East Florida. It had its side benefits even if Mark didn't see the potential in the mounds in the photos Clauson had taken.

My cell's jingle sounded and Reading's number shown on my LED screen.

"You rang?" I asked doing a poor imitation of the Adams Family's butler Lurch's greeting at the door.

"You busy now?" Reading's voice was way too formal. He wouldn't have responded to me in that way if something wasn't up.

"Aaaaaaaa … So what's wrong?"

"Nothing. Benson has invited us to eat with him. Can you make it? He wants to talk to you and Caralene about the campaign."

"Are you on the—"

"I'm not. I am with Benson, Caralene and Lisa. We'll all be together."

"You want me to be available, Reading." I asked, hoping for no … knowing it would be …

"Yes."

Thirty Seven

Robatowski's was a great place to meet to discuss Benson McGill's attempt to become Sheriff of Indian River County. The restaurant couldn't decide what it wanted to be and that thread was the one it held in common with Benson. Robatowski's offered Irish, Russian, and American cuisine. The menu was confusing because the featured items, Fettucine Alfredo, Chicken Parmesan, and Mussels Marinara, didn't fit the advertised ethnic billings. McGill was a parallel as a public official. A member of Vero's old guard, he was more at home at a bluegrass festival than at the social events held by the current members of the city's elite.

Like most of Florida, the town had changed drastically in the years after World War II and its long term residents found themselves an endangered species. Yankees inundated the state when it was 'discovered' by the millions that spent time during their military training in the warm-in-winter, sunshine state. They came back for that warmth, the fishing, the beaches, the slower pace and the natives found themselves becoming a minority of increasingly less importance. This is what created Benson's dilemma.

Benson McGill is a born politician. I'm sure he wet an index finger and raised it from his crib to see which way the wind was blowing. Possessor of a silver tongue, Reading says the man could sell Eskimo women bikinis in the dead of winter and an over-priced lifetime supply of condoms to their eighty year old husbands. Having progressed into his fifties, McGill's hair had enough gray interspersed to provide him a distinguished look. Patrician features reflected his intelligence and his ambition.

If Benson had his druthers he'd have been happy to see Vero Beach stay just the way his grandfather described the sleepy town as it was in 1945. Below his thin veneer, he was a Confederate flag-waving, red-necked Cracker without the prejudices that sometimes accompanies the type. Given a choice, Benson would have functioned as the stereotypical good-old-boy police chief. The police chief is appointed, not elected. He straddled fences between new and old and was selected for the office.

Being a political animal and very pragmatic, Benson McGill counted heads and realized that the power base in Indian River County had overwhelmingly shifted to its new inhabitants. He adopted their likes, dislikes, dropped his heavy southern accent, and swayed toward their point of view when possible. His popularity increased. The county sheriff was from the same good-old-boy mold, but he remained in office by maintaining a hard-core native Floridian base that never missed a vote. Benson saw the opportunity to move up a notch on the political scale and decided the time had come to bump Arlen Threep from office.

Reading had told me to join the group in Robatowski's back room. When I entered I was surprised by the large number of people seated at a long table. I recognized half or more of the faces. Two of the faces I knew were ones that I wished weren't there. Caralene's poker mask hid what I'm sure she felt. Mine didn't when we exchanged glances. The other face shocked me and made my skin crawl. Ted Prince. He was one of the wealthiest, politically powerful, handsome, slimy, creeps who lived in Indian River County. He was also one of the reasons I'd quickly left exotic dancing … stripping … as a way to make a living. The grin on his face was sickening. It was the same expression that the neighbor's male pit bull had when he chased every canine female that was in heat … with just a skoosh less slobber. I suspected at least one reason I'd been selected. I just hoped Reading wasn't aware, or could take the physical beating I intended to inflict. Two doctors' wives were there, Lisa Lister, a black Baptist minister, four police officers from the department and their wives, the leading real estate developer, and three lawyers. There were two men and two women I didn't recognize. After I shot Reading the *I'm going to kill you* look, and he returned a *What did I do now* expression, I sat down.

Benson smiled, "Sorry for the late notice, Chessie. It wasn't Reading's fault." Benson is quick at picking up those little human expressions that betray our emotions. He did a quick round of introductions. After Benson finished, it was clear why everybody seated at the table was there except for three of us, Caralene, Lister, and me. Everyone seated represented a block of voters – blacks, Hispanics, the society page leaders, blue collar reps, and the community's small business leaders. In addition, McGill was exhibiting his embracing of diversity: one of the police officers there was black, two of Cuban decent. A second thought reduced the mystery attendees to two. Why Caralene was matched with me was solved, she would be a "bright black light" highlighting Benson's very real commitment to the minority community. Pandering was in full force.

The meeting's participants associations answered everything except why Lisa and I were sitting at the table. I had the theory I had when I walked into the room and saw Ted Prince … that I was to be his entertainment, a *quid pro quo* for his financial and vocal support for Benson's candidacy. It was still a theory because I had no proof. My greatest question was why Lisa Lister was in the room. The remaining mystery, why Lisa and I were there, was sure to be solved by the evening's end.

When Benson's stated his reason for inviting Lisa it was to, "Consult with her on matters that affect the media. She's here strictly off the record. Her being here is our little secret and I must warn you that Lisa has informed me I'll receive no preferential treatment and certainly no open support. She has agreed to remain neutral and not divulge anything she learns as an insider."

What bull shit! Lisa was an aggressive reporter whose first allegiance was to her profession. If Lisa learned something that was "big news" she'd abandon the ship quicker than the crew and passengers on a sinking freighter that was two-thirds under. I knew that and I knew that Benson did. She was there for another purpose, but what was it? And, was I there as Ted Prince's potential playmate, a position (or positions) I *would not* accept, something else I was sure Benson knew, or was I there for a reason I couldn't foresee?

* * *

The meeting broke up. Reading, Lisa and I were discussing where to go for drinks when Chief McGill strode up to us. He smiled at all, said "Thank you all for coming," with what I perceived as false warmth, and reached out and to shake my hand. I responded grudgingly and had the unfulfilled desire to protect my crotch with my other hand.

"Chessie, glad that you could come and join the campaign!" I'd seen Benson's smile in documentaries featuring crocodiles. He looked at Lisa and Reading, the grin still in place. "May I borrow Chessie for a few moments ... alone? I promise I shan't be long." He didn't give them a choice.

He steered me to table in a private corner, asked one of the lawyers to act as a barrier so we could have a private discussion, and waited until he was sure we wouldn't be interrupted. I opened our conversation, "Shan't ... Benson ... shan't? Where did that come from? We're speaking one redneck to another. Shan't?"

I thought I might make him mad and he'd 'fire' me. Instead, Benson laughed. "Chessie, that's one of the things I love about you ... what you see is what you get." The smile faded to one that was barely perceivable. "I can level when I talk to you. You sure don't like Prince, do you? I don't blame you. I always look for a slime trail when he crawls off. It entered my mind that knowing Ted's fondness ... for sex ... and you ... you might get the misconception that I want you here for some kind of evil purpose." He leaned forward, "Believe me, I don't. The only thing I'd say is, don't be nasty to him even if the bastard deserves it. Do what you have to do to be civil, that's it ... regarding Ted. He's here because he is very influential within a group whose support I need. Or, at least, I need their money. He's also a buddy of the man that Reading fingered while getting the blow job and I'm hoping being exposed to Reading and you will get him to calm down that guy when I reinstate Reading." He paused and looked serious. "Let's talk about why I need your help. Let's talk a bit about what I might be able to do for you. We're adults, let's talk like them."

I'd heard many similar pitches in the back seats of cars. "Adults, okay. As adults in regard to what?"

"My winning this election." Benson leaned forward. "I have a good chance to win this thing. One of my lawyer friends is experienced in political races. He said I'm in good shape, but it will be close ...unless I can do two things. If I can do one of the two it should be an easy win. One of them is getting most of the women's vote, the second is some kind of big news event that makes me look good and old Threep not so good."

"Fine. How do I fit in? There are quite a few Vero ladies, well, let's just say they aren't impressed by me. And, let me give you some advice. You're not stupid, so don't underestimate Lisa Lister. If you're counting on her blowing up something you bring her, it won't happen."

"Oh, I know you're right about Lisa. She'll bring it to me ... but that's my problem. You happen to be my access to someone who can give me an opportunity to convince many of the women in this county to vote for me. Mrs. Weiss is president of the Indian River Association of Women. She's a strong leader and the women in the community love her. That group consists of a dozen women's clubs, lady's civic groups, and social sororities. Gloria Weiss is in love with archeology. That's all she talks about. My lawyer friend says that he has an idea of how to get to speak to all them and make Mrs. Weiss my biggest booster."

"Sorry, Chief. I don't know Gloria Weiss and I'm not an archeological expert."

Benson nodded. "True. But you have a friend that is. Reading has been talking about how you are volunteering on digs and that you have become friends with Dr. Mark."

"Dr. Card." The turn in the discussion caught me by complete surprise.

"Dr. Card, that's right. Seems Gloria Weiss knows all about him. See, if you can ask Dr. Card if he would make a few speaking engagements *with me*, I can get Mrs. Weiss to raise some money for his research, I get a chance to speak to the ladies, get Gloria's undying gratitude, and a lot of votes I wouldn't have gotten otherwise. Makes everybody happy." Before I could speak he raised his finger to his lips. "And here are a couple of things I can do for you. When I'm Sheriff, I can go through a review of your assault conviction, reopen it, talk to the right people ... and sponge away that felony ... reduce it to a misdemeanor, possibly get rid of it completely. After all, it was Threep who pushed to pursue the charges against you. He should have ignored those, and would have if it had been anyone but the Bradden boy. You should never have even been brought in. Tell me you wouldn't like to see Threep's nose rubbed a bit, Hmm? Let him bathe in the mud?"

I didn't like the idea of being bought, but the price was good. I stared at him, unwilling to commit. Revenge was something I hadn't considered. Remembering the humiliation suddenly made it important.

"You haven't said no," Benson said.

"I'll talk to Dr. Card about it." I suddenly thought of killing a second bird. "Benson what kind of story are you looking for from Lisa?"

"Something to make me look good; better than old Threep."

"Something like ..." I pretended I was thinking something up. "Say ... say catching a killer or uncovering a drug ring or a robbery gang?"

"Exactly like that." McGill smiled. "If Lisa gets wind of that." He whistled. "I'm in. You know something?"

"No. Well, not exactly. Can you let Reading work on something if I hear the right rumor? Informally, before he is reinstated? There's not a whole lot of time between now and election-day. Isn't he how you lined up Lister?"

"I cannot tell you I'll do that. If it got out that I had him back on the job early it could cause complications. Course, if he did things on his own so I had plausible deniability … and if I managed to get credit … I wouldn't object."

"I think we understand each other, Benson. This may be both our lucky day."

Things were looking up. Except the part where I told Reading and he would tell me to go to hell.

Thirty Eight

You probably aren't going to like this, no, that wasn't going to work. If I started the conversation with Reading that way, I'd never make it past his retort, *If you knew I wouldn't like it, why did you do it?*

I'd had two-and-a-half hours to come up with a way to convince Reading to do something I knew he wouldn't want any part of and didn't have much to gain. He could have a lot to lose. There were numerous approaches I considered. To the present, the only reaction I envisioned was ... "NO!" ... "HELL NO!" ... "NO FUCKING WAY" ... this to be followed by lectures on staying out of his business, not knowing what I was doing, how much danger I was in, plus many more I wasn't smart enough to think of and he would.

I wondered how much more time I had. It would take them thirty minutes to get to Lisa's apartment from Robatowski's, twenty minutes for session one, ten minutes between, thirty for session two, twenty minutes for drinks and some rest, fifteen for the final, and twenty to get home. He should be walking through the door. I sighed. Things would just have to happen as they happened. Worrying any more wouldn't solve a thing. I decided to see what email messages came in during the day.

"You have mail." My lap top always sounded enthused and happy about that. Usually, after I finished surveying the trash the net dumped in my mail box, I felt like it should sound discouraged and pissed. There was more dribble in my mail box than droplets on a barroom's toilet or bathroom floor.

Opening the mail disclosed over twenty new messages. I always sort through them, dealing with those that are garbage or ones I want to ignore by sending them to the trash bin. That usually gets rid of two thirds and I start on the ones worth opening. Tonight, I froze at one entry. It was from *Mary.Perez.2012@fasttrac.net.* I never expected an answer.

I opened the message and read.

> Hi Chessie,
> Thanks for returning my things to my mother's. I'll get her to send them to me. Say hi to Hootie and Reading for me, love them both. We are moving all over Oregon's back woods so it will work better to email your questions. No phone reception in the boonies.
> Thanks, Mary.

She was alive! I couldn't believe it. I was so sure she was one of Rooster's victims I never expected to see what I had on my computer. I mumbled, "Isn't that the shits."

"I don't know, is it?" Reading had snuck up behind me.

His hand leaned on my shoulder as I spun around in my chair. I punched at him somewhere, lightly, and scolded, "Don't do that, you always scare the crap out of me."

"Hey, you scare me just being around." Reading looked tired but relaxed. He generally did after leaving Lisa. "What's so shocking in your email it has you heading for the porcelain?"

"You know I was going to take the stuff Hootie gave me to Mary Perez's mother. When I did, I got Mary's email and phone number from her. Honestly, I didn't think I'd hear back from her. I got this." I pointed to my lap top's screen.

Reading read the note once and appeared to read it again. Finally he said, "Why didn't you expect to get an answer."

I frowned, "You know."

"No, tell me." Reading was going to make me wallow in my mistake.

"You can be such a turd. She's alive, okay. I didn't think she was. Feel good now?" I looked at my screen and started to delete it.

"Don't do that, Chessie." Reading was either teasing me in a way I'd not seen or was seriously contemplating something I'd missed. "Let me read the whole thing, including your note to her."

I stopped, and moved away so he could have access to the keyboard. He read my message and her answer several times before he answered, "You don't know that."

"Know what?" I asked.

"That she's alive." Reading moved away from my computer. "Look at it again."

"I don't need to," he frowned, so I added, "but I will." When I finished I had no idea what he had discovered that I hadn't. "Sorry. This tells me I need to email her if I want to get hold of her. That's pretty much it."

"Chessie, there's nothing in the answer that whoever wrote it couldn't get from reading your note. All you can say right now is that someone is answering Mary Perez's emails. Don't you think it's suspicious that she doesn't want to have any phone communications? You can easily fake an email response. It's one hell of a lot harder to fake a voice."

None of that had occurred to me. "So how can I find out?"

Reading hesitated then said, "You can use the ruse that the Navy code breakers used at Pearl Harbor. Put something in your response that's false and see if you get it back."

"Like what."

He thought for a few seconds. "Ask her if she remembers her date with me. If she does, it isn't her. We never had a date."

"Clever. I'll send it back right now."

"Good. Then will you tell me what happened at your cabinet meeting with the chief?"

I looked as tired as I could and lied. "Can we postpone this? I'm beat. Benson wanted to talk about me being friends with Doctor Mark Card and setting up some campaign events with Doc speaking to draw crowds. There are a few other things, but, really, nothing we need to speak about tonight. Take my word for it."

"You work tomorrow?"

"Yes, but I promise we'll talk tomorrow night."

He nodded and was happy. If I got an answer from Mary … or whoever … it would tell me what my next steps should be and if I had any leverage with Reading.

Thirty Nine

There were two good reasons for me to send an email to Mark. One was to get him started on getting approval for us to gain access to the Circle X Ranch. The other was for a replay of the bedspring tests we performed on my last visit. A third objective was getting Mark to give a few speeches and appear behind the same podium as Benson McGill. Knowing the constant need for cash the archeology department experienced and Mark's love of performing for an audience, I didn't see any challenge there.

I wrote the note asking for a chance to visit with him on the up-coming Monday or Tuesday. If Mark was able to expedite our getting on the property, I figured it would take two or three weeks at best to get the bureaucratic wheels turning. That would give me some time to nose around the court house and carefully trail Rooster a time or two more. My time away from dealing with the bait man directly, had decreased my respect and therefore my fear of the barbarian. I didn't see a great risk … he hadn't a clue I was following before.

I would also get an answer from Maybe Mary, the name I'd christened the person who responded to the emails I'd addressed to Mary Perez. Reading's ruse would tell us a lot. I believed it would confirm that Mary wasn't the person replying to us and my beliefs about the evil nature of the bait man.

Three days working on Hootie's boat would seem like an eternity. The good thing would be only eight days remained on Reading's suspension after the weekend. With the seasonal slowdown, I wasn't sure whether Hootie had ordered bait or not. I hoped he hadn't. Avoiding any meeting with that pile of slime scrapped from the bottom of humanity's cesspool made me happy.

One factor that would complicate and slow the weekend clock to an excruciating crawl was an unexpected quick response from Maybe Mary. Confirming Reading's theory that it could be someone other than Mary Perez returning our emails changed the urgency, at least in my mind. I saw any delay in bringing Rooster to justice as a potential death sentence for some unfortunate.

Forty

Hootie was late and the bait man was coming. I sincerely hoped Hootie would show before I had to face Rooster. Having to be close to the miscreant was bad enough with Hootie present. What would he say or do without Hootie to moderate the situation? What might I do or say to the son-of- bitch if he hassled me? I'd find out soon, Rooster's truck was almost to the fish camp store.

I watched Rooster swing down from his truck cab from my vantage point inside the store's front window. Rooster surveyed the parking lot, saw my pickup, and saw that Hootie's Jeep wasn't there. A smile formed on Rooster's face. More correctly, his expression was a leer. The lights in the store told him I was there. I didn't want to get caught inside by Rooster so I raced for the door and went outside, meeting him on the porch stairs.

"Store on fire, Chessie baby?" Rooster asked.

"No." I looked up the road for Hootie. There was no sign of him. I was on my own.

"What's wrong, sugar pants? Nobody here, but you and me. That bother you? You scared?"

"Scared of what? You? A middle-aged pile of manure? A loser? I don't think so."

We stared at each other, anger boiling up in me ... contempt and disdain emanating from him. His body blocked the stairs. I moved to one side and tried to pass him. Rooster shifted so he stood directly in my way. I tried to pass him on the other side. He moved so quickly I couldn't get around him. I shouted at him, "Get out of my way!"

"I don't think so." A strange expression appeared on Rooster's face.

"Get the hell out of my way, you piece of shit." I tried to shove my way past him. He laughed. I doubled my fist and tried to drive a forearm shiver into Rooster's bulk. I bounced off him like a rubber ball. There was no railing so I floated down to the ground with a thud, nose first.

Before I could roll over, Rooster pinned me to the ground. His massive hands drove my shoulders into the sand and his legs and body smothered me from the waist down. The stench from his body and the chum blocks caused me to gag.

He said in a low voice, "If you aren't afraid of me, you should be." I was as helpless as a newborn puppy. Rooster stated what I already knew. "I can do anything I want to you and you can't do anything about it. You think you're smart crossing me? Don't do that one too many times. If you do, I'll fix your ass so a person can drive a tractor trailer up it." He shoved me in the middle of the back as he climbed off. "Next time you *assault* me, remember what I said."

I got up, furious and scared. I'd done something extraordinarily stupid. *Never give an opponent the satisfaction of tears* my father drilled into me. I just had. I was the aggressor in a situation where I could ill afford that luxury.

Forty One

I seethed as we cast the mooring lines off of the boat. When Hootie arrived on the scene, Rooster auditioned for an Academy Award. He was courteous and a gentleman in every way. I had to suffer through Rooster's patronizing garbage, bowing and scrapping to me as though I'd just become the queen of England, while Hootie nodded his approvals. It was a struggle to treat Rooster civilly after our run in and one at which I failed. It made me look like a vindictive bitch. Were Rooster's actions a valid threat? I chose to treat them as such.

Willie Mitchell's girlfriend wrecked his car and Hootie had to pay for filling the diesel tank, putting both of them in a foul mood. When I tried to open my cell phone I found it was completely discharged. It took a full day of charging old Samsung in Hootie's store to find out the only people trying to contact me were people trying to sell me something.

I neglected to store a couple of chum boxes which began to smell before I jettisoned them over the side. This earned me a reprimand from Hootie and I responded with … more tears. My reaction made me madder. The day wasn't working out. I became short-tempered with my customers and cost myself tips.

Hootie left me to clean the boat by myself. It was his way of telling me I'd been a horse's ass, for he normally helped enough to cut my time by a third. Willie didn't even wish me good night when he left. I was feeling sorry for myself and felt sorrier when Mark answered my note. He postponed our meeting to Thursday, something that wouldn't normally affect me at all, but with all that had happened on this day, I took the delay as a personal rejection.

Reading didn't respond to my efforts to contact him. It was the final straw. I summarized my day's problems and placed them squarely on Rooster's smelly ass. There had to be some way I could ruin his day, too.

At ten PM, I thought it came.

Forty Two

Even my favorite TV programs were working against me. Reruns of *Bones* were ones that were from the earliest produced. I have trouble with Temperance's character in the first few productions. Cold is one thing, no pulse is another. I tried watching *Blue Bloods* and Tom Selleck's part was so small I lost interest. The *Law and Order* airing was Wolf at his worst. The remote's power button and my bed were looking increasingly inviting. My finger stretched toward *off* when my computer's mail box creaking sound-effect for my told me I had mail.

Scrambling out of bed, I tripped on a pair of my dirty shorts and came close to connecting my eye to the table my computer rested on. I clicked on my mail box, and the sender's address displayed: *Mary.Perez.2012@fasttrac.net*. I couldn't wait to open it.

The email read:

> Hi, Chessie,
> Tell Reading I remember our date quite fondly. I hope everything is going well for him.
> Mary.

I didn't need Reading's help interpreting the answer. Besides answering a question in a way that was clearly false, the wording was something a fifty-year-old-man would construct, not a twenty-something female. Quite fondly? Everything is going well? Not feminine, no curiosity, and definitely not worded by a person under thirty. I was almost gleeful ... Rooster had screwed up ... big time.

Now, how could I snare him? What was a suitable way to arrest him? SWAT teams armed with K-9 units, mini-cannons, and flame-throwers seemed appropriate. I couldn't devise a scenario that I believed was a terrible enough way to capture him. I wanted to be able to watch Rooster ripped to shreds ... the more blood-thirsty my hallucinations became, the more inadequate the punishment seemed. Rooster had become more heinous than Hitler and Stalin merged into a single personage in my warped judgement.

Reading's unwanted voice insistently demanding rationality wouldn't silence. It became louder and more demanding. It asked if my zeal to inflict pain and suffering on my hated enemy was worth the risk of allowing him to slip through punishment's web. That argument left me unable to fall prey to my more ridiculous fantasies, but the depth of my emotions kept me from abandoning them completely. Grudgingly, I began thinking of some way to get Rooster to incriminate himself ... without including Reading in my plans. My euphoria eroded. The more I thought, the more I realized what I'd learned hadn't told me near as much as I'd assumed. All that I'd really learned was that Mary Perez wasn't answering her emails. In fact, the more I thought about the way the emails were answered, the more I doubted Rooster had anything to do with responding to them. "Quite fondly" and "everything is going well" weren't the wording I'd expect to come from the bait man's brain. Reading's reading of the situation had to be correct. Rooster *was* a feather on the bird. However, that feather was one I wanted to pluck ... now! There was still over a week to wait before Reading was officially able to help. And would he? Probably yes, he'd help, but to what degree? So what, I told myself. As long as I didn't do anything to step on Benson's toes, and put Reading in a bad spot with the Chief ... Damn the torpedoes ... full speed ahead.

I needed to find out what organization spawned an evil as severe as the bait man. There were two whole days for me to plan for that. Two dreadfully long, excruciatingly long, never-ending days to plan, to connive ... to make mistakes.

Forty Three

After two days of some of the poorest fishing Hootie claimed he'd ever experienced, my patience had reached its end. I spent my time during the days listening to Hootie's customers complain about every topic that the imagination touches. How bad the fishing was, how bad a guide Hootie was, how bad a mate Willie was, (I'm sure I was the subject of the same people's gripes when I wasn't around.), how bad the bait smelled, how bad the evening news had become, how much the taste of a Big Mac changed, and the one thing everyone agreed on … politicians from the president down were fertilizer.

After racing home and avoiding Reading and his questions, I spent my time researching. The county property records were a reasonable place to start. Finding what I wanted in them seemed straight forward enough. There were plenty of "how to do its" available. The instructions were understandable and straight-forward. I tried a couple of sample runs and found out everything worked *unless* the property's owners didn't want anyone to know who its owners were. I had zero success, but I thought I would have better luck if I actually went into the court house, got some knowledgeable help, and could follow the chain.

I tried. The clerks were eager to help, but they couldn't invent information that wasn't there. It didn't take long to determine the only thing I was having success following was my tail. By 10:30 in the morning I was thoroughly discouraged.

Identifying the property from the maps and getting the legal description wasn't a challenge. Getting meaningful information past that point certainly was. The Circle X

Ranch was owed by an LLC named Special Medical Solutions which was in turn the property of Poof and was "an affiliated business, owned and operated within the corporate scope of another company, Overseas Enterprises, Inc." I didn't remember Reading mentioning anything about Poof or Overseas Enterprises when he talked about what Caralene had discovered. When I tried to find information through the Florida business records I came to a dead end. All references to Poof were referred to Overseas Enterprises, and those records were concealed behind the veil provided by a company registered in the Grand Cayman Islands. All attempts to get past the layers of curtains obscuring just about anything regarding that company were far over my pay-grade.

I elected to see if there was anything that might help me in other data bases, such as occupational licenses, regarding HM Bait Company. There wasn't. Its products and services were listed as "bait." All addresses were PO Boxes. Its owners were listed as a wholly owned subsidiary of Circle X Ranch Properties. The data was so general it was of no use. I'd circled the track again.

I decided to see if I could get information on Special Medical Services. Addresses were PO Boxes, corporate listing of phone numbers and emails were Cayman based. The terse legal description was: "Provider of special projects and products at the request and specification of its customers." That could be anything. Signatures, if any were required, were always the same, "J. Smith." One of the clerks assured me that proof of identification such as a passport or driver's license was required to sign the documents. That was less than helpful. Smith was a very small needle in a very large haystack.

Every road I tried to follow ended in a dead end, one with a tall concrete reinforced wall across it terminus. The only thing I learned that Reading hadn't told me in our previous conversation was the name of two more companies that were somehow wires in the iron web the master-minds behind the Circle X Ranch and HM Bait companies created.

I glared at the computer monitor I was sitting behind and mumbled, "Shit."

"Frustrating, isn't it?" I recognized the voice. It belonged to Caralene Wills.

I turned and starred at her. My mouth hung open like an empty jar. A surprised one.

Caralene looked at me with smug superiority smeared over her face. "Whoever constructed that jigsaw puzzle knew what they were doing."

"Yes, they did." I felt like I did when I was a kid caught stealing change from Mom's purse for the ice cream man.

"Did you and Reading talk about what I found out when I chased down the bait company and the man that was bothering you?" Caralene wasn't as sarcastic as I expected, which was the way I always envisioned her.

"Yes."

"You find anything else out?" Caralene appeared to be extending an olive branch … her tone was neutral, even a little friendly.

I refrained from snapping at her and making the face I would have normally greeted anything she said to me. "Nothing much. I found that there are two more companies involved I hadn't heard of before."

"Poof and Overseas Enterprises. I came across them, but I didn't have time to research them before Chief McGill caught me. I'd say some big time, big money law firm came up with the corporate chain. It will take time and money to pierce what you see they've constructed." Caralene pulled a chair up and folded her long lean ebony body into it. She was attractive, smart, and was my nemesis on the athletic fields we shared in high school. We didn't like each other then ... or since. I viewed her suspiciously. Did she want something?

"Is there a way to find out who owns all those businesses?" I asked.

It was Caralene's turn to look suspicious. "Yes. A damned hard and probably expensive one, but why? Reading said you were interested in finding out if the bait man had a record and is dangerous because he was threatening you. Charlie Cocker, right?"

I looked at her wondering how much I should tell her. Would she blab to the Chief and get Reading in trouble? She liked Reading but ... I decided to feel her out a little. "That's the way it started."

"So what changed?"

I hesitated. Why lie when the truth would serve better? "I can tell you, but you know the situation Reading is in. I can't see him hurt."

Caralene remained silent for a few seconds. She made her decision and spoke. "That's the reason I'm discussing this with you now. When McGill hired me, Reading was the only man in the department that tried to help me. I got a hell of a lot more support from him than I did from the brothers in the department. A few times he covered my mistakes. I won't let anything hurt Reading that I can help. I don't know that what you are doing will create a problem for him, but I won't allow the chance of that happening."

I stared at her, remaining silent. There was a hell of a lot more to Caralene than I ever suspected.

"Besides, I guess we're sort of in the same situation." Caralene leaned toward me. She focused on my eyes, reading my reaction to what she said. "With McGill tapping us to be in his campaign, I mean. Neither of us have a choice. With Reading being vulnerable and at a critical time in his reinstatement, you have to dance. I work for him. I can't complain about how Benson has treated me. Actually, it's been very good and very fair. I'd campaign for him *on my own*. I understand what he's doing. I just don't like being maneuvered and used because I'm black to get votes in my community."

I nodded, "I know how you feel."

"I saw Benson lead you off after the meeting. He can be ruthless and conniving." Caralene lowered her voice. "Don't let him try to make you do something you can't live with."

I was surprised. Even though I was sure it was because I was Reading's sister, she was trying to look out for me. "You mean did he ask me to screw someone for him? No. When I first found out I was being asked to serve, I guessed that was the purpose. Did he want something from me? Yes. I'm friends with a professor that is very influential with some members of the community whose support he needs. He wants me to arrange that."

Caralene leaned away. "McGill is good if you put him on a scale with the pluses and minuses. He just is a firm believer in the end justifying the means. You see what he did with us. I imagine we're in the same boat ... he needs something from us, he's willing to do something for us, but has a lever if we don't." Caralene smiled as I nodded. "Chessie, Benson tries to run the police operation without corruption, but he isn't above playing games to improve his position or keeping from getting cross-wise with people that could hurt him. It's like what he did with Reading."

"What did he do with Reading?" I asked. "I never could understand why Reading got suspended. It seemed severe for what he did. The things he did or didn't do … well, I thought some type warning was more in line."

"He didn't tell you everything. I know Reading keeps a lot inside his thick skull. You ought to know what really caused him to get suspended." Carlene looked around the room to be sure there were no listeners. "Reading didn't get suspended for the way he gave out traffic tickets or for not arresting the kid for trashing that guy's garage. What he did had to do with him arresting McGill's supporter and it goes further than I'm sure you know. What got him in trouble was he wouldn't play the game. You know about him collaring the man who tried to escape by running through lights and was getting a blow job when Reading caught up with him?"

"Yes."

"What you don't know is that McGill had Captain Willard pressure Reading to drop the arrest and tear up the paperwork. Reading wouldn't do it. There were drugs involved. Reading found enough marijuana in the car for felony possession. When the papers Reading filed disappeared, Reading prepared replacements. People that support McGill were plenty mad about that. They wanted everything to go away. The asshole he arrested was furious. Guess what happened next? The marijuana disappeared from the evidence room. Reading still wouldn't cave. Charges got dropped. The old boy ended up in divorce court, but not in jail. Now you know why Reading actually got suspended. The official reason was for making a charge without substantiating evidence. Officially, McGill wasn't involved until the end. Plausible deniability. Benson likes Reading so he salvaged him the best he could and still protect his career objectives."

"How do you know all that?" I asked.

"I can't tell you."

We left the records office together. I had not learned the things I'd came there to discover. The information I did get was more important. And, as Caralene and I walked through the front door, I knew I had one less enemy in Vero. Maybe I was going to gain something really valuable, a friend.

As I climbed into my F150 I decided it was time for Plan B. I would have to go back to following Rooster. Sooner or later I felt sure something that he did, someplace he went, or something he delivered would provide the information that we needed to unravel the mysterious fabric his job was woven into.

I needed transportation. Using my truck was out of the question. I had all of Monday afternoon to rent wheels to follow Rooster.

Forty Four

The sign said, Ruppert's Rent-a-Wreck. The part that appealed to me was the subtitle … Cheapest Rates on the Space Coast! The sign appeared to have weathered a hurricane or two. Ruppert definitely wasn't into increasing his overhead. The fellow who stood behind the counter was a short, balding man, fat enough to stretch the shirt he wore so tight I felt in danger of being wounded by flying buttons if he took a deep breath. That shirt was Clorox-spotted tan with the name Ruppert embroidered on the pocket. Ruppert was one of those people whose age could have been forty to sixty-five. His eyebrows were highly arched to the outside of his head and sloped down toward his nose making his face resemble a pit-viper.

His smile and cordial greeting were both forced. "Welcome to Rent-a-Wreck. We rent by the day, week or month. What type of vehicle would you like?"

"Something that will handle sand roads. A four wheel drive pick-up. Something like that." I looked at the lot where his vehicles languished.

Ruppert's eyebrows lifted and his eyes had a suspicious glint in them. "You got a pickup you drove up in. What's wrong with that?"

"Good question. The truck isn't a four wheel drive." I stalled for time while I concocted something. I decided to tell the truth … kind of. "I need to be driving a vehicle that people won't recognize."

His grin widened. "Meeting a boyfriend?"

"No, trailing someone."

Ruppert drummed his fingers on the counter. "I don't want bullet holes in what I rent you."

"I'll be shooting a camera not a gun. I'm going skunk hunting."

Enlightenment shone in Ruppert's face. "Ohhh, you're cheating husband hunting."

"You might say that." I figured that was as good as anything for him to believe.

"How long you need it for?"

"A week."

He nodded and said, "Got just the thing for you. See that gray Jeep Waggoneer? That's the kind of vehicle nobody ever takes a second look at. Four wheel drive. And notice the heavy tint on the windows? Made for your purpose."

I looked at the SUV sitting in the lot. It was non-descript and the windows were as dark as a hearse. "How much?"

"Five day week or seven?"

"Five days."

Ruppert gave me a quick size-up and pronounced. "Forty-two a day so that's $210. And that includes road service. If you break down I come and get you."

"Do I need to worry about that?" I asked.

"You're not renting a brand-spanking new Maserati." He reached under the counter, removed the keys and slapped them on the counter. "There's a hundred dollar security fee up front. If you leave your pickup parked here, I'll waive that."

The fence around *Ruppert's Rent-a-Wreck*, was high, topped with barbed wire, in good repair, and the two Dobermans and the Rottweiler in the pen near the gate looked vicious. "I'll leave my truck here. No one will drive it, right?"

Ruppert laughed. "I won't be renting your truck out. Might have to move it around the lot. Leave the keys. Check your mileage when you park it inside the fence."

I picked up the keys, said, "Bye," and started for the door.

"No bullet holes," he said jokingly.

I laughed and agreed, "No bullet holes."

Forty Five

The smell of stale cigarette smoke and Clorox grated on my nose and made the Egg McMuffin uncomfortable in my stomach. The problem—there was no escaping the smell in the Waggoneer. Mosquitos, sand flies, and deer flies filled the air outside the windows patiently waiting for them to open and serve me up as their morning entree. I'd parked the Waggoneer in the same spot on the power line road I'd previously used to wait for Rooster to leave on his morning runs. To be sure I got there before the bait man left, and to avoid Reading's questions, I arrived and parked before four o'clock. It didn't take long for heat to build in the SUV making it necessary to start the vehicle and run the air conditioning every ten minutes.

The world outside the car was more hostile than when I parked in the same spot before. Only a sliver of moon shone intermittently through the heavy cloud cover that creeped across the sky. The trees, bushes, and weeds were completely still, frozen by the lack of the slightest breath of air. Light fog I drove through on my way to the Circle X Ranch had thickened into an unseen blanket until I shined my flashlight disclosing a wall in front of me. I doubted I could see fifty feet. Fear that I wouldn't see the glow from Rooster's truck headlights struck me. I could well end up sitting all morning waiting for him after he was long gone.

I'd been parked for an hour and a half when I became aware of dull illumination in the car. There were headlights approaching from the rear. They were moving very slowly down the sand road through fog that made it hard to stay on the graded surface. I didn't expect company, and hadn't thought of how I should react if someone approached me this morning. During previous trips, I decided I'd tell anyone who stopped and asked that I was a bird watcher. The binoculars and camera setting on the seat next to me were great props. It was close enough to dawn to use that explanation.

The vehicle gradually took shape through the mist. It was a HUMV with its fog lights on, straddling the road as it neared, the driver decreasing his approaching speed with each foot he got closer to my Waggoneer. The HUMV stopped completely when its front fender was even with the rear door of my vehicle. After a few seconds, the bright beam of a spotlight flooded the inside of my car. I heard the HUMV's door open and close with a thud. I couldn't tell which thud was louder the door closing or my heart beating. The outline of a person walked next to my car and stopped at the passenger side window and tapped on it.

"Hello in there." It was a man's voice. "Are you having car trouble?"

"No, I'm fine." I decided I'd better give the man a reason for sitting in an unlighted car at 5:30 AM in a place so isolated. I cracked the window six inches and said, "I'm just waiting for the sun to rise."

"Waiting for the sun to rise?" The man bent over so his face was in the window. I turned on the interior light so I could see it. The face belonged to a man I judged to be in his fifties. He was handsome, with salt-and-pepper hair, nicely dressed, with a posture that had a distinctly military bearing. "What happens when the sun rises?" The man was more amused than concerned.

I held up my camera and returned it to the seat. "I've been told this is great place to see and get some pictures of sand hill cranes at sunrise. I'm an amateur ornithologist."

"Really?" The man smiled. "I'm sure you know this, but you're more likely to see one out in the pasture to the left. Early in the morning they'll be feeding there rather than near the creek." He waited for me to answer.

I held up the binoculars. "I didn't see a good place to park along the road. The fences are close and I was afraid I might get stuck in the ditch on the one side. When I see them come out," I waggled the binoculars, "I'll sneak down toward them."

"Makes sense. Be very careful if you get out of your car. This area has a large population of Cottonmouths and Rattlesnakes." He peered in the car. "I can't see what type shoes you have on. I don't suppose you have a pair of snake boots do you?"

"At home, not here. I'm a Cracker so I'm aware of snakes. I'm careful to stay away from weeds and bushes in striking distance of my legs."

He nodded. The man was friendly, but also very observant. His eyes systematically scanned everything inside the Waggoneer and that included me. "You should be okay, but I'd stay in your car until it's light enough to see things on the ground clearly." He started back toward his HUMV.

"Do you think the people would mind me easing through the fence to get a better shot?" I called after him.

He silently returned to the window and examined me more carefully. "Fences are put up to keep people out as well as to keep animals in. Out in those open fields you'd be vulnerable to a different type of shot. Not much defilade except palmetto. I wouldn't trespass."

His response using a decidedly military term for cover chilled me, goose pimples rising on my arms. "I noticed the fence on the one side is really high. Is that deer fence?" I asked, hoping to get more information.

The man looked at me for several seconds before answering. "Not deer. Part of that property is a sanctuary for exotic big cats, specifically, tigers. If you trespassed in there, I might be remembering you fondly." He smiled at the shock that registered on my face. "You think you'll be back tomorrow?"

"No. I'll either get the photos I want today, or if the birds aren't here, I'll look someplace else."

He seemed to like my answer. "Good luck. I hope you get some beautiful pictures of Grus Canadensis." The man hesitated then asked, "You are?"

"Ch—" I quickly changed what I was about to say. "Charlene. You are?"

"A friendly farmer." He smiled as he walked away.

As his HUMV passed I flashed my light on its side. A circle with an X inside was stenciled on the door. Dawn was easing over the horizon as I watched the HUMV cross the bridges remaining barely visible as it proceeded to the gate for the Circle X Ranch. The headlights illuminated the fog as the HUMV turned into the drive, stopped while the gate was opened and the vehicle passed through. I watched until the lights disappeared into the thick forest.

The spot I was parked in was no longer tenable. I started up my car and was ready to pull onto the road when I saw headlights emerge from the woods on the ranch drive. Through the mists I saw the white blotch and outline of Rooster's truck. After he closed and cleared the gate, he headed for Route 60. I followed with my lights off and hoped the mysterious man hadn't talked to Rooster. Yes, I sincerely hoped that. I stopped at the Circle X gate and waited for Rooster to make his turn at the highway. I could catch him without his seeing me. Or, at least, that's what I believed.

The truck's headlights turned east toward Vero and I eased along the sand road with my headlights remaining off. I prayed I hadn't aroused enough suspicion in the man that he phoned Rooster to mention me. When I reached the road, I turned my headlights on, and raced down Route 60 to catch Rooster. The box truck's familiar rear end appeared in the early morning light and my headlights when we got halfway to the I-95 Interchange. I was committed to following the bait man, I just wasn't sure I should.

Forty Six

The white box truck traveled north on I-95 until the Palm Bay exit. Tuesday morning traffic made trailing the bait man difficult. I had to scramble to keep up with him even running two red lights to stay in visual contact. Rooster was in a hurry this morning. His normal cautious driving habits altered to driving over the speed limit and aggressively darting through traffic. Either he was trying to meet a time deadline … or, he was aware someone was following him … me.

When Rooster turned into the emergency entrance driveway for East Coast Central Major Surgery Clinic, I briefly thought it might be for another reason; maybe someone was injured or sick. The truck raced up the drive and jolted to a stop outside the buildings glass front. As I guided the Waggoneer to the visitors' parking lot, Rooster's familiar form leaped down from the cab and raced … to the box truck's rear door. He rolled the doors open, pulled out a two-wheeled freight cart, and carefully removed one of the special looking containers I'd seen him handle at the Palm Beach airport freight-company. He positioned the container on the cart as though it contained eggs then pushed it through the sliding glass doors as fast as he could walk. Rooster was in the immaculate white uniform I'd seen him wear once before. What was in the container that created the need for such urgency?

I sat patiently in the parking lot thinking he would emerge quickly. He did not. Time ticked by slowly, decelerating as it became longer. It was an hour and ten minutes before Rooster reemerged from the hospital. His demeanor had changed. The cart he'd rushed inside now had four containers piled on the small carry platform.

Rooster's sauntering gait was completely opposite to his frantic pace on his arrival. He piled the containers and freight cart in the back of the truck, closed the door and then did something that frightened me. Instead of immediately getting into his truck's cab, he walked toward the parking lot a few steps. Rooster then carefully scanned the whole parking area looking for something ... me. I was sure the "friendly farmer" had a discussion with my nemesis. It was then I wished I could kick myself in the ass. The thought of at least trying to write down the license plate number on the HUMV should have crossed my mind. I blew it.

Rooster methodically focused on each car before going to the next. I was glad I had parked a couple of rows back and in the middle of a pack of cars. Usually, I'd have found an isolated spot that would be easy to leave quickly. I scooted down in the seat so it appeared no one was in my vehicle. I stayed below the dashboard level for several minutes.

When I raised my head and looked out my windshield, Rooster's truck was in motion rolling toward the clinic's exit onto the road. It was simply too dangerous to try to follow him while he was fully alert. I decided to sit and watch him. Common sense told me it was best to abandon following him for the rest of the day. The stubbornness in me said, "You have your money invested in renting the Waggoneer. Catch up with him later in the day." The stubborn me won over the logical me. I decided I'd wait in hiding by the interchange to I-95 where he'd exited. I might get lucky enough to pick him up there. By sitting in the parking lot for ten minutes after he left, I felt I'd minimize the chance of an encounter before I was ready. I watched Rooster exit the lot.

He turned left on the highway toward Melbourne. I assumed he was going somewhere for another delivery and that told me I had plenty of time. I decided to get out of the car and stretch my legs. The box truck turned right at the first intersection and disappeared from sight. Watching the traffic gave me something to do. Anyone trying to merge onto the heavily traveled road in the morning traffic faced a battle worth watching. Then I recognized the front of Rooster's truck pull up on a side street across from the parking lot. A chill went through me. There was only one reason for Rooster to have taken the route he had down quiet side streets, to see if someone was following him.

* * *

The realization was sobering. No doubt remained that Rooster suspected someone was trailing him. But had he learned enough to figure out who that someone was? I stood in the lot wondering if the "friendly farmer" had provided Rooster with enough of a description to identify me. I cursed myself for turning on the interior lights in the Waggoneer. It let me see what the man looked like and it also gave him the opportunity to see me clearly and in detail. I had to assume Rooster knew it was me. That meant he knew to look for the Waggoneer. A return trip to *Ruppert's Rent-a-Wreck* was on my afternoon agenda, swapping my rental was a necessity. Following Rooster any more that day was not.

My mind rebelled at wasting the day. What could I do? There were two places I could go and ask questions. I could visit the homeless shelter in Melbourne and the farm supply store and see if I could gather any information. Rooster was a regular visitor based on his interaction with those I'd observed on the times I trailed him in the past. Finding a believable reason for these folks to talk to me would be a challenge. I decided it was worth the effort.

St. John's Helping Hand House certainly wasn't in the high-rent district. It took a couple tries for me to locate it … my memory and reality, were a couple of streets apart. As I parked the Waggoneer in front of the shelter, I concocted a method of getting some information about Rooster from the people who ran the place. Lisa Lister had a series on "Community Angels"—I decided to masquerade as one of her producers.

A skinny man wearing filthy clothes, three days' of beard stubble, and smutches of dirt adorning his face stood in the doorway. He was in his twenties and leered at me without any attempt to cloak his thoughts. He blocked the door and forced me to say, "Would you please move." He sneered and moved out of my way. When I opened the door and passed him, he asked, "Givin' any free samples, cunt?"

I ignored him and looked for someone to talk to. Standing behind a counter was the elderly lady I'd seen embrace Rooster on a previous trip. She smiled as I approached. "What will you let the Lord do for you today?" she asked. It immediately made me feel guilty. The first thing I was going to do was lie to her.

"Get some information." At least my first three words were true.

"Information? About *St. John's Helping Hand House* or the folks who run it?" The woman's smile broadened. "I'll be happy to help you if you'll be so kind as to tell me why you're interested."

"Sure," the lie started, "I'm a freelance producer for the Vero at Sunrise Show. You know, the one which stars Lisa Lister."

"*OH*, I love that show and I love her!" She looked at me warmly. "What did you say your name is?"

I borrowed the name of one of the show's producers. "Sandra Seally. You are?"

"Lulubelle Jones. Everyone calls me Aunt Lulu."

"Well, Aunt Lulu, may I borrow a pad and a pencil? I'd like to see if we have a story here. Have you seen Lisa's series on community angels?" I smiled and hoped I didn't look like a crocodile looking for lunch.

Aunt Lulu scurried to her counter, found a legal pad and a pencil, and returned. "Here you are, dearie." She handed me the pad. "I thought that feature had ended," she said.

"I'm looking for stories for a second series. This new one will have a slightly different focus. Along with featuring places like *St. John's Helping Hand House* it will feature individuals who help your organization, contribute things like clothes. Angels to the angels so to speak."

"I have just the persons for your story: Tony Rossario, Charlie Cocker, and Edward … Well, I can't give you his last name because he doesn't want people to know how generous he is to us."

"We certainly don't want to expose anybody who doesn't want publicity. Let's forget Edward What's-his-face and concentrate on the first two. Let me get this written down." I began scribbling notes. "Tell me a little about both of them. What does each do for the shelter?"

"Tony owns four fast food restaurants. All the food that is fixed and left over he donates to us. It provides us with 70% of the food for our guests. And, he will hire some of our residents if we know them well enough to vouch for them."

"That's interesting, but tell me about the Charlie guy," I said.

"Oh, Mr. Cocker! What a wonderful man. He is our most reliable angel, if you'd like to call him that." Lulu's smile threatened to reach each ear. "He donates clothes several times a month, takes time to talk to each of our residents, particularly new ones. He actually takes them to doctors to be sure they're in good health, he arranges for them to get work, and he will help them with transportation to get anywhere in the country. Mr. Cocker makes sure they have some clothes for their start-over. He even buys them a new suitcase. He pays for it out of his own pocket and he's not a rich man!" She looked skyward. "He's a truck driver. Well, I say he's not rich, but that's not true. What he does makes him spiritually rich."

I listened incredulously. That didn't sound like the man I knew ... at all. "Charlie Cocker? Is that his full name?" I asked.

Her answer verified what I wanted to know. "Yes, but he likes to be called by his nick name, Rooster."

"Let's focus on him. What else do you know about him? Address? History? Anything? I promise anything you tell me won't be repeated to anyone except Lisa. Oh, I'd like your word you won't discuss what we're talking about with anyone, including Mr. Cocker, until I call you and tell you we're going to proceed with the program. I think you can see the problems."

Aunt Lulu's face became very serious, "I promise. I understand."

"Good. What can you tell me about him?"

As Lulu thought about my question, she became vexed and this showed in her expression. "I don't know that much about him, really. Let's see ... He was in the military for a long time. I know he was in Kosovo during all that trouble that happened there. He speaks about it from time to time. I'm not sure, but I think he might have been homeless for a while."

I asked, "Why do you think that?"

"His personal hygiene is lacking to the extreme at times. That's something we see here."

I nodded and said, "What else do you know?"

"I know the company he works for has an arrangement where he is on call seven days a week. I guess he makes good money because of that. If one of our people has a health problem that costs money, sometimes a fairly large amount, he has helped many times by pulling cash out of his pocket. He's done this for the two-and-a-half years I've volunteered here. One thing he does, is take an interest in newbies. He gets to know about them, to know about their families, he even gets their clothing sizes and buys things just for them. He doesn't care if they are male or female, black or white, young or old. He is a good man."

"If I decide I want to contact him, do you have an email or phone number?" I asked.

"No." Lulu looked dejected then a light shone in her eyes. "Let me check something." She went back to the counter and fumbled through some items in a drawer. Lulu smiled as she pulled out a slip of paper. She copied something on another piece of paper and hurried back to me. "I have his home address. I sent something to him he forgot. He lives in a little town named Fellsmere near Vero Beach." Lulu extended it to me then withdrew it while she asked, "You won't tell Mr. Cocker I gave this to you. He is a very private man. Tell him you got it from one of the people he befriended, okay?"

"Absolutely, and you promise not to tell him you ever talked to me, right?"

She smiled, said, "Absolutely," and handed the paper to me.

"Thank you, Aunt Lulu." I turned to leave.

"Don't pay any attention to the vile man outside, he might say something to you disgusting," Lulu said.

"He already has."

Lulu shook her head. "He's an example. Charley is even charitable to a reprehensible person like that. That man is waiting for Charley to pick him up. Mr. Cocker is taking him to the doctor's."

A shot of electricity hit me. I threw my watch toward my face and mumbled, "My, look at the time. I'm late for a meeting. See you." I ran outside and was thankful there was no white box truck in sight.

* * *

I expected my trip to the farm supply store to provide me practically nothing. Just the opposite happened. I'd been concerned about establishing rapport with the clerks and servicemen, however, that proved to be easy. I'd loosened the top three buttons on my blouse. No one even asked my name. All were male and happy to take a few minutes away from loading trucks and shuffling inventory. They referred me to a man named Hugo. I told him I wanted to find out about starting a fish farm, and if he had any customers who had an operation and would share information with me.

He grinned, "What kind of fish? Tropical or food?"

"Food."

"Got three of them. How big of an operation you planning? What are you raising? Catfish or Tilapia?"

"Tilapia for sure. Maybe cats if everything goes well. I'm looking at building twenty to thirty ponds." His eyes widened at my words.

"That's a big farm. Have you looked into getting permits for that? It ain't gonna be easy." Hugo looked impressed. He took his eyes off my boobs for a long enough time to see if I was serious.

"Can you help me with a name?" I asked.

"Lady, we got a customer that fits that description damned near exactly, but that won't help you one bit. Those people that run the place are real bastards. They won't even let us deliver to them. We thought we'd do them a favor and send our truck out to their place with a back-order. They have a guard on one of the gates. Scared our driver shitless. The guard was a military looking type and fired a warning shot as Felix drove up to the gate."

I opened my eyes wide and pretended to be shocked. "Really?"

"The guard told Felix to turn the damned truck around and not to come back for no reason 'tal. Our man was so flustered he couldn't maneuver the truck around in the space he had. The guard threatened to shoot him. Felix said some guy dressed like an officer showed up in a HUMV and allowed him to drive through the gate into a pasture and turn around. Felix got out of there and told our boss he'll quit before he goes back there."

"Where is the farm? Know any names?"

Hugo looked at me like I was crazy. "Out on Florida 60, past Blue Cypress Lake. It's named the Circle X Ranch. It's off Power Line Road. I don't know if there's a sign, but you'll see the cables. As far as names go, I know the driver who picks up the stuff they buy from us. His name is Rooster something-or-other. He isn't the type you invite to a Sunday school social. Only thing you'd get from him would be an indecent proposal." Hugo looked into the warehouse we stood in. He yelled at a man working fifty feet away. "Hey, Felix, what did you say that they called the boss man out at Circle X?"

Felix was a short, stocky Hispanic fellow who said, "I no go out there, Hugo. No way."

"Wouldn't do that to you, buddy. This lady wants to contact those people." Hugo waved his hand toward me.

Felix looked disgusted and said, "You no want to go there."

Hugo looked at me and I said, "I'd still like a name."

"Remember the name?" Hugo repeated.

"*Llama es* … I mean … his name is Harlan. The guard, he call the man colonel, too."

I asked, "Is Harlan a first or last name?"

Felix answered, "*No se.*"

Hugo counseled, "Look lady, you don't want anything to do with them. I've heard there's a government experiment goin' on out there. Mess with them … you'll likely end up gator food."

"Thanks, Hugo," I said and walked toward the dock.

"You goin' out there?" Hugo asked.

"Probably," I answered.

"*Vista, alli es un chica loco!*" Felix said loud enough for all in the warehouse to hear. I listened to the men laughing as I stepped down the dock stairs.

Forty Seven

I didn't have a chance to even say hello to Ruppert. He greeted me with, "Miss Partin, I know you want to swap vehicles. I have a different one ready to go for you."

I'm sure my jaw dropped before I asked, "How did you know?"

He laughed. "You'll never make it as a spy. I got a call from your dude asking about the Waggoneer. If it was my property. Who rented it from me? Those kind of things." Ruppert saw my alarm, so he reassured me, saying, "Don't worry I didn't give him your name. I told him Barbara Streisand was slumming down here. He didn't think it was as funny as I did." He tapped his fingers on the desk and shook his head. "Didn't take very long to catch on to you. Your man called before 9:00 AM. If you're thinking about being in the private eye business you probably should keep your day job. Your husband sounded like a nice guy, but I have to ask: any bullet holes?"

"No bullet holes. How did he trace the car to you so fast?"

"That is not a problem. If he has any friends in law enforcement, that's a 'while you wait' phone call." Ruppert grinned, "It was a good thing you realized you'd been spotted. I assume you want a different vehicle. You don't strike me as the type of woman who gives up." The expression on his face finished his thought, *even when you should.*

I nodded, knowing he was right. I couldn't give up.

"I've got a Jeep CJ-5. Its painted olive drab. You can park her in the bushes and blend right in. She's an oldie, but goldie. One thing, can you drive a stick?" Ruppert looked at me like he expected a *yes*. He already had the keys in his hand.

"No problem."

He grinned, tossed the keys to me, and motioned for me to throw the Waggoneer keys to him. I did. Ruppert said, "The plastic windows are pretty weathered on that rag top. You can see out well enough to drive, but it will be damned hard to recognize you except by looking in through the windshield. I'll let you have it at the same rate, but remember ..." He waited for me to complete his sentence.

"No bullet holes." I smiled at him. "Thanks, Ruppert."

He laughed and yelled, "Be more careful when you follow. I'm running out of the type cars you want."

Forty Eight

"What is that Jeep doing in your parking place?" Reading got halfway through his spaghetti and meat balls before asking me the question I expected when he walked through our duplex's door. I'd been lucky the night before with the Waggoneer … he never saw it because he'd spent the night at Lisa's.

I was ready with an answer. "I'm checking some possible archeological sites for Dr. Card. I don't want to mess up my truck."

Reading nodded as he twirled his fork in the spaghetti. "Where's your truck?"

"I left it at the rental agency. It's safe there."

Reading looked at me with his truth verification stare. He laid his fork on the side of his plate after loading his mouth with pasta. "You on the college staff now? You get reimbursed for renting that thing?"

"I hope I will, but I don't know. *Little Brother*, it's less expensive to rent that Jeep than to pay for a paint job for my 150 or pay to fix something that gets tore up underneath it. I am sure of that."

He considered my words for a moment then said, "That makes good sense, Chessie."

"Thanks, Reading," I said sarcastically.

"Of course, that wouldn't be the case if part of your looking for sites was out trespassing on the Circle X Ranch property."

"I promise part of my plan isn't to crash through a fence out there to go snooping. I don't want any bullet holes in the Jeep or me."

Reading nodded without any show of humor. "You might want to check voice mail. I believe I heard a call come in for you from Mark Card when I stopped by to eat lunch."

* * *

The voice mail was what I wanted to hear. Mark said he would be happy to look at the aerial photographs I had of the Circle X and said there was another delay in beginning work on the Okeechobee site. Since there was no hint of when the FDLE would remove the crime scene classification, Mark said it would be something he could try to expedite. Mark asked for a time and date for us to get together. I answered, the coming Monday. In between, I had Wednesday and Thursday left on my rental to try to learn more about Rooster, "the friendly farmer," and their pals by shadowing them. Since they were aware someone was watching, it would be fool-hardy to continue trailing Rooster or watching the ranch for an extended period of time. Sooner or later I'd end up in a serious jam, maybe in one of Rooster's bait blocks.

I felt I'd learned quite a bit during the day and I wanted to be sure when it came time to share it with Reading I wouldn't forget something important. Since I didn't know what would become worth investigating, it meant I had to document everything.

I started with Rooster's rushed trip to the hospital and his complete change in urgency after he'd made his delivery. Writing that I was sure Rooster's detour proved he knew someone was following him, irked me. Admitting why he knew he was being followed was even more difficult. I documented the sequence where the friendly farmer had caught me and warned Rooster of my presence. Stupid! I detailed my visit to the homeless shelter, particularly what I learned about Rooster's actions and that I had a home address for him in Fellsmere. Then I wrote about my visit to the farm supply store. The armed nature of the effort to keep people away. The rumor the ranch was some type of clandestine military installation. The fear that the truck driver had of the ranch.

I decided I needed to write about my getting the aerial photographs and the large sophisticated compound they disclosed. I noted the answer I'd received from whoever was faking responses from Mary Perez. When finished, I had good reminder notes ... and I'd preserved the information for Reading if something happened to me. That thought made me shiver.

Forty Nine

Parking on the power line road or in an isolated location on Route 60 was a no-no. I knew that even though I'd changed vehicles, a warned Rooster and his cohort would be wary of anything out of the usual. I believed I had an answer. An abandoned gas station/convenience store at one of the county road intersections on Route 60 served as a public parking lot. Truck drivers driving big rigs rested there. People carpooling parked there. One Jeep CJ5, a commonly driven vehicle for the area, parked among the other cars wouldn't draw a second glance. The disadvantage was I would only be in a position to see and follow the bait man if he drove east on the highway.

By 4:30 I was sitting in the parking lot among a number of people waiting for their carpool rides. Light rain made seeing the white box truck more difficult, but it also made it less likely that Rooster would pay any attention to the roadside.

The drizzle continued. Light traffic on Route 60 meant I could see well enough to be sure that Rooster's white box truck hadn't passed me. Time rolled by. Cars accumulated in the lot as car pools assembled and departed. Dawn arrived. Six AM and no Rooster. I began thinking how I would use the day if Rooster didn't pass me by 7:30, the latest time I thought he would be on the road to make deliveries. I decided I'd visit the medical facility and find out what Rooster might have delivered there. I could also visit the address I had that was supposedly Rooster's home. The last of the car pools left. My watch's green LED said 6:40. When I returned my gaze to the highway, the silhouette of a box truck began to appear in the haze and light rain. Using the binoculars to get a closer look, I strained my eyes until I could see that the truck color was light blue not white. Swiveling the binoculars, I looked to see if the bait man's box truck was coming down the road. My eyes widened. Coming through the rain was a gray HUMV. I focused the glasses on the HUMV's door. It finally got close enough for me to see the circle with an "X" in it stenciled on the door. My hands were on the ignition keys before I'd consciously made the decision to follow it.

* * *

My first order of business was to get close enough to see and then record the HUMV's license numbers. Though the traffic was light, the HUMV moved at a fast clip, eighty or faster. I had to push the Jeep to ninety to catch up. Even running at that speed, I didn't get close enough to read the plate numbers until we were four miles from the I-95 Interchange.

"Florida license plate number, XSR 176," I said as I simultaneously scribbled those numbers on a slip of paper resting on my steering wheel post. Not wanting to create any suspicion, I dropped back slightly after securing the information. Blue lights flashed behind me and I heaved a sigh of relief as the highway patrolman zoomed past. The universal reaction when a police car appears, for traffic to slow to the speed limit, slowed the HUMV making it easier for me to follow.

I hadn't been able to tell anything about the person driving the HUMV other than it was a male. Rain lessened, then disappeared completely right after I followed under the I-95 overpass. The "friendly farmer," if it was him, was driving the HUMV into downtown Vero Beach. I kept waiting for the HUMV to make a number of sudden turns and become difficult to follow, but the driver continued through town, taking the simplest route to get to the 17th Street Bridge. We crossed the Indian River and drove to the beach turning south on Ocean Drive. Though I kept a car or two between us, I kept watching for some sign that the HUMV driver realized he was being tailed. I saw none.

Four miles down the beach road, the HUMV's left turn signal flashed and the vehicle turned into a circular driveway leading to a palatial beach front home in one of the area's truly exclusive neighborhoods. I drove down the road and made a U-turn. By the time I approached the building's front where the HUMV stopped, a man was climbing into the passenger side of the car. The name on top of the mail box in front of the house read, "Dr. James Orella." I pulled into a driveway several lots down. The HUMV immediately returned to Ocean Drive, turned right behind some very slow moving traffic, and passed in front of me. The "friendly farmer" sat behind the wheel. The man next to him was gray headed and looked to be in his fifties.

As I stared at them, a voice came from outside my door. "Can I help you?" A woman in a sun-suit smiled at me. She had a garden rake in her hands. I hadn't noticed her when I slipped into the drive. I unzipped the window so I could talk to her. She relaxed when she saw I was a woman. I thought I was going to lose the HUMV so I decided to try to get some information about her neighbor.

I smiled and asked, "Do you know where Dr. Orella's office is located?"

"Are you looking for a GP? I know three that are taking patients." The lady was trying to be helpful.

"Dr. Orella doesn't take new patients? Someone told me he is very good." I hoped the woman would volunteer information.

"I understand he is a splendid surgeon, but he only does consulting of some type. I think he does heart surgery or brain surgery. I'm not sure what he does. I just know he doesn't have a regular practice."

"Thank you, I guess I'll stay with the doctor I have now," I said.

I eased the car back on the road. The HUMV was barely visible ahead of me and I thought sure I'd lose contact with it. I was able to see the vehicle turn left. When I made the turn I was surprised to still be able to see the HUMV. In a few minutes, I felt sure the driver was retracing his steps back to Route 60. Crossing over the 17th Street Bridge confirmed my thoughts. Within ten minutes we were passing under the I-95 overpass, headed east toward the Circle X Ranch.

The question was obvious. Were the doctor and the "friendly farmer" friends or did the surgeon have some business at the Circle X Ranch? I stayed a quarter of a mile behind the HUMV until it turned down the power line road. I continued past the road and considered what to do next.

Fifty

"Dearie, I've lived here all my life and I never heard of that road." The waitress at the Saussie Pig Barbeque took another look at the slip of paper Aunt Lulu had given me with what I'd hoped was Rooster's home address. She saw the disappointed look on my face and quickly added. "It could be. We have lots of streets that are numbered like that. Let me ask those officers. They'll know." She pointed to four men dressed in law enforcement uniforms seated at one of the tables, munching on sandwiches and sipping coffee. She asked, "Can I borrow that address and show it to those boys? They'll probably know where it is, if anyone does."

I handed the paper to her and watched her walk to where the lawmen sat. My attempts to find Rooster's house failed. It wasn't on the map app on my phone. Trying to find the street by wandering the small agricultural town whose street grid was partially laid out on a numbered grid system proved a waste of time. I was unable to get instructions when a tried a convenience store clerk who spoke Spanish much better than English. Fellsmere wasn't a big town and I now had a better knowledge of it than I'd ever need. The Saussie Pig was my last shot at finding Rooster's house, if it existed. Within several seconds, a tall thin officer dressed in a uniform I didn't recognize accompanied the waitress back to my table.

"Arcel here knows where your address is. He'll give you directions, dearie." The waitress smiled and eased away saying, "I'll get the pot and freshen your coffee."

"Mornin', Ma'am." Arcel's speech drawled out to an extreme even for the Cracker community where *Old South* was still spoken. The patch on his arm identified him as a member of Agriculture Security – Private Law Enforcement. "You a wantin' ta go ta this here 88th Terrace address?" He smiled, exposing tobacco stained teeth with a few shreds of pulled pork wedged in them, providing evidence of his lunch order. He handed me Lulu's note with the address on it.

"Yes, sir." I smiled and did my best to look friendly.

"Hain't that hard ta find. You all just get on the road out front. That's Fellsmere Road or Florida 514. Head on west back through town. The road makes a big old curve ta the southwest by Maple Street. Keep on a goin'. You'll be out of the main part a town. Look for the street sign that says 141st Avenue. Turn left on that road. It goes off at an angle. Once you get on that, go 'bout a mile and quarter and look for a sand road with a big homemade sign sayin' Pump House Road. You can't but turn right on it. You okay to there?"

"Yes, sir."

"You drive down it 'bout another half mile. On your left you all will see a sign that says Bush hog work done here and under that you'll see 88th Terrace hand painted on the same board."

"Don't forget to tell her it's a gated community, Arcel," one of the other officers quipped. The remaining two men laughed heartily.

Arcel grinned at me. "You are in the country, ma'am. The type gate they are talkin' 'bout is made of four strands of barbed wire wrapped to a post and pulled tight across the road. You'll know you're in the right spot. It's the first road ta your left and it's the only road with a cattle gap. Good thing you got a Jeep. There's lots of loose sand on that road." Arcel made a strange face at me that was half smile and half *your crazy.* "How well you know those folks back there?"

"Not at all."

"Hmm. You might want to remember they's six houses back there and hain't none of the folks livin' there that are real friendly. They hain't what I'd call house broke."

I swallowed hard before I said, "Thank you."

The officer said, "Good luck," and returned to his pulled pork sandwich. The manner in which he wished me good luck led me to believe I'd need it.

Fifty One

Arcel's directions were excellent. I pulled the CJ5 to a halt opposite of 88th Terrace. The gate made of rusted barbed wire didn't have a Keep Out sign posted on it, but nailed to one of the posts a sign said Private Road, Guests and service groups only, Use at your own risk. Down the road were a number of homes that had been built on subdivided tracts, my guess each parcel was five acres. Herefords and Brangus cattle roamed what amounted to open range inside the fence. Some houses had small fenced areas around them to protect shrubs and small vegetable gardens from destruction by the cows. Homes were as varied as the imagination would allow. They ranged from mobile homes surrounded by junk cars on concrete blocks, rusty farm equipment, and refuse of every category to a large brick, two story structure landscaped immaculately which would have fit nicely in an upscale gated community.

I scanned the property for several minutes. No one moved about, the only evident life were the twenty-five or so cattle. All the community's mail boxes were lined up on road where my Jeep idled. Names were on all of them except the street number that corresponded to the one Lulu designated as Rooster Cocker's. It took several more minutes for me to summon the courage to get out of the Jeep, lift the loop of barbed wire that held the gate stretched across the road, and pull open the wire that kept casual drivers off the property. I carefully laid it down, ran back to the Jeep, pulled it inside and, after some internal debate, closed the gate behind me.

I drove along the sand road trying to locate Rooster's house number. To my shock it was my last guess, the large brick home. I drove past the driveway going back to Rooster's house, then made a U-turn a few hundred feet past Rooster's property. There were no vehicles or other sign of life there. The house was at least a hundred feet from the sand road. My nose was itching and my intuition told me there was something important I could learn by sneaking a peek inside. I did a quick 360 degree head swivel, turned the steering wheel, and drove the jeep up the concrete driveway.

I opened the Jeep door cautiously and made a careful scan of the neighboring homes and Rooster's house. There was more distance than two football fields to the closest neighbor. The only movement on the ground continued to be the cattle grazing. Vultures circled in the sky above me. Was that an omen, a warning to get my rear back in the Jeep? I believe in such things, but chose to ignore the harbingers of death riding wind currents overhead.

Though sure Rooster was somewhere driving his truck over a Florida highway, I couldn't be sure that there wasn't someone inside the bricks. The drive ended in a circle with a lush island of palms and shrubs in its center. A spur off the driveway led to a free standing two car garage. Its door stood open and there were no vehicles inside. Oil stains on the drive near the front door were evidence of where Rooster normally parked when home.

Stepping as cautiously as I would have in a palmetto field full of rattlesnakes, I walked to the front door. Stained glass panels flanked the ornate and massive oak door. A heavy polished brass knocker served as the doorbell. After a deep breath, I banged the knocker five loud times. A minute passed and I repeated the action. No one answered my summons. Was it safe to snoop? Apparently, no one was home. Before I decided to walk around the building and peek in windows, I did what Reading would have told me to do: ask myself, "What are the risks?"

It was then the fact the date was 2016, not 1916 hit me. Surveillance cameras! Panic ensued. I frantically searched the eves, around the doors and windows, but couldn't find any. My shoulders relaxed as the fear subsided. Why would anyone worry about people trespassing here? With all the built-in deterrents, only a fool would invade the property. That was a sobering thought. I was far enough away to see anyone coming to check me out as long as I remained vigilant. Though it was surprising to me that the security mindedness of the folks running the Circle X Ranch hadn't rubbed off on the bait man, I welcomed it. It should be safe to make a quick clockwise tour.

I walked around the corner of the building and immediately became disappointed. The windows closest to me were above the level I could look through without standing on something. Quickly, I moved toward the rear of the house. Close to the building's rear corner I found a window that would allow easy peeking. There were bars on it. I peered inside. The room contained a bed ... that was all. The sheet rock walls had been damaged in a number of spots. It was more what I'd expected to see in a place Rooster would live. I continued around the corner to the back of the house.

As I did, I almost crashed into a large cage built against the house wall. Dogs! It was empty, but the structure was impressive. The framework was heavy galvanized pipe sunk into concrete flooring. The chain link fencing disappeared into the poured cement. It was large, at least stretching back from the building by twenty feet and I guessed it to be fifteen feet wide. A roll-up shutter covered what I assumed was an entrance to the inside of the house.

Two facts struck me. One was that the entire top of the cage was covered with chain link. Rooster really wanted to keep his dogs under control. The second was there was no door or exit from the cage other than into the house. He didn't want anyone to let the dogs out. It was strange I hadn't heard them bark, and I deduced they might not be there. The cage reeked of Clorox.

Passing the cage, I approached and looked through the barred window on the rear door to the home. Inside I saw a modern kitchen with stainless steel appliances and a bright cheery yellow paint job. The two rooms I'd viewed so far were almost like two different people owned the place. Then I noticed a rumpled and shredded rug on the floor. Why was that there? I couldn't see into the far corner, but could see windows I could look through on the far wall. I continued on my circling.

The side window disclosed little, other than all the windows had bars and to confuse me further, an attractive breakfast bar was in the corner I couldn't view from the back door. Was someone living with Rooster? The décor wasn't what I visualized as something he'd select. Other than getting a better view of the ripped and ragged rug there was nothing of interest. I moved on quickly, realizing I needed to leave as soon as possible.

The next windows I came to provided a view of a great room. What I saw inside confounded me more. The room had rich looking wooden paneling on the walls, leather sofas and chairs, and featured a huge fireplace with an imposing mantel. It was what adorned every space on the wooden paneling and perched on tables around the room that fascinated me. I stared through the bars at a collection of mounted animals and big game trophies of which a museum would be proud. I recognized an onyx, Cape

Buffalo, moose, Big Horn Sheep, leopard, and lion, among many more. A twenty-foot long snake skin stretched above the mantel. Smaller taxidermized animals from the common place, such as a raccoon, to exotics, like a kangaroo, stood about like guests at a cocktail party. I was so intent I was oblivious to motion in the room until my view was suddenly blocked.

Orange, black, and white filled my vision. Big brown eyes stared into mine. Behind bars and glass, a tiger's face was a foot from mine. Its low growl and my high-pitched scream were simultaneous. I jumped back from the window and focused on the bared teeth of the huge animal. My heart beat so hard I thought my chest would explode. I wanted to run, but my feet were frozen to the ground.

"I see you've met Oscar," a voice came from behind me. My head jerked around to the sound. A tall jovial looking man stood fifteen feet away, a large smile twisting his lips. Middle aged, he had a farmer's build … hard muscled … and the Stetson he wore verified my thought. "He's a real big shock when you aren't expecting him." The only thing unfriendly about him was the high powered rifle slung over his shoulder.

I closed my eyes, my head started to swim, and my knees told me they wanted to fold. I mumbled, "Dear, God!" I felt the man's hands help support me as I fought for consciousness. It took twenty or so seconds, but my mind cleared to the point I could hear the man repeating, "Are you okay, are you okay?"

I sucked in air and said, "Yes, I'll be fine now." Concern in the man's face reduced my fear of him.

"I have to ask who you are and what you're doing here." The man sounded apologetic.

I shook my head, buying a second or two to devise a story. One came to me. "I'm an estimator for a pest control company. They sent me here. I think it must be the wrong address. They told me a shut-in elderly couple would be here."

The man chuckled and said, "Yep, you got the wrong place. The son-of-a-bitch that lives here isn't that. My wife saw you knocking on the door and told me. She thought you might go inside. I grabbed my gun and came over so you wouldn't end up as Oscar's dinner."

My tale satisfied him. I tried to look contrite and asked, "Would you please not tell the owner I was here? I don't want to get in trouble for trespassing."

He laughed, "Fat chance of me telling him a damn thing. There isn't a person in this neighborhood that talks to the guy that lives here. Most of us wouldn't piss on him if he was on fire to put it out. I know I wouldn't. Ever since he bought this property from the guy that owned it before him, he's been a problem. Shoots people's dogs that come up to his house, things like that." He grinned. "You were never here."

"Thanks."

"No problem. And, don't worry about anyone else telling him. Besides not liking the man, the bastard doesn't show up for days at a time. Sometimes, he comes long enough to feed Oscar and then he leaves. He comes and goes at strange hours, mostly in the middle of the night. My wife says he loads and unloads a bunch of stuff. She has nose trouble when it comes to other peoples' business. Everything from bags of white powder, to big white boxes, even things my wife thinks are sides of beef that he slings over his shoulder. I kind of wish Hell would open and swallow him."

"It's a shame to lose a good neighbor for a bad one. How long has he been here?" I was fishing.

"Two years. He rented from Harlan the first six months, then he bought it. That was damned disappointing. We liked the Harlan guy. Kept to himself. Made no waves, even when the cattle ate half his landscaping. He just put up electric fences in the shrubs. He was some type of retired government or military big-wig. Had money to burn. That man was kind." He shrugged his shoulders. "The man who has the place now stinks, both figuratively and actually. He enjoys killing and doesn't mind people knowing it. I think he likes intimidating them. All those trophies in the living room are his. Most of the neighbors think he is involved with cocaine or something else in the drug trade."

"What was the man's name who lived here first."

"You mean the man that built the house or the one who sold it to Charlie, the asshole that lives there now?"

"The one who owned it before the asshole."

"Harlan was his first name. I think his last name was Madden or Minstrel. I'm not good with names. I remember it started with M, that's all I can swear to." He looked at me with a *why do you want to know* expression. "You could stop at the Miller's place," the man pointed at a house close to the gate, "They were pretty friendly."

"That's all right. I don't really care." I looked in the window, the tiger's face was gone. My excuse to leave was, "I need to get going, if I want to get paid." I walked toward my Jeep. The man accompanied me to my vehicle, speaking continually about how much the neighborhood disliked the man I knew as Rooster.

Fifty Two

I pulled the CJ5 into the parking lot on Route 60 where I'd started my day. It was only two o'clock and I needed to figure out how I could put the three or four hours I had left in this day to good use. One way was to find out who the mysterious man was that drove the HUMV. If it was Harlan, I guessed that he was the central figure in the whole affair.

I remembered Ruppert's words, "That is not a problem. If he has any friends in law enforcement, that's a while-you-wait phone call." I had a new friend who might trace the HUMV's license plates. Brother Reading could do it, but would he? I decided to try Caralene first. The police station was on my quick dial list.

Irene, the receptionist, recognized my voice and said, "Chessie, your brother's not around. You want me to leave a message on his desk in case he comes in today?"

"No. I didn't call to talk to him. I want to speak to Caralene Wills."

"Caralene?" She didn't say it, but her question, *whatever for,* was in her voice.

"Yes."

"Okay. I'll try her extension."

After a couple of rings, Caralene answered. "Sergeant Wills, investigative support." There was a split-second pause before she asked, "I don't recognize your phone number, who's calling?"

"It's Chessie Partin. Have you got a few minutes?"

"Uh-huh. Just a second. Irene, get off the line. If there is anything you can know about I'll tell you later." After a couple seconds of silence, there was a faint click. Caralene said, "She's off. What do you want?" Her tone was more curious than suspicious.

"How did you know she was on the line?" I asked.

"That's just Irene. She's got the curiosity killed the cat disease. If it might be gossip, she likes to listen in. She probably thinks she'd find out something about the chief's running for sheriff. Is that what you want to talk about?"

I tried to think of an approach and couldn't. "No. Remember the other day when you helped me over at the court house? I was wondering if you could find something out for me that has to do with that?"

"Depends. What do you want to know?"

"I have a license plate number for a vehicle that belongs to the Circle X Ranch. I'd like to know who it's registered to."

There was a hesitation. "What are you doing girl?"

"I got behind a HUMV that had the Circle X markings on it while I was driving through town. I thought that would be another way to find out what we were looking for the other day."

Caralene paused again. "Okay, give me the plate numbers. It's probably registered to the Ranch, but I might have a way around that."

"It's Florida plate XSR-176."

"It will take a few minutes. You want me to call you back?" Caralene asked.

"Yes."

"Okay. It may take a while." Caralene hung up.

While I had my phone in hand I decided to call Mark Card and set up a time and place to meet him. I got his answering machine and left a message. "Mark, this is Chessie. Can we meet at your office at ten on Monday? Let me know if this is a problem. See you Monday, I hope."

After I placed my phone in my bag, my mind entered the whirlwind that had been my day. I took a deep breath and began to reflect. From my unexpected luck at being able to find a link that could identify the mysterious owner or manager of the Circle X to the terror of having a tiger snarl at me from only inches away had me unsure what might happen next.

My phone buzzed. It was Caralene. After hellos, Caralene got right to the information. "The plates were registered to the ranch, but I know a few tricks. I got into the insurance coverage that is required and who the primary driver is. Your man's name is Harlan Mengel. If you want, I'll see if I can find anything out about him."

"Yes, I'd welcome that."

We hung up and I waited for either the HUMV or the box truck. Neither passed traveling in either direction by the time I left at 6:30. I wondered how Reading endured stakeouts. I was bored to tears when I left for our duplex.

Fifty Three

Reading's pickup was in his parking place in front of our home, but a note waited for me on the kitchen table.

Chessie,
> *I'm with Lisa. She is interviewing Katie Perry at a concert in Ft. Lauderdale. See you tomorrow AM. Irene tells me you have been speaking to Caralene. What's going on? If it has to do with the election, make sure you get permission from McGill before you two do something on your own. If it has to do with Rooster <u>don't do anything</u>.*
> *Reading*

I sighed. Tomorrow I'd be up and gone before Reading forced himself out of bed, if he made it home. Lisa would be lobbying for him to spend the night with her somewhere, anywhere, and I knew that was likely *not* to be in our duplex.

There were only five days left of Reading's suspension. I didn't want to explain everything to Reading until he was legally able to help. There was no good reason to tell him, or that's what I convinced myself. Why complicate matters unnecessarily? The chief had expressed a strong interest in the results of exposing Rooster and whoever else might be involved. "There's no way I'll screw up enough to get caught," I told myself out loud hoping the sound of my voice would allay the nagging feeling I was about to enter mistake city. I believed proceeding with something was warranted.

Those thoughts forced me to think about what I would do tomorrow. I had the Jeep for one more day and it was hard for me to abandon using it. I was sure neither Rooster nor the man I now knew was Harlan Mengel had connected me to the Jeep. If I was very careful I could follow one or both if the opportunity presented itself. The outfit I'd worn the first time I'd tailed Rooster was in the utility room and I knew where Reading had a fake mustache stored; that would protect my identity from anyone, except a person who walked up to my vehicle and looked in from a few feet away. It was my last chance. I'd do it. Sitting in the parking lot on 60 reduced the probability of hooking up with one of them so I decided I would stay mobile so either way they choose to turn onto Highway 60 I would be able to see them and hook up. There were breaks in the median within a tenth of a mile on either side of the intersection with Power Line Road. I'd simply make a circuit from turn lane to turn lane until one of the vehicles appeared … or didn't. I'd worry about that if it happened.

Fifty Four

The hairy strip pasted above my lip itched. Reading's fake mustache and wig under the floppy straw hat were additions to my disguise that made me feel confident that no one would recognize me. They were uncomfortable, but I believed necessary to not screw up. It was only 5:30 in the morning and it already bugged me.

I'd filled the Jeep with gas, stopped for an Egg McMuffin, and prepared for a long morning. It was an hour later than I wanted to be driving the skinny race track like route that acted as the top of a "T" created by the Power Line Road's dead ending into Route 60. One or both of my targets might have already left. I consciously asked if I'd subconsciously been so tardy that I would miss my connection. "Good," I told myself, "If that's true, it wasn't meant to be." Traffic was light to nonexistent, so I was confident I'd be able to spot either as they drove up the Power Line Road and turned on the main highway if I hadn't missed them.

I'd made fewer than a dozen circuits when I spied headlights turn on the Power Line Road from the Circle X Ranch drive. As it neared the intersection, the running lights that alerted drivers of its presence told me the box truck would be my target for the day. I finished the circuit I was on and trailed the bait man's vehicle by a couple hundred feet. The day started uneventfully at 6:05. Or so it seemed.

The truck traveled east toward the I-95 Interchange. Rooster had returned to his normal driving habits, he kept his speed at or under the limits, his road etiquette impeccable, his turn signals busy indicating every lane change and when he reached the interchange, his intent to go south on I-95. A line of traffic formed behind me and I couldn't help thinking we looked like a mother duck with her ducklings trailing close to the rear. It would be light soon and the glare from the idiots headlights following me would disappear. That couldn't happen too soon.

I expected Rooster to exit at the road that went to the fishing docks like he had the previous trip when I'd followed him. He didn't and continued south to the Interchange for Florida Highway 70. He turned east on the road with little on its sides other than cattle pasture and dairy farms. I knew this road because it was the highway I used to go to Dr. Card's Okeechobee archeological dig. Light from the rising sun streamed through my Jeep's rear window replacing the headlights that sat on my tailgate on I-95.

Rooster continued to maintain his driving habits that made him super easy to trail. I wondered why. My guess was he drove so conservatively to keep from being stopped and eliminate the possibility of a patrolman rummaging through his truck and discovering illegal cargo. I stayed a respectful distance behind the white box truck, dropping back as much as two-tenths of mile once we passed under the Florida State Parkway and entered cow country. There were few places for him to leave the highway without my having enough time to react. I focused completely on him. We'd driven three or four miles when his brake lights came on and soon his flasher blinked on and off indicating a left turn. I increased my speed and nearly caught him as he turned south on the side street. A sign read McCarty Road, a paved, but narrow road and, with the exception of a trailer and a run-down little house near the intersection, lined with nothing: Nothing being unimproved pasture consisting of palmetto and pines with a few scrubby stands of oaks and cypress heads scattered through the table flat land. That laid behind barbed-wire fence that lined it. A horn tooted behind me. A red pickup sat on my rear bumper. He wanted to get where he wanted to go and Rooster and I limped down the road at thirty-five miles-an-hour. He could pass or wait, "Screw him," I thought.

Less than a mile further, Rooster slowed as we approached a narrow bridge over Termite Creek, hardly an inviting sounding place. The forty-foot wide stream's black waters made a sharp turn to go under the road before heading east toward the Atlantic. Jungle-like growth made the shorelines impenetrable.

Rooster crept over the bridge. He drove at fifteen miles an hour for another couple hundred feet before turning on his left turn signal again. A green street sign named the sand road he was about to turn down Twin Creeks Drive. The box truck turned as slowly and deliberately as a whale surfacing to breathe. An alarm went off inside me and I decided not to follow. As I continued forward the red truck that was following me turned and darted down the road behind Rooster's truck. A sickening feeling swept over me. Had the follower been followed? How could that be? I was sure there was no way to know what I was driving. The box truck and the red pickup stayed in my side view mirror for seconds before they disappeared as they drove into thick woods. My heart raced. After I continued for a quarter of a mile, I stopped and watched to be sure neither reemerged on the road.

Had I been discovered? If I had, the best thing for me to do was go home. My heart was still pounding. It had to be a coincidence. I sat on the road for ten minutes before I decided it was worth the risk to make the trip down Twin Creeks Drive.

Before I started, I used my cell to access Mapquest and look at the road I was about to drive. Twin Creeks Drive was a dead end. There were a number of side roads shown; most were probably access roads to ranches. All of these dead ended with one exception, a farm lane that twisted around like a tortured snake, crossed another branch of Termite Creek and ended by emptying into a highway named Eleven Mile Road. Every lobe of my brain told me looking for Rooster on that road was foolish except the retarded one that said, "Hey gutless, this is what you came to find out." Of course, that lobe won. I wouldn't risk taking chances. If I saw either truck on the road, I'd turn around and scram. My hand turned on the ignition without further thought. Logic would have ended my escapade before it started.

The Jeep rolled back to where Rooster had turned and I followed where he'd gone like birddogs following quail. On mindless instinct. The densely forested property to my left bordered the creek. On my right ranch land spread from the road alternating in improved and unimproved pasture. My head swiveled back and forth to try to catch a glimpse of the white box truck's form. I passed a couple of houses but I saw no trace of Rooster or his vehicle. Judging from the map on my cell phone screen and the curves I'd already negotiated, I was two thirds of the way to the end. My possible escape route turned off to my right, looked like a well maintained graded road, but I could see a sturdy wood gate across it fifty yards in from the road I traveled. I hope it wasn't locked if I had to use it.

Heavy woods flanked both sides of the Jeep as I approached a blind curve. After making the turn, the road suddenly entered an open area with grassy pasture on the right. On the left a large number of small fish ponds were arranged in rows. A driveway led back to a small farm house and a number of pole barns 200 yards off Twin Creeks Drive. The large weathered sign's lettering proclaimed Zelda's Tropical Fish, wholesale only. Parked by one of the barns were Rooster's truck and the red pickup. I suppressed the urge to slow and instead sped up until the road reentered dense forest and became invisible from the fish farm.

My heart raced. I hadn't seen humans standing around, but I hadn't gotten more than an extended glance at the house and pole barns that were packed with farm equipment that could hide a number of people. What next? I looked at the map. The last thing I wanted was to be caught with Rooster and his friend between me and escape. The map showed I was approaching the road's end, a place I definitely didn't want to be cornered. When I found a place wide enough, I maneuvered the Jeep the 180° I needed to head away from a potential trap. I slowed my Jeep to a crawl as I approached the point where a curve and woods obscured peoples' view of the road from the fish farm. Inching the CJ5 along I advanced to the point I could see the sign and driveway … finally the farm, house and barns. In the ten minutes since I had past the fish farm the red pickup had disappeared. No one was visible anywhere that I could see.

Having Rooster in a position to cut me off with his truck wasn't going to happen. I backed up the Jeep far enough I could get up to a reasonable speed going forward and then raced across the exposed section of road until I was out of anyone's sight from Zelda's. A set of ruts headed back into heavy forest 150 feet after my vehicle wasn't visible. I stopped, backed into the unfenced farm lane just enough that I wasn't easily seen by someone traveling the road. In seconds I positioned the Jeep as far behind clumps of palmettoes as I could. The JC5's olive drab finish worked well as camo. I swallowed hard, said a prayer, grabbed the binoculars and the cell phone, and climbed out of the Jeep to make my way through the woods so I could spy on Rooster.

Large red gum trees at the property's edge provided an excellent place to hide from eyes in the house and the barns. Rows of small ponds between me and the buildings offered an unobstructed view. Only two or three scrawny bushes hung to the side of a couple of the fifty or more tiny lakes. Rooster's truck remained parked in the same spot with no one visible and no activity. I pressed the binoculars to my face to get a closer look. The yard around the house where the box truck was parked was more dirt than grass. Rooster's freight cart leaned against the tail gate.

The Red pickup was gone, I assumed off the farm. I swung the binoculars on the pole barns which were packed with all manner of machinery, tanks and containers. Behind one of the barns I made out several shipping containers. Several pallets covered with tarps were stored in the pole barn closest to the truck.

As I sighted on the farm house, Rooster, a man wearing jeans, a tee shirt and a military fatigue hat, and a stout woman dressed in a sack dress walked out the front door. They laughed as the man vanished from sight behind the house and Rooster picked up his freight cart. Rooster and the woman strode to the pole barn nearest the truck. The woman pulled back the tarp exposing a pallet with neatly stacked white plastic packages about a foot square and three inches thick. Rooster promptly loaded as many of the "bricks" as he could on the cart, hauled them to the box trucks rear door and loaded them inside. Was this the smoking gun? I snapped eight pictures with my cell phone.

Motion at the side of the house drew my attention. The man who accompanied Rooster and the woman from the house drove a "gator" utility vehicle past the box truck and among the ponds. He seemed to be checking the small lakes, but he moved rapidly and generally in my direction. I wasn't willing to take the chance. The pictures in my cell phone were potentially the most important thing I'd learned. That was enough. I rapidly retreated to the Jeep, hopped in, retrieved the Mapquest map on my cell, tossed it and my binoculars on the seat next to me, pulled back onto Twin Creeks Drive, and drove toward Highway 70.

Exhilaration, created in equal parts from snapping photos of what I believed were drugs changing hands and from getting away without being discovered, swept over me. I checked my rear view mirror on a long stretch of straight road, as I passed the escape farm lane I'd found on Mapquest. No one was chasing me. My shoulders relaxed a second time. Another three-quarters of a mile and I'd be safe.

The color red flashed in front of me from one of the farm roads a hundred yards ahead. It was the pickup truck that had followed me when I turned off 70 and I'd seen parked in the fish farm. More alarming, the truck swerved and stopped ... angled across both lanes of the road, blocking it. Terror and panic seized me as my knuckles turned white while they choked the steering wheel. I glanced at the map on the cell phone screen on my cell phone, slammed on my brakes, and made a U-turn so sharp and fast I almost rolled the CJ5.

As I raced for my escape road, I glanced in my mirror. The red pickup was in hot pursuit. When I slowed to make my turn the truck closed the distance between us at an alarming pace. He was so close that when I turned into the ranch road the pickup zoomed past before making a panicked stop in a cloud of dust. I saw the red through the dust cloud circle around to give chase. There was no decision to make regarding the gate. I had to crash through and hope the wood wasn't reinforced in some way. Wood planking shattered and exploded as I smashed through. I checked my rear view mirror. The truck stopped at the scattered mess of splintered one by sixes.

When I looked through my windshield I realized I was headed straight for a barbed wire fence and that the farm road made a 90° left turn. I made the turn on two wheels. Crack … Whap. Someone had just shot at me. I swiveled my head away from the farm road long enough to see a man standing next to the red pickup, a rifle in his hands. My eyes returned to the road. I waited for the second bullet and an impact on my body. It never came.

Fifty Five

My lone-wolf attempts to follow Rooster were done. When I finally reached the safety of a restaurant parking lot, I discovered what the whap sound was when the man shot at me. A neat set of holes had been made in the rear plastic roll up windows when the bullet entered on one side and exited the other. I guessed the high-powered rifle was a .308. That reinforced my decision. After I quit shaking.

Little brother Reading was completely correct in his analysis. I swam in the deep end of the pool without a life vest.

The questions about what I'd do the rest of the day were answered—get my rump and the Jeep back to the rental agency, pay for the damage and rent, go home, and lock myself in until Reading showed up. Too many things were happening not to be honest with him. Fear stimulated questions without answers in my mind. Had the red pickup been sent to see if Rooster was being followed? Would the man in the red pick-up have recorded the Jeep's license number? Would they lie in wait for me, possibly at the car rental agency? I stopped thinking. There were too many possibilities.

What would Reading do, I asked? He'd expect anyone with the foresight to arrange for someone to tail the tail to make an all-out effort to discover who was following. They could try to intercept me or they could guess that the Jeep was rented at the same agency and force the information out of Ruppert. I decided I should get back as quickly as possible, but avoid back tracking on the route I made following Rooster that morning. If they deduced that I'd swapped cars at the agency, the easiest thing for them to do was lie in wait for me there. That meant simply driving up to the agency's front door wasn't smart. Parking a block or two away and carefully looking for someone staking the place out was prudent. If I didn't show up, they could convince its owner to cooperate in other ways and identify me. That was a problem I'd have to figure out later. I left the parking lot with those intents.

My cell phone's jingle sent me digging in my bag halfway back to Vero. Reading's number registered on my screen. I pulled off the road to avoid the disaster that driving in heavy traffic on US1 and talking on the phone might cause. By the time I found a place to pull off the road, the call went to voice mail. I listened and heard Reading scream, "What in hell have you done? Where are you? Get in touch with me damned quick. You've got the Feds calling McGill about you. Get home now."

The shit had hit the fan.

Fifty Six

Reading had spent the first five minutes of our conversation yelling very uncomplimentary comments at me. Most all of them were true. Any defense I would have tried to make would have been a futile sham so I elected to keep my mouth shut. I tried to look contrite and ashamed. Actually, I felt like most criminals—terribly sorry that I got caught. I couldn't muster up a bit of remorse for having tried to roast Rooster.

Keeping silent shook my brother. My usual response to an attack was to counter at least as vehemently as the initial assault. He hesitated several times, waiting for my explosion or for me to say something in defense. When he'd vented and I hadn't retaliated, he finally asked, "Damn, Chessie, do you see what your meddling has done? It's probably screwed up any chance of actually coming up with a case against Rooster. He has to know about it now. I know you don't think of things like this, but I'll probably end up getting fired. Do you give a shit?"

I took a deep breathe. "I screwed up. If I thought I'd get caught and cause all this grief, you know I wouldn't have done anything. I tried to think ahead and be sure what I did wouldn't create problems. I guess I'm not as smart as I thought. As far as your boss is concerned, let me go in with you and explain you didn't have anything to do with what I did. Reading, I wouldn't do anything to hurt you … not on purpose. Let me try to make this right."

"You'll get that opportunity. Benson told me to talk to you, find out all you did and what you know and then for us to come into his office for a talk." It was Reading's turn to sigh. "I'll get my day in court so to speak. I'm surprised he didn't just fire me right away." We both sat in silence.

Finally, Reading asked, "Have you talked to Benson about Rooster?"

I thought for a second. The time demanded complete transparency. That's something I'm not good at, but I decided to try. "Yes and no." I saw the steam reforming in Reading's boiler and quickly held my finger to my mouth to shush him. I said, "Let me explain before you start."

He nodded. Not willingly. He'd have preferred to strangle me.

"When we were at his campaign meeting at Robatowski's, he said he was looking for some kind of an event to help get publicity for him. Something to help get him elected. He hinted, but didn't say, that's why Lisa was there. That's when I asked him if I knew something that might lead to solving a murder or might be part of a big drug case, would that be the type thing he wanted? He weasel-worded his answer, but the bottom line is that's exactly what he wants. He made it clear I was on my own, but he'd like it to happen. I asked about you and he said *no* until after you are reinstated. That's why I went ahead on my own."

Reading's expression changed slightly, but it changed. "Tell me everything you know. Everything." When I got up from our kitchen table, he snapped, "Where are you going?"

"To get some hard proof. Photographs of the Circle X Ranch, the home address of Rooster, and an email I got from whoever is faking being Mary Perez. Isn't that what you always tell me we need? I took notes so I don't miss a thing. You'll know everything I know."

Reading put his hands up in front of his chest. "Sorry, that's what I say."

* * *

Reading carefully examined everything I showed him. He listened intently to everything I had to say. From tigers in windows to my photos of white packets of powder being exchanged. From stories about Rooster's kindness to indigents to the hatred his neighbors had for him. From HUMVs to mysterious medical doctors. From emails from fake senders to bullet holes. When we finished Reading took one last look at the aerial photos of the Circle X Ranch then stated his opinion, "Chessie, you are very lucky to be alive. We'll take all this when we have our meeting with Benson ... we have to meet him yet tonight."

"What about returning the Jeep to the rental company?" I asked. I wasn't looking forward to what I thought was coming.

Reading shook his head, "That'll have to wait. I'll return it for you tomorrow. Benson is paying overtime to some people to have this meeting right now. That's where we're going to be."

Fifty Seven

It was almost six when Reading and I entered Benson's office. He was business-like and I'm sure he'd practiced his facial expression at many poker games. We sat down and he asked, "Fill me in on everything. All of it. Don't leave out a thing even if we have to be here all night."

Benson listened to the details attentively. It was the longest period of time I'd ever seen him refrain from making some lengthy comment. He asked short concise questions and there were few of those. Both Reading and I expected him to be angry and to show that anger in his expressions and words. There was none. It shocked me and I could see Reading didn't know what his boss was thinking. The photos and emails caught his attention, but he was definitely listening for something ... I just couldn't tell what. I began and ended my discussion with an impassioned plea separating Reading from my actions. If the words had any impact on Benson, I couldn't tell.

When I finished, the chief remained silent for a full minute. He looked at me, shook his head slowly and said, "I never want you mad at me." Benson grinned and looked at Reading. "Is she always so dedicated to things she gets focused on?"

The chief's smile relaxed Reading. "Oh, yes. That's for good *or* for bad."

"You know, I don't care for somebody trying to do my job for me." Benson smiled as he spoke. "In the situation you find yourself, Chessie, I can understand that." The smile faded. "But the fricking phone call I got from Washington ... that frosts my ass. Those bastards stuck their nose in my business and they shouldn't have. What they did and how they did it tells me there is something or somebody they're protecting. The bitch was from the Department of Justice," Benson feigned throwing up at those words, "and she emphasized it was an informal call. That's the tip-off right there." His smile returned. "I'll take care of those folks. We'll tell them one thing and do as we please."

Benson got up from his desk and walked to his office door. He told his secretary, "Ellen, would you find Caralene and have her come in to join us? And, ask her to close the door when she gets here."

He walked to where Reading was seated and spoke directly to him, "Your sister is a good saleslady. I believe her ... and even if I didn't ... there is undoubtedly something that bears investigation here. You can suit up on Monday. I'll have your badge on my desk when you come in." Benson sat at his desk and addressed me. "You have to understand two things, Chessie. What we believe is true and what we can prove is true aren't always the same. What we want to do as law officers and what the law allows us to do isn't always the same. Jurisdiction, things like that. You can do some things that your brother and I can't. If we did them *we'd* be breaking the rules."

Benson looked up as Caralene entered the room and closed the door. "Have a seat," he said and motioned to a chair next to his desk.

"Caralene is part of our little task force that will informally investigate this business. So are you Reading. And, so are you, Chessie ... if you want to be. In fact, I'm counting on you doing some things we can't. It won't be official, at least not until we have proof so strong we can break through walls people might try putting up. That's short of doing things that could get you hurt or killed. Interested?"

"Absolutely." Reading told me later that I looked like a cat ready to pounce.

"When I told Caralene about our meeting she said she was doing some research for you. I told her to go ahead. Tell us what you learned, Caralene."

Caralene smiled at Reading and nodded to me. "This is about Harlan Mengel. I checked out something for Chessie and his name surfaced." She made a point of her next statement. "I volunteered."

Benson grinned, "No problem, Sergeant Wills, you were just following your law enforcement instincts."

Caralene couldn't restrain her eye-roll completely. She said, "Harlan Mengel, is a retired military man. The man is a West Point grad. He served in a number of capacities, most of which were involved with logistics. Many of these had to do with medical support. His primary responsibility was medicines and anesthesia supplies."

The chief said, "That means opioids."

"Yes, sir," Caralene said, nodded, and continued with what she'd discovered. "He was involved in the conflict in the Balkans in the late 1990's. His rank was colonel. He was assigned to investigate atrocities in the area. Kosovo is mentioned repeatedly. Then in 1999 he falls through the cracks. He was assigned to liaison with some kind of a CIA project. Everything is classified. Nothing shows up until 2005 when he officially retired."

She hesitated. When no one asked questions she continued. "Since he left the military, he's been the manager or owner of a number of businesses. Most of them have to do with medicine. Some agriculture ventures have been included. With the exception of the first couple, it's hard to find out much about them. He made prosthetic's and supplied special parts and components, but the information doesn't specify of what. Evidently he's very wealthy, though it appears he is good at hiding it. The man maintains close ties with Washington big wigs. Many of the law firms he deals with now were individuals he knew in the army. He doesn't have any criminal record."

Benson asked, "What do you think his involvement is?"

"I think he owns and runs all the businesses we know have something to do with the Circle X Ranch." Caralene showed no doubt. "One other thing. The man who started this whole thing, the bait man, Rooster. I think I found a possible connection. There was a list of his staff, those who served under him in Kosovo. One was a lieutenant named Charles Rocker. His description fits the man we call Rooster. A group of Kosovo militants captured him and he was branded in some manner. It didn't say where. I thought about the "R" on his head. Anyway, he escaped. He was charged with rape and was court-martialed, but wasn't found guilty. He ended being dishonorably discharged. After that, he dropped off the face of the earth."

Caralene's word's registered with me. I remembered something I learned in a forensic archeology class that had to do with that period in Albania and Kosovo, but it escaped me. I dismissed my memory for later thought.

"There's every reason for us to investigate what's going on." Benson puffed up like a toad. "Murder and drugs; those are reasons. There's a multitude of reasons we can't. Start with jurisdiction. We can't prove anything that has happened was in my area of jurisdiction. The Circle X is in the county. We don't have a body. Those photos of white packs of powder being loaded in the truck could be sugar … who knows. You seeing teeth would get a laugh from a judge, not a search warrant, even if the ranch was in my jurisdiction. What evidence we do have isn't enough for warrants. Even the Boyd boy's car, the one piece of tangible evidence we might be able to link the Perez girl to, is in Sheriff Threep's impound lot. He won't give us access. So here's what we can do. Caralene, you try to find something that will let me claim jurisdiction of what's happening out there. Anything you can find … no matter how flimsy … let me know about it. I need a reason to get my nose in this. Most of the things that would help get information on the case, whatever it maybe, the department has no jurisdiction over. That means you, Chessie. Are you willing to do the *safe* things you can? Follow-up with the homeless shelters, visit the clinics and hospitals, see if you can get any information about the bait man. If you can get onto the property with Dr. Card, do it. Whatever you do, don't even think of trespassing on the Circle X." He turned to my brother. "Reading, your first assignment is to supervise what's going on with both Caralene and your sister. Help them both." Benson looked at me. "That means being sure Chessie stays alive. If something sinister is going on out there, we're going to sniff it out, pin it to the wall, and bury the people responsible for it under the jail."

I smiled and added, "And, get you elected as our new sheriff."

Benson tilted his head to the side and said, "If that happens I won't cry over it."

Fifty Eight

The next morning I arrived fifteen minutes late for work. I was driving Reading's pickup and he would return the Jeep, pay for the bullet holes, and retrieve my truck. Being late wasn't accidental. It was planned. I hoped that Rooster would have made his delivery and left by the time I pulled into Barnes Fish Camp. I'd still have to wrestle with the bait and chum boxes, and Hootie would be pissed at me. That would be fine if it meant I avoided Rooster.

The white box truck was still in the parking lot as I drove down the drive. Hootie and Rooster stood next to it. Rooster held his clip board. If I drove slow enough he might leave before I had to park. After Hootie had signed the delivery slip and disappeared into his store, Rooster continued to stand next to his truck.

The bait man waved to me as I passed. His evil grin told me I wouldn't be able to avoid exchanging words with him. After I parked, I decided not to back off and avoid the confrontation. Hootie's presence in the fish camp store insured my safety. As boldly as I could muster, I walked within a few feet of Rooster on my way to report in to Hootie. I was determined not to speak first. I shot him a disdainful look.

The big man remained motionless as he leaned against his truck … the evil smile remained. Instead of the usual verbal barbs, he didn't utter a word. Instead his lips pursed like he was throwing a kiss. Then his lips moved, mouthing silent words. As near as I could tell they were, "You're dead."

My bravado fled and I was sure my countenance gave that away. The truck door opening sounded like a buzzer, drawing my attention to his only words "So, you're driving a truck today." If Rooster's intent was to scare me shitless, he succeeded.

Fifty Nine

My trip to East Florida Sciences University was pleasant. It was good to be driving my F150 again. Reading returned the Jeep to *Rent-a-Wreck,* pleasantly surprising me with a bill for only $125. I was disappointed when Reading didn't get to meet Ruppert. The clerk manning the office told my brother that he'd received an email to sub for him for several days.

The Atlantic remained calm all weekend making it an exceptional trip for the guests, which in turn made for especially good tips. They paid for the bullet hole expense and left me with my normal income. Three days on the water reduced my fears.

My resolve and zeal to fulfil my commitment to Chief McGill's investigation team returned. I plotted ways of maneuvering Mark into approving our trip and expediting the paperwork. It didn't prove necessary.

"You're right. This definitely is manmade and is in precisely the right location for a settlement. Notice the circle the mounds appear in. That fits my theory that one of the unique things the Ais culture did was to build mounds in a circle around their villages." Dr. Card the archeologist was speaking, not Mark my boyfriend. He had several of the aerials spread out on his desk and he shifted his excited focus back and forth. "Where are these from? I know you said close to Blue Cypress, but can you show me?" He pulled a road map out of his desk.

I traced Route 60 with my finger until I reached the Power Line Road leading to the Circle X Ranch. "There." My finger circled around the area I knew the ranch was located.

"Great! I'm positive … but I need to verify it." Mark got up and went to a file cabinet, opened it and thumbed through folders until he found what he wanted. He returned to his desk. As he sat down he said, "If this is where I think it is, our job is practically done for us."

"Why do you say that?" I asked.

"There are areas called Antiquities Protection Zones. They were set up by the state to keep archeological sites from being destroyed." Mark opened the file folder and unfolded a topographical map. He placed it over the photos. "Land owners that have property in areas where there are suspected artifacts are given the opportunity to sign a document that requires them to report and protect any finds and it gives us the right to examine areas that may be a site. They get a nice tax break."

The power transmission lines and road were shown on the map. It clearly displayed the drive leading to the ranch and a single small house, not the spread I'd seen."

"It's different," I commented.

"This map is from 1996," Mark explained.

I could barely contain my excitement. I stabbed my finger on the ranch road. "That's it. The Circle X. There's the entrance."

"Fantastic. Let me check." Mark thumbed through the filed papers. He grinned. "That's in the area and the owners are signed up. It's owned by a corporation and there's no contact information here, but that's just a phone call to Tallahassee."

"How long will it take to process the paperwork?"

"Today." Mark smiled. "I have the forms here. I fill them out." He pulled a blank form from the folder with a flourish. "And I approve it."

"How soon can we get on the property?" I asked.

"A couple days I imagine. I have to fax a copy of the form to Tallahassee, get the contact information for the person to speak to, tell them we're coming, and set up the time and day. I'll make the call to Tallahassee right away." The archeologist morphed into my boyfriend. "Anything else you'd like to do while you're here?"

"I'd like another look at your collection of orchids at your place."

Mark smiled. He didn't have an orchid collection.

Sixty

Mark bubbled with enthusiasm while I cringed with mixed feelings of apprehension and excitement. He drove his truck along Power Line Road toward the Circle X entrance. The gray HUMV waited for us. As we approached, the man who had introduced himself as the "friendly farmer" and who I believed was Harlan Mengel stood inside the gate at the padlock and twisted the key as we made the turn into the drive. The man swung the gate open and then motioned for us to enter. As Mark's truck passed through the gate, I had the strange feeling I'd reached the threshold of Hell. Our host closed the gate and locked it behind us.

It was the first time I'd had a good look at the "friendly farmer" in daylight. He was average height, muscular but trim, and I had to admit, kind of good looking. His salt and pepper hair and a mustache gave him the air of a distinguished gentleman. He had piercing brown eyes under heavy brows. There was a facial resemblance to Richard Gere, he of *Pretty Woman* fame. He walked with the confidence and posture of a man used to command.

Mark put the window down to talk. He said, "Hi. I'm Dr. Mark Card. Thanks for letting us have access to your property."

"Welcome to the Circle X Ranch, Dr. Card. I'm Harlan Mengel. I manage this operation. As Miss Beck told you when you made the arrangements for your visit, we're happy to have you here. I've arranged to be your guide and transport for as long as you require. We have a swamp buggy that will facilitate your visit to any portion of the property with the exception of the restricted areas. Some of the land is impossible to access in a normal four wheel drive like yours." Mengel spoke with the polish of an experienced lecturer.

"Restricted areas?" Mark asked.

"Yes. These are in accord with the agreement we signed. The restricted areas are minimal and I'll explain the need for this as we travel to your area of interest. If you'll follow me, please, we'll proceed to the location where the swamp buggy waits."

He smiled at me and said, "Good morning, miss," as if he'd never seen me before, but I caught the flash of recognition in his eyes before he walked back to his HUMV.

While we waited for Harlan to lead us to the swamp buggy, Mark spoke. "I know that face, I just don't know from where." He shook his head. "A professor from Cornell? Maybe? I'll ask later." Mark spoke more to himself than to me.

How could Mark know him? I remained silent as I thought about how I'd handle any questions about Mengel and our previous meeting, should the subject come up.

Mark broke the silence as he started his truck to follow the HUMV. "Get a load of these fences on either side. They're so high it's like driving in a canyon. I've never seen a deer fence that high or topped with that much barbed wire."

I paraphrased what I'd been told. "Fences aren't only to keep animals in, they keep people out."

"If that's true here, and I'm sure it is, they don't want anyone near this place." He whistled. "I guess we'll find out soon."

We traveled a well maintained sand road in far better condition than the Power Line Road. We entered the thickly forested area and heavier dust rose from the

HUMV's tires. Mark hastily raised the window while we both choked in the gray-white cloud. The HUMV moved steadily, emerging from the woods into an area of improved pasture. The inner gate the farm store driver described lay 200 yards ahead. The guard house looked like an enlarged phone booth you'd see in a museum. An air conditioner stuck out one side, but I saw no evidence of electric service. When we were close, a guard dressed in military fatigues stepped out of the miniature building and opened the massive gate, one as high as the adjacent fence. When we drove through the gate, the guard, a large man, powerfully built, with the cold eyes of a killer, waved us through.

"Damn, did you see what he was carrying?" Mark sounded excited.

I looked back quickly. The man had weapons slung over his shoulder and on his side. "You mean the guns?" I asked.

"Guns? Chessie that guy was carrying enough firepower to stop an elephant. He had a MAC 10 mini machine gun on his hip and that high power rifle might have been a .45-70!"

The HUMV pulled into the field next to the chassis of a modified truck. Six foot high wheels, seats perched where a cab used to be, and a ladder built onto the side were all typical of the custom vehicles used to drive through swamp and terrain other vehicles couldn't handle. Mark wheeled his truck next to the HUMV. As I started to open the door, a large sign printed in bold red letters caught my attention. Caution! Dangerous exotic animals may be present. Stay in your vehicle! "Mark, did you read—"

"Yes. Now we know why the guard carries an elephant gun. There might be one here."

Mengel was already standing next to the swamp buggy. As we approached the vehicle, Mengel spoke to us. "Once we get on the buggy and start traveling it will be difficult to hold a prolonged discussion. Let's get some things taken care of before we leave this area." Harlan pointed to the sign. "You noticed the warning. Good. We have some large cats on the property. They're held in a specific area and not allowed outside their compound. The fences you see are a fail-safe, just in case what has never happened ... does. We have seven tigers, two jaguars, and five lionesses. They're not house pets. We have no illusions about that."

"Is collecting animals your hobby?" Mark asked.

"No. Those cats are part of projects we do here. They're many and varied. I saw your eyebrows rise when I mentioned restricted areas. Let's deal with that." Mengel smiled and pointed down the road to the very large complex I'd seen from the air. It seemed completely out of place in the pasture near the woods that bordered one side. The main structure, twice the size of a football field, was painted in blotches and slashes of green, olive drab, tan and brown. Camouflage. A few smaller out-buildings and a house or office were satellites for the huge facility. The airstrip, hangers, a twin-engine plane, air socks, and orange balls marking tree lines lay beyond.

"The restricted areas are anything within the confines of the fence that surrounds the complex you see and the big cat containment area. If you insist, I can put the cats in cages and you could look there, though I can assure all you'll find there is cat scat." He waved his hand at the camouflaged building. "What we do here is research and we produce very special products. One of our larger customers is the government. We work with the Defense, State, and Justice Departments." He paused and smiled.

"Some things I can tell you about, some ... I can't. Examples. We are working on developing cattle for the State Department for countries that have need of specialized breeds to thrive in the environment they exist. We are working on ways of increasing the pounds of fish a pond can produce. We manufacture vaccines." He stopped smiling. "There are many more I can tell you about and we do other things that are classified." He paused like the polished orator he was to shift the direction of his talk. "Actually, commercial customers make up sixty per cent of our base. We perform breeding trials, produce medicines, provide all sorts of specialized items for med facilities, produce and sell eatable beef and fish, even fish bait and fishing products as you're partner here knows." Mengel smiled at me and nodded. "Miss Partin, did you get your photos of the Sand Hill Cranes?"

My mouth went dry. "Yes, but not the day you saw me." I tried to keep my composure which felt both its feet were on ice. Mark looked at me with surprise, but didn't comment.

Mark asked, "This isn't what I'd visualize as a location for a government contractor. I'm curious, how did you establish your business ties to the government?"

Mengel remained quiet for several seconds. He finally nodded as he made a decision. "It's not information you need for your archeological survey ... but I'll answer one question. I spent twenty-six years in the military. I have many good friends still there. My companies do excellent work. When you have connections and you produce the results people want, they talk to others, good things happen. Also, there are times when it is impossible to get a project funded, it's politically unpopular, that kind of thing. I can do things that need being done ... shall we say informally.

Of course, my services are extra valuable for that reason alone. You do understand?"

"Makes sense," Mark said. I remembered what Caralene said about his assignment to the CIA during the final years of his military service. That could mean he'd do anything.

He pointed to the top of the swamp buggy. "Shall we get started?" Mengel scrambled up the ladder as easily as a monkey climbs a tree. He leaned over the edge of the platform he stood on. "Be careful coming up. People have fallen off this thing." He extended his hand. "When you get three or four rungs from the top give me your hand. I'll help get you into your seats."

Mark said, "You go first, Chessie. If you lose your grip I'll break your fall."

I nodded, wishing that I hadn't come. The man who was our host had delivered his message to me. *You are playing the mission impossible game. Quit or be destroyed.* I wasn't looking forward to the next few hours. The steel pipe that formed the ladder should have grimaced as I ascended because I gripped it so hard. Mengel grasped me by the wrist and helped me into the old sofa that sat on the hunting platform. Mark climbed the ladder and was in the seat next to me before Mengel turned around.

Harlan smiled and said, "Miss Partin, you look stressed. Don't be. Stay seated and *don't do anything foolish* and you'll be perfectly safe."

I nodded. Safe? Bull shit!

Sixty One

"According to Miss Beck the area shown in the photos you sent is right there." Mengel pointed to a rise in the land a few hundred yards ahead. Our conversation was very limited. The engine noise from the muffler-less buggy limited it to Mark's occasional question and Mengel's short answer. Mengel warned us, "Hang on, the area around that spot is actually an island in a marsh we'll have to drive through. It's deep and uneven in places."

The vehicle slowed and Mengel shifted into low gear. Water squished from under the huge tires as the swamp buggy eased down into the grass and weed covered marsh. Wake began pushing away from our path as we entered deeper water. Soon we were driving in three to four feet of water. A gator hurried away and a moccasin bared its white mouth at us displaying its fangs. The snake refused to move until treads came within inches of touching it.

Mark removed a small camera from his pocket and snapped pictures. The intensity in his eyes told me he was excited about the site's potential. "Perfect," he kept mumbling.

The vehicle lurched sideways and down on one side. I clawed the sofa's arm to stay in it. As quickly as the swamp buggy had tilted, it righted itself. It was beginning to crawl out of the water. Mengel looked at us and said, "Pot holes can make riding exciting." He steered to within a few yards of one of the mounds, stopped, and shut down the engine.

Mengel said, "I assume you'd like to get down and examine the mounds, Dr. Card." Mengel put his hand up as Mark rose from the sofa. "Be very careful down there. Look." He pointed at the side of the mound closest to us. "See it?"

"No. What do you see?" Mark asked.

"See that clump of wild rose? Watch under it. You'll see it move."

Both Mark and I pinned our eyes on the bush. He saw it first. Mark said quietly, "Shit, that's a big one!"

"I'd say over six feet," Mengel guessed.

As he spoke, there was a slight movement and I recognized the form and markings of a huge Eastern Diamondback Rattlesnake.

"The rainy season forces rattlers to seek higher ground. I'm sure there are several around here." Mengel opened a long metal box behind the sofa and removed a twelve gauge shotgun. "We'll take some snake repellent with us." He put a handful of shells in his pocket as he spoke. Mengel glanced at me and saw my terror–filled eyes riveted on the snake. "Are you going to accompany us, Miss Partin?"

I shook my head violently because my tongue wouldn't function.

Mengel nodded, "If you change your mind, be very careful where you step." He turned to Mark. "There are shovels and other tools in a storage box mounted to the chassis if you want to use them." Both men swung their legs over platform's edge and climbed down the ladder. I was left with mosquitoes for company.

* * *

Mark and Mengel slowly examined the mounds as I watched and swatted at insects. They gingerly stepped over some spots. Most likely due to snakes or fear of them. Mark scratched surfaces with a trowel and put a few items in plastic baggies he always carried. From his posture I perceived he was losing his enthusiasm. After they'd been on the ground a half hour, Mengel handed Mark the shot gun, walked back to the swamp buggy, and climbed up beside me.

Mengel smiled and said, "I'm going to move this to the other side of the mounds. There are some rattlers down there. I'm moving the buggy so Mark doesn't have to walk through them twice." He started the engine.

We passed Mark who was intent on examining something he'd exposed and continued another thousand feet stopping a few yards from the highest pile of earth on the little island. Mengel turned off the engine and stared at Mark as he wandered slowly around one of the mounds. He spoke to me without looking my way. "I would have thought someone who was born here would have made their peace with snakes."

I watched Mark take a quick step backward and detour around something lying on the ground. I said, "Some things you never get used to, no matter what."

"I understand. We all have things we can't tolerate. For you its snakes. For me it's sharks. I'm sure you've seen my plane. I'll fly an extra hundred miles to avoid flying over the ocean." Mengel turned and locked his pupils on mine. "Things don't have to be large or fearsome to create terror in an individual. Our mutual friend, Charlie, is terrified of wasps. He was captured and kept in a crate infested with wasp nests. Needless to say, he was stung. The man can't stand to be near them. Rooster and I have been together a long time. He reported to me in service. I'm responsible for the orders that caused him to end up in that crate. Rooster and most of the men who work here have been with me twenty years or more. When you have been in battle together there's a bond, one you can't break, and one others don't understand. I feel responsible for them and they're loyal to me. We take care of each other." He looked back at

Mark. "I see Dr. Card has seen enough of these mounds to learn what he needed."

Mark worked his way back toward the buggy while keeping his eyes glued to the ground, watching where he was about to step. Mengel yelled to him, "Dr. Card if you're finished, let me drive over to you."

"Yes, that would be fine." Mark stopped in his tracks and sounded very relieved.

Sixty Two

"It's not at all what I thought." Mark's disappointment showed in his face as well as his voice. "Those piles of dirt are just that. My guess is someone brought a backhoe in there and dug watering holes in the marsh area so the cattle would have a place to drink when the water table dropped in the dry season."

"You can tell that from just walking around them?" I asked.

Mark laughed, "I had some help. Four by fours were driven in the ground where they wanted each pile. The Ais didn't have saw mills or Coca Cola bottling plants. I found a bottle near ground level in one of the test plugs I made."

Mengel shouted over the engine noise, "Is there any place else you'd like to look?" The driver's seat was located in front of the passenger's sofa and made communicating hard.

"No." Mark was disgruntled. The arrangement of the mounds had elevated hopes of confirming his pet theory about Ais communal patterns. No joy.

"If you're ready to head back, I'd like to take a couple extra minutes. I have something I have to check while I'm in this area. Okay?"

"Fine," Mark said.

We crossed the marsh, exiting in a different direction. The swamp buggy managed to get through the bog without the frightening tilt we experienced on the way in. Motor noise acted as an alarm for the wildlife. A covey of quail rose, a mother turkey and her half-grown young scurried among the palmettoes, deer stopped drinking from a pond, raising their tails like white flags as they bounded away, and feral pigs grunted their displeasure as we passed. We'd traveled over a mile when I saw where I thought Mengel was headed. Four posts arranged in a rectangle, each with a red pennant fluttering from it, stood in the middle of nothing.

Inside the post's perimeter were a multitude of purple and pink flowers. Hundreds of flower covered shafts poked straight up toward the sky. Each tube was three to four feet tall and came from a small base roughly a foot and a half in diameter. Mengel stopped the vehicle a few feet from what was obviously a garden plot.

Mark smiled and said, "*Digitalis purpurea.*"

"Excellent, Dr. Card. Otherwise known as Fox Glove." Mengel looked over the 100' by 200' cultivated area.

"You make medicine from these?" Mark asked.

"Yes, among other things," Mengel answered.

"Why are you raising it so far away from your compound?" I asked.

"Good question, Miss Partin. This plant requires acid soil, lots of humus, and semi-dry, partially shaded conditions to thrive, but there is a more important reason. Are you familiar with wine production?"

"A little," I lied.

"Then you know the wine's taste is strongly influenced by its environment and the soil the grapes are grown in. These plants are in this spot because there are chemicals that occur here that intensify the properties we want when we harvest them. To simplify, these plants are grown on what amounts to botanical steroids. They are 450% more potent than those grown in a random spot."

Mark whistled, "That mean they're that much more deadly than randomly grown Fox Glove plants?"

Mengel nodded, "And, they have the potential to increase the potency of medicines we may choose to make from them."

Mengel started the vehicle, shifted into gear and headed in the direction of the compound. We skirted a cypress head and when we emerged we were within a hundred yards of the fish farm ponds with the compound visible in the distance. Mengel drove the swamp buggy onto a road that bisected the tiny lakes and led to the buildings far ahead of us.

One of the narrow lakes was completely surrounded by an eight foot high chain-link cage and covered with a tin roof. When we were close, I asked, "What's in there?"

Mengel let the vehicle idle next to the cage. He said, "It's a State Department project. The fish in there grow fast, can survive in low oxygen, and reproduce at a prodigious rate. However, we don't want any of them getting out, the species isn't indigenous, and we don't want anything getting in that pond."

"What kind of fish is it?" Mark repeated.

"A variety of Piranha." Mengel started the buggy down the road.

The mile plus ride back toward Mark's truck was relatively conversation free … the noisy engine restricting us to short questions and shorter answers.

One of those exchanges turned out to be particularly instructive. It provided me with an idea of the scope of what was contained in the walls of the imposing building behind a twelve foot high fence with its coils of razor wire "hair" growing on top.

Orange windsocks, aerials, heavy duty power cables, and other items I didn't recognize adorned the top of one of the outbuildings inside the fencing. It was far from the air strip so I didn't understand the need for the wind direction finder.

"Mr. Mengel, what's that little building with the air sock?" I pointed at it.

"That's our utility shed. Our water plant and our auxiliary power generator are located in there. We have to be self-sufficient here. Refrigeration can't be interrupted."

I persisted, "Why do you need the air sock?"

"Gaseous chlorine."

"You use that much water?" Mark asked.

"Yes."

As we approached Mark's pick-up some of my raw fear had dissipated, but I was still apprehensive. Harlan Mengel had delivered his message to me. In capital letters.

Sixty Three

Reading listened. As usual, he tried to maintain the expressionless mask he prefers to wear. When I told him what I saw, and particularly, what words Harlan Mengel and I exchanged, the mask disappeared and all manner of emotions and surprise appeared in its place. He sat, silent and pensive after I finished.

I waited for his thoughts until my patience waned. I asked, "What do you think? I knew we were taking on something difficult, but is this mission impossible?"

Reading, said nothing. He got up from the kitchen table, went to the refrigerator, and removed six cans of beer. When he returned he said, "This is a six-pack kind of problem." He pushed a couple cans toward me and said, "Break your diet."

"What's Benson going to say when he hears?" I asked. I guessed he'd back-peddle or bail out completely.

"That's harder to figure than you might think. Benson McGill is a pragmatic character and a political animal, but there's a stubborn streak in him that runs wide and deep." Reading ran his index finger around the rim of a beer can several times. He popped the can open and took a swig. "Down deep he's as red-necked as you get. If there's ever a time machine invented, he'd probably volunteer to fight with Lee at Gettysburg." He took another swallow. "I believe he won't be willing to give up easily. He'll see it as a possibility to increase his political position *if* he can protect himself and shift most of the risk."

"To us?"

"Or whoever. He'd throw us under the bus, but he'd try not to. That's about the most you can expect out of a politician."

"How do you fight the ties and power Mengel has? I have to admit what I saw and heard has me overwhelmed. McGill could take one look and ... bail." I was close to abandoning my place in the effort.

"It is a possibility. But, he might see the same possibilities I see. Mengel's position may be far less invincible than you think it is." Reading emptied his beer, crushed the can, and popped the top on another. "Chessie, did you ever wonder why he made such a concerted effort to convince you that you were powerless against him and his friends, whoever they may be? If Mengel had the unlimited power he hints at, he'd simply kill you."

Reading made sense, but he hadn't seen what I saw. "I don't believe it's all a bluff. You'd have to see—"

"Chessie, I didn't say it was all bluff. I do believe he has limits and he knows that he's exceeded them. That's why he wants us to stop pushing." Reading maintained eye contact with me. "Well, are you going to stop pushing?"

"I honestly don't know." I really didn't.

Sixty Four

I wasn't the only one who was unsure of pursuing Rooster, Mengel, and the nameless shadows that protected them. Reading set up a meeting with Benson. When he learned the extent of power Mengel claimed, his resolve was shaken. But, as Reading had surmised, the chief was unable to walk away completely. He told us to let things cool off for a week before we resumed chasing. I believed he needed the time to determine if he wanted to wash his hands of the whole project.

Benson wasn't the only person who was on the verge of quitting. The only thing that kept me from being the first rat to leave the ship was the fact *I was responsible for opening the can.* I felt like I'd dragged Reading, Benson McGill, even Caralene into what was my rumble. My feelings about Rooster hadn't changed. He was a human refuse heap and I still believed he was responsible for Mary Perez's disappearance. A little doubt had creeped in, but what bothered me most was that the doubt was more a product of my fear of the consequences if I persisted and lost rather than any loss of conviction about the bait man's guilt.

I wished fate would send me an omen.

Sixty Five

"What are you doing this morning?" Reading asked. He was back in uniform. What he wore provided him with a comfort zone. I couldn't help thinking of him as an oversized Linus wearing his security blanket. I chuckled.

"What's funny about that?" He looked perplexed.

"You make a funny looking 240 pound Linus."

"What are you talking about?" Reading was just young enough that he wasn't familiar with the *Peanuts* comic strip.

I decided to avoid the whole explanation. "Skip it. You asked about my agenda for today. I don't know. We need toilet paper and a few things from the store so I thought I'd pick them up later." Reading didn't respond to my pause so I went on. "There are a lot of things I need to think about. I do my best thinking on the beach. I'm going to walk over there after I get back from the store. Two things you can be sure of, I won't be anywhere near the Circle X Ranch and I won't be following Rooster."

Reading nodded. He stared at me for several seconds before saying, "Why don't we swap cars today? I'd be more comfortable if it was harder for someone to follow you. And, you need to abandon the idea of any long walks until this whole business shakes out. You're too vulnerable out walking by yourself. You can't stop what's happening to us by walking away any more than you could stop the world turning by pretending there's no night and day."

Sobering. Reading's words slapped me. Exit wasn't going to be easy or safe. Facts, not desires, controlled where I was. In reality, I had no say as to whether I could claim a do-over and change history I'd created. That truth was something I couldn't ignore when I plotted where my course should lead. I asked, "You think I'm in real danger?"

"Hell, yes. Chessie, you always tell me that I believe what others tell me too easily. Because Harlan Mengel puts on a show for you and makes you believe you'll be safe if you shut up and go away, doesn't mean that's his intent at all. Everything you've observed about him and Rooster should tell you just the opposite." Reading looked at me, reached across the kitchen table and put his hand on mine as I raised a fork loaded with scrambled eggs. "This is one of those times that being trusting, being gullible ... is being hurt, being dead." He reached in his pocket and tossed his pickup keys on the table next to my plate. "Where are yours?"

"In my room, on my dresser."

Reading got up, stood for several seconds, then leaned toward me and placed his hands on the table. His face ended three feet from mine. "Call me every two hours. Always tell me where you are and where you're headed. Stay in public places where there are plenty of people around. Don't let anybody convince you go anyplace with them. I'll be identifying your body if you do. No texting. I want to hear your voice."

Sixty Six

Reading's warning weighed on me. I left at the same time he did. We shared our paranoia as we snuck out of the house, scanned every driveway on Banyan Road for an auto that shouldn't have been there, and took circuitous routes to get to the main roads we needed to travel.

There was no reason to believe that Rooster, Mengel, or anyone associated with them had the foggiest idea of where I normally shopped. That didn't keep me from driving far out of my way to avoid the Publix where I normally bought groceries. Pulling in and out of the parking lot made me so apprehensive I thought about returning home and barricading myself inside, until the realization that catching me at my home would be one of the easier places to abduct me. It would be safer to stay in public places until Reading returned to our duplex.

Driving around in Reading's 150 made me just a few shades less concerned about being followed. I reasoned that if Mengel and company were efficient enough to nose out all the information they had on me, they probably had the same information on Reading. They were sure to have his license plate number, the description of his truck, all things they needed to find me. Maybe the answer was to rent another car. Without coming to a conscious decision, I steered Reading's pickup to *Rent-a-Wreck*. My paranoia remained. I circled the rental agency four times looking for someone sitting in a car or loitering who might be waiting for my possible appearance. I didn't see anyone. When I finally drove in and walked inside, I was surprised. Ruppert was not behind the counter.

"Hi. Is Ruppert around?" I asked.

"No. Can I help you?" The boy behind the counter looked like he found his way in the rental company while on lunch break from his junior high class.

"When will he be back?"

The boy shrugged his shoulders. "I don't know. I'm a temp. His relative's hired me. He had to go out of town unexpectedly."

The possibility slapped me across the face like a dead mackerel. "Has anyone talked to him?" I asked.

"I don't know. Do you want to rent something?" The boy looked bored.

"No. I'll come back later." I couldn't escape quickly enough. Carelessly, I pulled in front of a car as I pulled out of the agency's lot. Luck was with me because the other driver swerved and avoided hitting me. I drove down the highway for a few blocks before pulling off on a side street. I made another quick turn, parked at the curb, and waited for a vehicle I knew would follow. My heart did gymnastics in my chest. My fears were confirmed by Ruppert's disappearance. Five ... ten ... fifteen minutes passed before I could relax. I wanted to go hide, but how and where?

As I sat in the pickup, my mind was made up for me. Reading was right, the choice wasn't mine. Mengel and his henchmen would come after me until I was removed as a threat to him and his operation. Doing what, I wasn't even sure. The only choice I had was to fight or cower in a corner until he squashed me. I chose to fight. Reading had said be careful. I would be. There were two places I might get some additional information without raising alarm flags if I was very, very careful. I pointed the F150 toward Melbourne and the St. John's Helping Hand House to have a conversation with Aunt Lulu.

* * *

The possibility that Rooster might show up while I spoke with Aunt Lulu was a real one. That was the last thing I wanted to happen. The phone number for the shelter appeared on my cell phone screen and I called the number.

"St. John's Helping Hand House, let God and us help you." It was Lulu's cheery, familiar voice.

"Hi, Aunt Lulu. Do you have a few minutes?"

There was a slight hesitation. "Yes."

"Do you remember me?" I dredged up my AKA from my previous visit. "This Sandra Seally from—"

"Oh! Yes I certainly do! From the TV station. How are you my dear?" The excitement I counted on was there.

"If I stop by, would you have time to talk to me, for say, fifteen minutes? Now there is one thing, I don't want to be there if Mr. Cocker might stop in. We absolutely don't want him to know anything until we make the final decision to run the story. You understand? Do you expect him today?"

"We don't expect him today. There's no … let's call them unfortunate guests … staying here right now, so he wouldn't have a reason. He always calls before he comes, anyway. You'd have at least an hour to leave before he'd be here."

"Good. See you in a half hour."

* * *

It was a sleepy day in Melbourne when I pulled up in front of the St. John's Helping Hand House. Lulubelle Jones waited right inside the thrift store/homeless shelter's front door, a willing accomplice of what she wasn't aware.

After we exchanged greetings and walked back to her cash register, she said, "We may get interruptions, dearie, but I have plenty of time and it has been slow." She opened a folding chair for me and sat on her stool behind the register. "Now, how can I help you?"

I opened a leather-bound note pad and said, "I have some questions. I might ask you to repeat things once in a while. I don't take shorthand."

"Oh, that's not a problem."

"Okay. Can you tell me some of the things that Mr. Cocker does to help St. John's Helping Hand House and the people that stay here? And can you tell me a little of the details of each item?"

"Where do I begin?" Aunt Lulu beamed as she spoke. "He makes sure that everyone who comes here for help leaves in good health. That's one of the biggest things. When a new person comes in, Rooster asks that we call him. He has an arrangement with this doctor. He takes them to the doctor's office for an exam. If they need medicine, Mr. Cocker gets it for them. When they leave here, they are as healthy as they can be ... given the circumstances."

"Do you know who the doctor is?" I asked.

"Dr. Orella."

The name froze me. "Dr. James Orella?" I asked.

"I think that's right." Lulu shook her head. "I've only seen him once. He came here when one of the women Rooster and he were caring for had a problem. He drove a red Porsche. The man looked very well-to-do."

I wrote Orella's name on my pad and the question, Why is a high powered surgeon doing a GP's work? "What are some of the other things that Mr. Cocker does?"

"He finds work for them. He tries to get them back home if they have a family. That's particularly true of individuals that have serious problems who would find it difficult to do well on their own. He buys a bus ticket and off they go to people who love them. Most of them he helps restart their lives. Mr. Cocker has friends at a number of companies who hire these people. He makes sure they have clothes while they're here and clothes when they leave. A lot of them have nothing when they come to us. In honesty, we wouldn't let them leave here without the essentials, but Mr. Cocker says we bear enough burdens. He insists he pay for the clothes and anything else needed while they stay here."

"I'd like to talk to one of these people? Do you have ways to contact any of them?" I asked.

Lulu shook her head sadly. "We very, very seldom do. Since I've been here, I only know of two who have contacted us to thank us. The best way would probably be through Mr. Cocker because they become closer to him than to us. He tries to do something special for each person and they bond with him. You would have to ask him and I know you can't." Aunt Lulu's face turned sad. "That may not help much, either. I asked Rooster if he hears from them and he said almost never." She shook her head. "It is so sad. Humans are less faithful and appreciative than most family pets."

"Do you have any records with any of these peoples' names, maybe where they came from?"

"Oh, no." Aunt Lulu, smiled sadly. "Many of the people we serve don't want others to know who they are. We don't ask anything but a first name and that they attend prayer meetings while they're here. It's slow right now, but in season we may have as high as twenty people staying. They come and go, Sandra. Some just want a night out of the cold. Some are happy with the life they lead."

"How many people do you serve in a year and how many are helped by Mr. Cocker?" What Rooster spent per person was significant.

"We average somewhere near four hundred souls a year. Some are repeaters; I really don't know what our actual count is. As far as Mr. Cocker's efforts, my best guess would be sixty to eighty."

"That's a huge commitment." I spoke to myself as much as to her. My suspicious nature had to ask. "Has Mr. Cocker ever told you why he does this? That appears to be a major expense for a man of limited means."

"Yes, I have. Mr. Cocker told me he did horrible things when he was in service and this is his way of atoning for his sins." Aunt Lulu put her hand over her mouth and looked alarmed. "I shouldn't have told you that."

"Believe me, the station has no desire to make a villain out of someone we want to nominate as a saint." Those words came hard. It was difficult visualizing the Rooster I knew as sorry about anything he did. "That's all I need to know for now. I'll be back in touch with you."

"Oh! I've spoiled it for Mr. Cocker with what I said." Aunt Lulu was distraught.

"No, no, no. I just have to go to other places," I said.

"Are they the other shelters that Mr. Cocker helps?" Aunt Lulu asked.

"No," I said and then asked, "How many other homeless centers does he work with?"

"At least four that I know about. I can find out for you."

I was still digesting the first piece of information when Aunt Lulu asked her question. Four more at the same numbers was roughly an additional 280 people. That was staggering. Lulu repeated, "If you want I can ask Mr. Cocker all the places he helps. And if new people come here I can try to find out their names if you want. Should I call the TV station?" That woke me from my shock.

"No, don't do that. Give me a piece of paper." I wrote my cell phone number on the paper she gave me and said, "Only call me on that number." I made a mental note to rerecord my voice mail and eliminate my name from it.

Sixty Seven

No one would confuse the facility I entered with a welfare clinic. The lobby screamed money. The East Coast Central Major Surgery Clinic had an imposing appearance as its name implied. It was the last medical facility destination where I'd followed Rooster. Statues, fountains, fancy tables and ornate furniture covered marble floors. Numerous painting and pictures smothered the walls.

Three people waited at the reception desk so I indulged a hunch. One fifteen foot section of pictures hung under an umbrella of words in gold lettering that stated: *Physicians that regularly utilize our clinic's facilities.* I was not surprised when I found, Dr. James Maxwell Orella, among the photos on display. Orella, if the picture was recent, was an older surgeon … my guess sixty … whose bedside manner would be described as snake-like if the expression on his face was an indicator. He had a Latin look about him.

"May I help you?" The receptionist gained my attention.

I smiled, she frowned. She probably paid more for the dress she wore than the five best that hung in my bedroom closet. Hers were probably acquired at Marcela's … I bought mine at Penny's and Walmart. She didn't get past my jeans and fishing shirt to make the decision I wasn't in the right place. Then it might have been balcony envy. The skinny broad could have used her chest for a carpenter's level. That brings the cat to the surface in some women who do without. Her smile was so strained she could have used fishhooks to keep the corners of her mouth pointed up. She repeated, "May I help you?"

I smiled, stood straight up, which thrust my chest forward. She frowned. Yep, boob envy. I said, "I'm just curious. I pass this place most days when I go to work and wonder what you folks do here."

Haughty is the best way I can describe her reply. "This is a highly skilled surgical clinic. We only accept referrals."

"And that means what, you specialize in patients referred by proctologists?"

She didn't appreciate my humor and her frown deepened. "No, madame. Highly sensitive plastic surgery, brain and heart surgery, reconstructive trauma surgery, transplants, and high risk orthopedic surgery *all* are preformed here."

"Really." I stared at her chest. "You ever been a patient here?"

"No! Do you have any other questions?" she asked with undisguised contempt.

"Just one. Is the Dr. Orella who practices here the famous brain surgeon?"

"No." The woman raised her chin and looked down her nose. "Dr. Orella is a fine heart surgeon. He's one of the very best transplant specialists in the world." She took a deep breath. "Is there anything else?"

"No. I'll leave you to whatever." I walked out biting my tongue. I so wanted to tell her, "You should consult with whichever physician specializes in personality replacements and get help."

The walk back to my truck found my mind spinning. How did the pieces fit together? Were there connections or were all the things I learned random and without relevance to the others? Mengel could be making some type of special digitalis from the Fox Glove plants I saw on the ranch. That would fit. Emergency deliveries. Express transport all over the world. Yes, that fit.

Did that mean Rooster and his activities were separate and apart from Mengel? Was Mengel shielding Rooster because of their long relationship? Was Rooster even more of a mental monster than I thought or was he schizophrenic with intense good and evil extremes?

I removed my phone from my purse. I'd forgotten to turn it on when I changed the voicemail message after leaving the shelter. There were several messages. Three were important. First, a text from Reading: *B home @ 6. C U then.* An email note from Mark Card: *Please call me as soon as possible.* Then another text from Reading: *B xtra careful.* His two texts were a half hour apart. I decided to call Mark that evening, but Reading's warning sounded urgent. My plan changed. Instead of returning to Vero on I-95, I chose back roads that wouldn't lead to a chance encounter with Rooster. That's when fate struck.

Sixty Eight

Steam rose from the pavement caused by a passing shower as I drove toward home. The afternoon sun's glare penetrated my windshield and caused me to squint at objects ahead. I was close to Vero and I intended to go to MacDonald's to kill time until Reading returned to our duplex. When I first saw the familiar form appear in the thin mists ahead of me I thought I must be hallucinating. Setting in a vacant store's parking lot a hundred yards ahead, was Rooster's white box truck or a clone. I slowed to catch the license number. I felt a chill pass through me as I read the familiar numbers.

What was he delivering? To a vacant store? When I got close enough to see it, the truck's hood was up. The truck was broken down and Rooster wasn't visible. Slowing to the point the drivers behind me started blowing their horns, I couldn't see anyone in the vicinity. Was this an opportunity or a trap? I drove a quarter of a mile as I weighed the risks and the rewards before I made the inevitable "U" turn. There was no way Rooster could have known I would choose this road to drive home.

The store where Rooster's truck broke down was familiar to me. An old lady ran a combination art gallery and painting school in the building and I took a course there. I knew another parking lot was in the rear. No one would see my vehicle if I parked there. Traffic on the road was heavy, so I'd be 'safe' stopping on the pretext of rendering assistance. I might get lucky and find something. *Might get lucky* isn't worth incurring risk, but I ignored my better judgement. I was in the store's rear, getting out of the pickup and making the decision to leave my purse in the cab without second thoughts.

I walked around the store cautiously. Peeking from behind the corner, there was nothing to see. Swallowing hard, I squared my shoulders, told myself I wouldn't take foolish chances and keep my foray quick. I walked to the passenger side cab door and hoped that the stress of breaking down would create a lapse in Rooster's vigilance. If he left the truck's cab doors unlocked, I'd be shielded from the view of passing traffic. It would give me access to his paperwork, and the information I might discover would justify the chance I took.

Once last survey assured me I was alone. I scrambled up the step by the door and peered in the cab window. Rooster's clipboard lay on the seat. It was stuffed with delivery papers. The lock button told me it would be futile, but I tried the door handle and got the expected result. Locked. All those papers made me salivate. I circled the truck's front and approached the driver's door. I hoped for a better result, though I knew repeating the same thing over and expecting something different to happen was Einstein's definition of insanity.

Taped in the window was a paper with Rooster's sloppy cursive scrawled message, *Engine failure, will have truck moved before dark*. Those words had the same effect on me that an addict in withdrawal would experience if he found one last pill in his stash. I had until dark.

Trying the driver's door handle repeated history. Hoisting up and looking at the clipboard felt akin to holding a prime rib, rare with horseradish sauce, in front of a starving woman, laughing at her … and taking it away. Even without intent Rooster frustrated and infuriated me. "There must be a key hidden somewhere on this thing," I mumbled.

I dropped off the step and retraced my way around the front of the truck, checking each wheel well and the hood light for the spare key I was sure was stashed someplace. No luck. The alcove under the gas cap provided no success. A second tug at the passenger door handle reconfirmed Einstein's genius. I slid my hand along the metal truck body frame as I walked to the truck's rear, hoping to find a magnetic key caddy. Nothing.

However, my luck changed when I rounded the back of the truck. The padlock that kept anyone from lifting the truck's rear door was missing. If there was a hidden key, that's where Rooster probably kept it. I climbed up the rear of the box like I'd watched the bait man do many times. Within a few seconds, the latch was open and I was rolling the door up. I stepped inside as cool air from the refrigeration rushed past me into the sunlight. A sign over a switch next to the door said Interior Light. I turned it on. After stepping inside, I hastily rolled the door down.

The sight of the inside of the door whispered in my ear, *Hey, dumb butt, you're confined. Want that? Really?* I tried to think rationally, a difficult process when my desires pull in different directions. No one would be back until dark. The spare cab key was here. I'd limit my time and get out. Twenty minutes. I wasn't wearing a watch, but my hand on my pocket reminded me my cell phone was in my purse … in my pickup. Looking around the inside of the box in the dim light I confirmed there were many promising items to check, incuding a stack of the specialized shipping containers I'd seen Rooster handle, paper work stuck between boxes on pallets, and a pallet-load of the plastic bags of white powder. The truck hadn't been stopped long since it was still cool from the refrigeration; I should have plenty of time. *Damn the torpedoes, full speed ahead,* came to mind.

I started by scrutinizing the plastic "bricks" of white powder. Cocaine would be the smoking gun we needed. A printed block on the packet read, Pond Clean - Algaecide - Safe for fish - No heavy metals. A bunch of the printing was too small to read easily. That's what it could be, but someone wouldn't transport cocaine with that printed on the packaging. I used my car keys to punch a small hole in the bag and took a *gentle* sniff. It definitely wasn't cocaine. The irritation in my nostrils made me happy I'd been cautious. I guessed it was what the package label read.

Pink pieces of paper protruding from between the cardboard boxes beckoned. The first shipping papers I scanned came from a chemical supply house that contained two pages filled with lists of chemicals that might well have been written by a resident of Saturn. I couldn't recognize any of the items. What was recognizable: the total of $3,700 on the second page. The sheets found their way into my pocket.

The next papers I looked at were from a medical supply company. Some items I recognized, some I didn't. What in the hell was Tubocurarine? Another item had a note with the instruction, *"for experimental treatment of bovine spongiform encephalopathy only."* That sounded like something for cattle with Mad Cow Disease. Also listed were forceps and scalpels of various descriptions, surgical sponges, disinfectants, plus many more items. These joined the other papers in my pocket.

The stack of seven specialized shipping containers was pushed against wall at the front of the truck box. Each container had a safety belt circling it. A label glued to each container said Property of Special Medical Solutions.

Stenciled on top was, Refrigerated container – do not open – **KEEP THIS SIDE UP** – valuable perishable products. It only took a few minutes to determine how special the containers were. When I tried to lift one, my back groaned; they were heavy! The words, Battery Compartment stenciled on one end of the container told the story. The unit had some type of mini-cooler built in. The lid had a handle with the word Empty on it. I moved a slide mounted over it which changed Empty to Active. Sophisticated! It sure wasn't a beer cooler.

The safety belt that should have circled the unit on bottom was loose and I stared. One end disappeared under one of the front wall panels. How would you maintain cold temperatures with a crack opened to the outside? I rested my hand on the wall next to the panel as I bent over for a closer look. To my astonishment the panel swung open. It was a door to a concealed compartment. That shock was secondary to what I saw inside.

The compartment was four feet deep and as wide as the truck body. I shuddered when seeing shackles bolted to the walls that could be used to completely restrain two people. When I walked inside, the door swung closed behind me. This could only be used to transport kidnapped prisoners. Stains on the floor left from efforts made to clean them provided another chapter. I said, "Oh, shit," in a whisper. I wanted out. As my hand reached for the door, I felt more than heard the rear door of the box truck roll up.

Sixty Nine

"I left the fucking light on!" Rooster shouted. "No wonder the battery died. Look how damned dim it is."

A voice I didn't recognize responded. "I don't think the light would drain the battery that much. Let's get the new battery installed. I need to get back to the ranch and, if the battery isn't the problem, you need the time to get the diesel repair guy here. You going to try to make your pick-up?"

"Hell no!" Rooster uttered some unintelligible obscenities and the lights went off leaving me in total blackness. As my eyes strained, my ears told me the box truck's rear door rolled down, ending with a bang that vibrated the floor. I stood frozen by fear, by indecision, and by the ramifications of my short sightedness. I tried to look at the situation like I thought Reading would.

I didn't want to be discovered so I elected to remain perfectly still. If the van started I could work my way to the rear, pull the door up at the first stop, and jump out. If the truck remained inoperative for a period of time, I'd have to open the door, jump, and run like hell for the traffic driving up and down the road. I might even be lucky … Rooster could leave, I could race to my truck, and drive home thanking God every second of the way.

My wait was short. The grinding of the starter ended with the hiccup the engine made as it started. Within seconds I lurched into the closed door which was shut securely. I told myself not to panic. The concealed latch was somewhere near waist high on the right side of the door on the other side of the wall. It made sense, if there was a way to open the door from the inside, the latch would be mounted on the side of the wall in the same location.

The truck stopped and I wobbled like a bowling pin. I extended my hand to the door, slid it to left until it touched the false panel divider. Pushing against the next panel with one hand while sliding it downward, produced a click before I moved a foot. I pushed with my other hand and the door swung outward.

Easing out the door took me from one inky blackness to another. As I eased the door closed, the truck started forward and I stumbled into one of the pallets loaded with boxes. There was a sharp pain in my ankle and when I moved it I felt some object come out from where it had stabbed me. Looking would do no good until I could get to the light switch. It wouldn't be good. Blood squished in my tennis shoe.

Trying to stand and make progress to the light switch by the rear door was slow and precarious. The truck's constant slowing and accelerating combined with minor movements, like changing lanes, made standing in a boat in a gale less challenging. I worked my way back until I cleared the last pallet-load of boxes, taking brave steps until I felt something solid. I grasped anything I could hold. Luck was with me; my fingers clutched one of the door's roller tracks. Luck remained a lady for I was on the same side as the light switch. Holding the roller track with one hand, my free fingers fumbled around the wall searching for the switch while my mind sent conflicting memories of where it was located. The thirty seconds it took seemed more like thirty years. Light flooded the inside of the box truck. Everything was the same as I'd last seen them. I sighed; the first part of my getting away worked.

I looked at my left ankle. Clotting blood covered one side while it rolled down the inside and outside of my Nike. A trail of blood drops and smears led back fifteen feet to where a red nail protruded an inch from the pallet. I had a Scarlet O'Hara moment and mumbled, "I'll worry about that tomorrow." That fifteen feet felt like a football field when I crossed it in the darkness.

The truck started forward and I realized I'd missed my first opportunity to get out. I said, "Shit!" found the bar that unlatched the door, and grabbed the handle used to pull it up. They provided stability as the truck moved. Things were looking up. The next complete stop the truck made, I was ready. That didn't take a long time. I could feel the deceleration and braking as the vehicle reached a complete stop.

I pulled down hard on the latch bar ... and nothing happened. I moved my other hand to the latch and frantically pulled down, shook and jerked the mechanism. It remained as immobile as Gibraltar. Slowly, the fact that Rooster had placed the padlock back on the door crept into my mind. Despair and anger fought for control of me. I fought tears. I'd done this to myself. After a deep breath, a strange thought entered my brain. *I wonder if the fish will like the taste of me in a chum block.*

Seventy

At quarter past six Reading's cell phone rang. He'd just made up his mind to take action about Chessie. She was supposed to call him more than five hours ago. Caller ID showed Caralene Wills.

"Hey, Reading. Sorry to bother you at home, but I have some man calling trying to get your phone number. He says its life and death. Says he's Dr. Mark Card. Can I give him your number?"

"Yes, and if his number shows on your screen give it to me."

Caralene rattled off the number and Reading scribbled.

"Why are you still at work, Caralene?"

"Those two wonderful letters, O.T."

"Mercenary. How long you planning to stay there?"

"Until eight. Why?"

"I might need some help. I'll let you know. Is Benson around?"

"Yes. What's up?"

"It's not a problem … yet. I'll call if the plane crashes. I'm hangin' up. We wouldn't want to mess with Dr. Card's life or death. Have him call."

Reading hadn't disconnected thirty seconds when his cell's screen lit and phone rang.

Dr. Card didn't waste time or words. "Is this Reading, Chessie's brother? I'm Mark. I'm Chessie's friend and she's in my archeology program. Have you heard from her this afternoon?" His thoughts and words gushed out like oil from an uncapped well.

"No. I haven't. I assume you haven't either and that's why you're calling. Do you want me to relay information to her?"

"Yes! Tell her to stay far away from Harlan Mengel." Card's delivery had elements of fear, anger, and urgency.

"Why?"

"Reading, I know you can't put a man in jail for what he's been, but that guy should be there. Or even better, in a box buried underneath it."

Patiently, Reading searched for reasons. "You have to know something you're not telling me. Can you share that?"

Card hesitated then said, "The only reason I'm reticent to … when it comes to Chessie's safety it doesn't matter. What do you know about our visit to the Circle X Ranch?"

"She said she told me everything."

"Did she tell you that I thought I recognized Mengel? I couldn't remember from where at the time, but I was sure I'd seen his face." Card took an audible breath and continued. "It bothered me, I kept thinking about it, and I finally remembered. That man was the shadow behind some of the massacres and atrocities in the Kosovo war."

"Shadow? I don't follow. Was he convicted of something? War crimes? Murder? Information I have was that he was still in service then."

"He was a bird colonel I believe. The stated reason for him being there was as an observer. Observer of what? Slaughter? As far as I know, he was never tried or convicted of anything. The rumors I heard had to do with some type connection between him and the CIA. The CIA had tentacles in that blood bath, I've heard on both sides. Secrecy shrouds the whole thing."

"How was he involved?" Reading asked.

"The details I know are because of the forensic team I served on. In 2003 our team was part of a UN effort investigating mass graves. There were Albanian informants that provided information on where the sites were and what happened there. What I'll tell you now is rumor, but it's rumor from the mouths of people that claim they were present at some of the killings. Mengel was somehow involved with the selection of victims for the Yellow House."

Reading asked, "Yellow House, what's that? I'm not familiar—"

"Few are." Mark's voice showed the emotion he felt. "The UN and most governments are willing to have it swept under a rug rather than face the ugly truth of what happened. I saw the results and I'll never be the same." He paused to compose himself. "The rumor is that the Albanians helped finance the war by selecting prisoners, taking them to a place just across the border in Albania, and removed their organs for sale on the black market. That place was the Yellow House. Hundreds, if not a thousand, had this fate. Harlan Mengel was accused of being the person who helped choose the victims, arrange for the sale of the organs, and he arranged for the disappearance of some of the bodies. Those he did have never been found. That's allowed the Albanian authorities to deny the crimes ever happened. The whole thing stinks."

Reading murmured, "Shit." He asked Mark, "Are you sure it's the same man?"

"Absolutely. I saw files with his picture in it many times."

"Thanks Dr. Card. I'm sure you understand. I have to hang up and get started on this."

"Sure. If there is anything I can do, call me."

"If Chessie contacts you, find out where she is and call me or the Vero police station."

After the call with Mark, Reading immediately called Caralene. He said, "Is Benson still there?"

"Yes," Caralene answered.

"Tell him I'd like him to stay there until I get in. I should be there in twenty-five minutes or less. Oh … if you can, will you stick around?"

"Sure Reading, what's up?" she asked.

"I'll tell you when I get there. There could be a hell of a lot more to this business with the bait man and the Circle X Ranch than we dreamed. And Chessie's in terrible danger."

Seventy One

Whipping myself with the many mistakes I made wouldn't do anything to help me survive. As the box truck rolled toward the Circle X Ranch, I knew I had to visualize the various possible scenarios when the trip ended.

It made sense that Rooster would drive the truck inside the innermost fence and park next to or in the large warehouse style building. I believed I'd be able to tell when we arrived by feeling the difference when we drove on the sand roads, and the number of stops Rooster made after that. My logic told me three: One at the farm gate, one at the guard house, and one to get inside the razor wire topped compound fencing.

The next question was where would I be safest when Rooster or someone else lifted the box truck door? That was an easy one. I had to hide in the hidden compartment. There was nothing to unload there. If I was discovered, I'd be in no worse shape than being caught in the box itself. I had to stay undiscovered for as long as possible. The longer I stayed free, the stronger the probability Reading would marshal help and come to get me out. How I was going to do that was something I'd have to do after I survived the first opening of the truck. I turned the lights off, felt my way to the rear of the truck, entered the captive's compartment, closed its hidden door, and waited in the threatening black silence. Fear gripped me to the point I wasn't sure my heart would survive until I at least had the slim chance to escape the truck.

We turned off on a sand road and the truck traveled to and stopped at what I visualized as the gate to the ranch. It continued and then stopped at the guard house. The truck then drove for less than two minutes. Faint buzzing sounds of an alarm horn sounded while the truck slowed to a crawl. A siren's screams rose and fell. The buzzing silenced. I visualized the truck entering the razor wire fence and finally entering through a door to the inside of the huge building. If that was true, I was in the belly of the beast.

If Rooster was used to easily overpowering his victims, I'd have none of that. He'd have to kill me to imprison me. Dying was a probability. I committed myself to doing as much damage to my enemies as I could before the inevitable. That thought changed my focus. I should have thought ahead and looked for weapons when I was in the light. Too bad. I'd blown the opportunity, so what. I had to work with what I could find. If I found nothing, I still had my Marine Corps training to use against my antagonist. Doing nothing wasn't an option.

Keeping my hand on the wall, I dropped to my knees and worked my way around the periphery of the room, one hand keeping contact with the wall, while the other groped for anything that I might use as a weapon. I'd reached the corner when I felt something metallic. My fingers quickly explored two circles with a couple of links of small chain between. Handcuffs! They weren't much, but they were better than nothing. The truck eased to a stop and the engine went silent as I took a firm grip on them.

The cab door slammed. Would someone open the rear door or simply leave the truck as was until the next day? My heartbeat increased to a NASCAR rate. Rattling at the box truck's rear door told me I had minutes or even seconds to live. The sound of the door being raised relieved rather than increased my fear. Resolution was far better than being suspended in the hell of indecision.

The next thing I heard was the rumble of a pallet jack rolling over the truck floor. A voice I didn't recognize said, "You want it all off?"

Rooster growled, "Yes, it isn't going to do us any good inside this damned truck."

"Throw a pallet up."

Rooster's response was unintelligible. I was sure it was obscene. There was a bang caused by a pallet being tossed in the truck. The jack maneuvered and stopped right outside the door to the compartment I hid in. I heard a grunt followed by the unknown person's voice saying, "How much do these things weigh?"

"Forty-seven pounds," Rooster replied.

"Damn, how much when they're not empty?"

"The stuff we ship in them doesn't add hardly anything." Rooster sounded impatient. "Get your ass in gear. I have to go home to feed Oscar."

I listened to the shipping containers being stacked on the pallet and noise of the jack on the floor moving them to the door.

"Hook this fork lift to the charger. The gauge is in the yellow," Rooster said, making it clear by his tone he was unhappy.

The jack moved around with stops in between. I visualized the man who produced the unseen voice moving pallets to the back edge of the truck and Rooster operating a fork lift and removing the loads from the truck. After four or five repeats, the voice asked, "Anything in the cage that needs unloading?"

"No," Rooster growled. "Leave the jack on the truck. I'll need it tomorrow."

I heard the man reposition the jack and jump down from the truck. It was what I didn't hear that made me happiest. The rear door was not pulled down. It was the conversation I heard next that was the most helpful.

"What parts of the security system you want on?" the voice asked.

Rooster's voice was fading, but understandable as he walked away from the truck, "Turn on the perimeter fences and the meat room section. Leave the rest off. Doc isn't cutting tonight so we don't need most of them. That way I won't have to return here if Warren sets one off accidentally. Oh. Don't forget to feed the cats."

I knew I'd be alone except for a guard, there was a security system, but much of it turned off, and I needed to stay away from the perimeter fences and the *meat rooms* until I was ready to attempt getting out. It reminded me to be careful what door I opened because the kitties I might find would be large, unfriendly, and hungry. That was a lot of good information, but what *were* the meat rooms?

Seventy Two

"That's what he said," Reading had just completed relating what he'd learned from Dr. Card, that Chessie was missing, and Reading believed the two things were related.

Caralene's face showed emotion, something it seldom did, and Benson shook his head, whistled and said, "Damn, we're in the deep end of the pool." Benson looked at Caralene. "Could you try to put a locator out on Chessie's cell and—"

"I didn't think you'd mind so I already have that started. The cell phone shows it's turned on and located along the Old Dixie Highway south of Sebastian near where it dead ends into US1. I sent Sullivan up there in an unmarked car to see if he can find it. Since that's out of our jurisdiction, I figured that would be best."

Benson nodded. "How long ago?"

"Ten, maybe fifteen minutes. He'll call me on my cell when he gets there." Caralene hesitated and added, "I started to try to check some of the things Reading told me about Mengel while Reading drove in. It supports what Card told him by the absence of information I found when I tried to check. Everything about Mengel from that time period is classified or missing."

"Body parts! That's so much worse, and bigger, than cocaine or an individual murder." Benson shook his head. "We are looking straight in the face of mass murder. It's under my nose, but out of my jurisdiction. Damn." He hesitated. "We can't leave Chessie in their control *if* they have abducted her." He spoke to himself as much as to Reading and Caralene, "How can we do this and still have some legal basis to interfere?"

"What about contacting Threep? Get him to either work together or let us go in," Caralene suggested. "Maybe you could—" Her cell phone rang. She held her hand up, answered her call, and, after a question and answer series, she said, "It was Sullivan. He found it. The cell was in your pickup, Reading. The truck is parked behind an old vacant store. You'll have to replace your passenger side window. Sullivan broke it to get in. Chessie's purse was in there with the phone in it. Money and ID were in there along with other personal stuff. He said the engine was stone cold so what ever happened was a few hours ago."

"Shit! Reading you said the last call you got was after noon so that means she's been in their control for six hours, maybe more." His eyes told Reading that she could be toast already. "Getting Threep involved is going to be very complicated. Hell, with me running for his job, he'll be suspicious. You can't blame him. He'll have to be convinced. Besides, there is a possibility he knows what's going on out there, or more likely, doesn't want to know what's happening. Those ranchers are the primary ones that keep him in office. He won't step on their toes without being careful. That will take time we don't have." Benson sighed. "Calling the feds could be the worst thing we could do: Mengel has pull there and we don't know how much. I make a call to them and if the right person finds out and makes another call, we won't see Chessie again." Benson shook his head. "I'm open to suggestions."

Reading nodded. "I have one that's pretty obvious. I need some volunteers to go in there with me. Not as members of the Vero Department, but as my friends searching for my sister." Caralene removed her badge and placed it on Benson's desk. "I can—"

The chief cut the conversation short. "Who do you want?" He spoke as he went to a closet and unlocked it.

"Brock, Stephens, and Sullivan. Wills can coordinate for us," Reading said.

Caralene snorted. "Coordinate my black ass. If I go, I go in."

"You heard the lady," Benson said and scratched his head as he opened the closet. "I'll get in touch with those men and ask if they're willing. Then—"

"Sir, they're on the way in now. I thought it might be better if I asked. It keeps you from being compromised." Reading made no apologies.

"That's smart." Benson motioned to the open closet. "Take one gun case for each person going with you. Those are Thompson's. They're old, but you can't get a better weapon for working up close. The brown box has 150 loaded clips in it. Take it." Benson hesitated then said, "Now the conditions. As of right now, I don't know what you're doing and none of your volunteers think I do. When you get inside, hopefully before the shooting starts, call me. I'll call Threep and ask for an immediate meeting. See where I'm going? You have a legitimate reason for going in there. There isn't a person in this county who won't understand you going in to save your sister. Or, blame me for supporting you. If and when you find Chessie, call me, I'll have the cavalry ready to go. How long before you're ready?"

Seventy Three

Hiding in the inky blackness of the box truck's hidden compartment was nerve wracking and made worse because the decision of when to leave the relative safety of my hiding place was mine alone to make. After an eternity of silent waiting, with no indication of any activity outside, I eased my hand down the wall to the door release and pushed. The panel popped open two inches.

The interior of the truck and inside of the building it was parked in were dimly illuminated. I peeked through the opening looking for any movement, listening for noise, being aware of anything that might indicate the presence of people. The little I could see assured me humans weren't around. I could see the interior of a cavernous warehouse. Faint buzzing and whirring sounds sounded like AC units or something similar. A couple more minutes built up enough courage in me to swing the door open and emerge.

Cautiously, I stayed pressed to the truck wall as I eased to the wide opening at the rear. In front of me were pallets loaded with all matter of material. Most items were in cardboard boxes. A hundred or more of the special refrigerated shipping containers were stacked in pallets in one area of the room. Conveyor systems were scattered in various places around the huge space. Offices and storage rooms stretched from wall to wall on one end of the 150-foot-wide building. Lights illuminated one office, but I couldn't see anyone through the glass windows that formed half of the front wall. It made sense the guard Rooster had mentioned would be headquartered in that space. If he was walking his rounds, it meant I should stay in place until he returned. The office light could just have been left on and if I waited for the twelfth of never, I'd be wasting valuable time. Waiting fifteen minutes seemed reasonable. With no watch, the only way to approximate the passage of time was to do a second count. I started, *one Mississippi, two Mississippi,* but boredom and loss of focus made me start over a couple of times. I decided to make a guess and trust to fate.

Little noises drew my attention at first. The whirring of the AC and refrigeration units were all I could discern, until a sound I recognized got my complete attention. A big cat's roar exploded the quiet. A number of overlapping guttural growls followed. The tigers were hungry. I peeked around the truck's wall in the direction from where the animal noises came. Another roar came followed by two more. Movement caught my attention. A door opened on the building's wall, and the guard emerged. I thought I heard him laugh, but it was so faint I couldn't be sure. Low rumbling growls came from that direction. He'd been teasing the cats. I thought about a Jim Croce song and words from it, *Don't step on Superman's cape.*

I had the advantage now. The guard didn't know I was present and I could watch and avoid him. The man carried a weapon, but in the light conditions and from the ninety foot distance exact identification wasn't possible. It was some type of a fully automatic, from the profile and its small size it looked like an Uzi. It had an unusual strap dangling between his wrist and gun. I didn't want to be on the wrong end of the barrel of that weapon.

The guard sauntered directly to the lighted office. He was tall, thin, and disinterested. He didn't look for anything except the office chair he was thinking about parking his rear in. I watched as he unlocked the entrance, entered the office, placed his weapon on a table near the door, turned on a TV and sat down with his back to the window and door. That gave me something to smile about.

I eased my way out of the truck and moved around the side that hid me from view of the office and the guard. My first look of the other side of the building came from where I stood. A wall was about twenty feet in front of the truck. Over half of it was windowless with one double door located in the this section. The remaining expanse consisted of multiple cold storage locker doors and, nearest to the external wall, a thirty foot section of windowless space with one door providing access to the area. That door shielded something special if the safety lights, elaborate latches, and safety devices indicated its relative need for security.

I was out of the truck safely. The guard had just completed his rounds so I had a period of time to find a safe place to hide and find a weapon. If possible, a phone would be good. Time was crucial. How much time did I have between the guard's rounds? How much time would it take for my disappearance to be confirmed? How much time would it take for Reading to come for me? How much time did I have before I had to make the decision to get out by myself? Time was something I couldn't waste.

I slipped around the front of the truck and saw the guard still seated, his feet resting on the desk in front of him, fully engrossed in the TV program. The area between the truck and the wall I hadn't had a chance to see before moving around the van was devoid of hiding places. Three huge overhead doors provided access to the building for trucks or other vehicles. Parked next to that wall, between those doors and the office the guard sat in, were four ATVs and the swamp buggy I'd ridden on less than forty-eight hours before. One of those might be my last hope of escaping. I fervently hoped the keys were left in their ignition switches.

Time was wasting. Finding a place to hide was imperative. Remembering Rooster's reference to leaving the alarm systems on for the meat rooms, common sense suggested avoiding the refrigerated doors in front of me and I decided the door with all the security items attached should be low on my list. The distance between where I crouched and the double door that offered the best chance of shelter was around seventy-five feet. The problem: What if those doors were locked? The open spaces of the warehouse offered no place to hide and the doors leading to the big cats were a ludicrous choice. I took a deep breath, remained crouched low, and swiftly moved to the double doors. I pushed on the bars mounted on one of the panels. To my surprise the door swung open and I stepped into a long hall. It was brightly lighted and I pushed the door closed to keep the guard from noticing. He remained clueless.

As I stood there, heart pounding, I recognized the odor I smelled every time I was in Rooster's presence. I truly was in the belly of the beast.

Seventy Four

"Shit, shit, shit! This is taking too long." Reading looked at his watch. It was six hours since Benson had given his limited approval to launch a rescue attempt. Now, Reading waited on a farm lane a quarter mile from Power Line Road. All five members of his volunteer commando unit were ready to go, but becoming more apprehensive by the minute. They'd just completed a squabble over who would wear the three night-vision scopes available.

One asked, "Is this going to happen for real?"

Reading answered, "Yes, soon as Chief McGill contacts Sheriff Threep."

"What are we waiting for? Old Threep is an asshole. He'll sit on his butt and want to do nothing." Sullivan wasn't a patient person. "If we don't get started soon and if what you told us is correct, your sister will be fish bait before we get to her."

"I'll try again," Reading said. He called Benson. Their conversation was brief. After the call, Reading told them, "We go in an hour, regardless."

"That's what McGill told you?" Sullivan asked.

Reading shook his head.

Seventy Five

The hall was over a hundred feet long. Numerous doors emptied into the corridor. The two located on the right side of the hall had red lights mounted above them, but the lights weren't illuminated. Six doors were located on the left side, some with windows, some without. I'd tried the first two doors on the left side. Locked! They were doors without windows and it discouraged me. What if they all were locked? The third door wasn't. Behind the windowless panel was a locker room that smelled of disinfectant. A row of a dozen metal closets lined one wall. Fresh scrubs hung on five of them. There was no place to hide. I tried to get into the individual lockers, but every one was locked. I quickly moved on.

The next door had a window in it, was unlocked, and was empty. I crossed the hall to one of the doors that had a light mounted above it. There was no window. I turned the doorknob, pulled the door open and stepped inside the dark room. As the door closed behind me, I felt for a light switch. My fingers found one and bright lights illuminated the area. Immediately in front of me, behind glass panels and glass sliding doors, was as complete of an operating room as one would find in the most innovative hospital. Tables, with trays of tools covered by plastic, stood surrounding an area that was the focus of a complex lighting system. An x-ray machine was visible through an open door inside the operating area. Two conveyor belts exited the room through its rear wall. Microscopes and many other expensive looking pieces of equipment sat on tables at various locations around the room. A waste container with a bio-hazard symbol on it sat a few feet from the sliding doors. Shelves loaded with small bottles and boxes stood against one wall. A stack of the special shipping containers rested on a platform next to where I visualized the doctors standing to operate.

Outside the glass panels and door, stainless steel carts, three feet wide and eight feet long were arranged in a neat row of seven. Each had four wheels and troughs that completely surrounded the structure that was the right height to have served as a gurney or an operating table. Nothing else shared the portion of the room the carts and I stood in except the strong odor of chlorine. When I tried to enter the operating room I found the doors were locked. Standing at those doors, the realization of what I was seeing was undeniable. Harlan Mengel's main business wasn't animal experiments, medicines, beef cattle, fish farming, bait, or anything legal. That was camouflage as surely as the paint on the outside of the building I was trapped in. His illegal enterprise wasn't cocaine, or smuggling some other commodity. Nor was it murder, other than the fact murder was incidental to his real interest. I was looking at the heart of an organ harvesting business.

I backed to the door, turned out the lights, peeked outside and slipped into the hall. I'd just gazed at the devil's home and realized that it would be the last thing I ever saw if I ever returned. The urgency to find a hiding spot and weapon increased tenfold. I raced to the next door, one with a light above it, on the same side of the hall. The door knob turned. I jerked open the door and stepped inside, finding the lights and turning them on in the same sequence of motions and gagged violently.

The smell that always accompanied Rooster was mixed with the smell of chlorine creating a vile concoction that could scarcely be considered air. What I saw was as offensive to my eyes as the atmosphere was to my nose. Conveyor belts entered the room from three different locations. All three fed a huge cylindrical machine that straddled another conveyor. On that belt, molds used to make chum blocks were lined up. The meaning was clear. A mixture of fish and beef parts were being added to human bodies to serve as a method of disposing of murder evidence without leaving traces. Surrounding the stainless machine was a platform with a ladder up to it. Sitting on the platform, I saw the bottom of a table that had handles extending over its edge. Among the handles I saw a knife blade. A weapon.

I climbed the ladder as though my pants were on fire. The table had several knives, a meat clever, and a hatchet sitting on it. The hatchet head fit in my rear pants pocket and wouldn't impede my ability to move. A knife with nine inch pointed blade was formidable so I snatched it from the table. Before I scrambled down the ladder my eyes were unable to avoid the temptation of looking into the six foot diameter opening of the cylinder. A massive set of blades mounted to a screw-like devices cut and mashed anything fed into its maw into two inch cubes that dropped through the hopper on the bottom into the molds. I shuddered and looked away before my dizziness changed to a full-fledged faint. When I fully regained my senses, I had made it down the ladder and was at the exit. The stench and the thoughts of what transpired in this room overcame me. I vomited. They'd know someone had been in the room. It didn't matter. I needed to find a place to hide and hope someone came to rescue me. If they didn't, it truly didn't matter.

I checked the hall for the presence of the guard before darting out, crossing to and entering a room on the opposite side. When I turned the lights on, I found I was in a room with clothes hanging on hangers suspended from pipe racks. The one on the end caught my attention. The stains on the front of the man's work shirt were vaguely familiar then I saw the name *Ruppert* stitched on its front. I could feel my hair stand on end. I looked for and found a tee shirt with a unique blue tint. On its front the words *Tips for Tits* was printed like an epitaph. It was difficult for me to know whether my fear or anger was strongest. There was no place to hide. I had to leave immediately or my clothes would join those on the rack.

Peeking into the hall before I stepped back into it, I accelerated my efforts to find a place to hide. I raced to the next door and found it was locked. The next door was also locked, but it had a window in it and enough light filtered through the glass for me to see it was an office. A phone rested on the desk. I inserted my knife blade in the space between the door and the jam and tried to push the lock bolt back. It wouldn't budge. Help was ten feet away and it might as well have been ten miles. Reluctantly, I ran to the next door, and the next, and the next. They were all locked. I'd made the cycle of all doors in the hallway. I decided that I had to check to see if the guard was still in place then check the rest of doors in the warehouse area.

Pushing the double doors open just enough to view the office on the far side, the guard was still seated in the office. His posture in the chair suggested he might be asleep. I squeezed through the doors, crouched down, ran to the truck and hid behind it. I looked closely at the area I hadn't visited yet. Five freezer rooms were close and weren't worth investigating. One of those had a sign above it that read Flash Freezing, protective clothing required! The one remaining door on that wall was the one with security devices attached. It would be my last resort.

There were only two doors on the exterior wall. One I'd seen the guard come out of had something to do with the big cats. There was another thirty feet away that had nothing indicating there was anything special about it. That would be my first choice. I poked my head around the truck's front fender. The guard hadn't moved. I trotted to the door and prayed I'd find that safe place to hide.

Seventy Six

Reading put the cell phone in his pocket and said, "Let's go." No one asked if Chief McGill had approved as Reading turned the ignition key in the delivery van borrowed from the impound lot.

When they arrived at the Circle X Ranch gate and after Reading parked the van, he said, "Okay, if any of you have second thoughts, now is the time. I'll understand." There was only silence in response. After several seconds he opened the van's door and picked up a bolt cutter from on the floor next to him. He said, "Let's get this done."

Reading cut the chain on the gate, it fell to the ground as the metal framework swung open several inches.

Caralene played her flashlight beam over it then a few inches to the side. She said, "Look at those tire tracks. Someone has been in here since it rained. That's in the last hour."

All knew what that could mean. "We'll drive instead of walk. I won't turn the lights on. We can get out before we get to the guard's shack."

As they climbed back into the van, all knew time was urgent … and getting more so.

Seventy Seven

It was locked. In black stenciled lettering the words, Hazardous materials storage, were on the sign next to the door. I glanced at the guard. The only change was that he had slipped into a deeper sleep judging from his body that slumped deeper in his seat and his arms that dangled limply at his sides. I decided to check the door I'd seen him exit earlier and I knew had some connection to the big cats. It might offer possibilities.

I ran to it, checked the guard one last time and carefully pulled the door open. It was inky black inside, the dim light from the warehouse produced suggestions of what was inside rather than clear visions. To one side light exposed a continuous row of vertical metal bars. Cages? Keeping one foot in the doorway to keep it from closing, I eased inside and allowed my vision to adjust. The strong smells of cat urine, feces, and rotten meat assaulted my nostrils before my eyes began capturing what the room's interior looked like.

What I'd entered was a wing built on the main building. There wasn't sufficient light to see into the deep recesses, but what I could see was chilling enough. Lines of bars disappeared into the dark on both sides of a wide aisle. In the aisle, metal carts built low to the ground were spread around at random. My guess was they were for feeding the animals. I was sure that part of the main course was human flesh. The cats, the piranhas, the chum blocks and who knew what else were an elaborate and efficient evidence disposal systems. I didn't want to disturb the cats if they were in the cages so I didn't even look for a light switch. It was impossible to find a hiding place because my foot tethered me to the door. Placing the butt of my knife between the door and the jam on the hinge side, I allowed the closer to pinch it in place and free me to do a little exploring.

As my eyes adjusted to the light, I peered into the cages as I walked past. The first two I checked didn't have a cat in them; the third did. Simultaneous to seeing the black outline lying on the floor, I realized that a chain-link fence served as the outer wall and the gates were open to the outside. The animals could come and go at will. A wall was at the end … no door … nowhere to hide. I'd passed ten cages, five on either side of the aisle. Only three of them had animals in them. If they noticed me, they didn't show a sign. Curiosity made me try to lift the latch on a cage door. To my surprise it wasn't locked. The door immediately tried to swing open. I pushed it closed and the latch eased down. I was wasting time.

Noises behind me caused me to freeze as I walked toward the door. Two distinct sounds co-mingled. One was the sound of sandpaper rubbing steel. The second … a deep rumbling purr … one a house cat couldn't make. Slowly, my head and shoulders swiveled. In the dull light orange, black, and white stripes stood thirty feet behind me. The tiger's head was buried in one of the steel trays licking the bottom. Zing! The cage door where I'd lifted the latch was open. I remembered a TV program about Grizzly bears and a caution that the worst thing to do was run from them. Running or quick moves triggered what the commentator said was a predator response. Dinner time. I hoped tigers reacted the same way. I turned slowly and backed toward the door. My knife had to be removed from its place as a wedge in the jam. The fifteen feet I had to cover was like fifteen miles in my mind. Finally, my hand touched the door. The tiger's head remained inside the tray.

Deliberately, I turned, removed my knife by opening the door as little as I could to free it. As I turned to back out of the door, the door closer emitted a puff of air with a, *shhiiisssshh* sound. The tiger's head came up immediately and its glowing eyes focused on me. Panic took over. I stepped out of the room as fast as I could and slammed it behind me.

Putting my shoulder to the door, I waited for the thrust of the tiger crashing against it. It never came. Instead, I heard a low rumbling growl followed by silence. I looked at the door latch. No wonder it was so heavy duty. The next person who was unfortunate enough to open that handle would be faced with a deadly surprise.

The fact hit me … I'd completely forgotten about the guard. The thought made me spin around and look at the office. My breath escaped in a relieved sigh. The guard was still in the sand man's land. It was unbelievable that he wasn't making another round … hours had elapsed from the time he entered the office and settled into his chair. One door left I hadn't explored. I raced to it. In addition to a heavy duty lockset, door latches were available to be put in place if needed. I asked myself, "For what?"

I felt for the hatchet handle, confirming it was there and could be removed quickly, then tried the door lever. To my surprise it was not locked. One of three latches was in use. I opened it and prepared to enter. I looked at a light over the door. It remained unlighted. The guard remained zonked, so I pulled the door open and entered what I expected would be complete darkness. To my surprise, the large room was dimly lighted.

The room was unlike anything I'd never seen. All walls had doors spaced six feet apart with a viewing window in them. Eight of these doors were on each side wall and four were across the back of the room. Most of the viewing windows were dark. Four of them, scattered in different places, were lighted and in addition, a small circular light was illuminated above each of those doors. I would check them, but not before I made sense out of what I was looking at in the room's center.

It was like a first aid room without walls. In the center stood an examination table with the back raised. It looked like the standard item one would see in any doctor's office with one exception; the heavy restraints attached to it. Racks and stands for IV bags clustered around it. Three large tables with electronic devices, screens, LED readouts and monitors, surrounded the chair. Sheets were stacked on one of them. Two of the metal Gurney-like carts I'd seen in the operation room were a few feet away. Cylinders of some sort of gas with regulators, tubing and masks stood a few feet from the head end of the chair. A cold shiver passed through me. This is where the victims were prepared for the surgery that removed their organs.

It meant ... I shuddered again ... the humans who would be murdered were kept in this room, alive, until their heart, lungs, liver, kidneys, and whatever else the ghouls running this place could steal from them. I rushed to one of the lighted windows.

I eased my head into a position to look into the room. It looked like a cell. But I lost interest in the details of the six foot by eight foot cubicle when I saw what was on a rack style bed. A naked woman lay on the mattress, her eyes closed, apparently asleep. Anger controlled me. Who could do this to another person? I knew who! I grabbed the door knob and tried to open the door, but it was locked. The deadbolt must be, too. If I could wake the woman, maybe we could force it open. Beating on the door didn't wake her. I raced to the next lighted window.

Another naked body lay on the bed. I gasped. It was Ruppert from the car rental agency.

Before I realized it, I screamed at him, was shaking the door, and trying to turn the handle at the same time. It wouldn't budge. Beating on the door, as I peered through the window, I saw his eyes try to open then relax again. He and the woman had been sedated.

"Think. Chessie!" I chastised myself. How could I get them out? The windows had wire mesh in them so breaking one wouldn't help. If I did get in, the deadbolt would still prohibit me from getting Ruppert out. The hatchet would break the window and I could possibly break off the door knob. There was still the deadbolt. "Damn," I mumbled and looked at the door again. Hinges! I could use the hatchet to knock out the hinge pins then I could open the door the opposite way it was intended. Within seconds I had the hatchet in hand and in sixty seconds more the pins lay on the floor. I used the hatchet to pry the door open. Success!

Failure! As soon as the door separated from the jam a buzzer started blasting in two second bursts. The light above the door flashed on and off. I'd set off an alarm. What Rooster referred to as the *meat rooms* was now apparent.

Seventy Eight

Reading and Sullivan crawled along the fence on either side of the sand road ninety feet from the guard shack. Fifty yards behind, Caralene and the other two volunteers knelt in firing positions, their Thompson M1A1 sub-machine guns aimed at the unsuspecting guard. Confident ninety rounds from their three magazines would destroy the man if he resisted Reading and Sullivan's attempt to capture him and the guard post without violence, they hoped pulling the triggers wouldn't be necessary.

As they watched, red lights and a gong began sounding from the compound far beyond the guard house. Flood lights changed the area around the buildings ahead of them from night to day. A floodlight drenched the sand road and all five volunteers in light. The guard didn't see them. His focus was on the compound. While Reading and Sullivan got to their feet and rushed the shack, the guard threw a switch and continued to stare at the buildings inside. Five steps before they reached the guard, he picked up a phone and was speaking as they ripped open the door and wrestled him to the ground. Blue lights turned on around the gate.

Reading screamed, "Stay away from the fence. It's electrified!"

Seventy Nine

The guard wasn't in the office. Frantically, I looked around the warehouse. I couldn't see him. Common sense told me he had to be coming straight for me. I jerked the door closed. There was no way to lock it so I searched for a place to hide. I ran and tried three of the cell doors; all were locked. I was running out of time. The only place to hide was behind or under the furniture and equipment in the center of the room. As I ran to the cluster, the sheets on one of the tables caught my attention. I snatched three of the sheets off the table, opened them and threw a cloth over each table, covering the equipment as though the sheets were protecting it. After adjusting each so they were close to the floor on all sides. I dropped to the floor and rolled under the one where the sheet was closest to touching the concrete. After positioning myself so the door was visible through the two inches between floor and sheet, I closed my eyes, prayed, and hoped my heart would slow before it gave out.

Fear that I would be caught before I found a place to hide, quickly transformed to fear of the unknown. No one came as quickly as I expected. I waited … and waited. A second's duration as a unit of time increases geometrically as the tension increases from waiting for the inevitable. At first, I was confounded. Why wasn't the guard opening the door? Though I'm sure it wasn't more than ten minutes, it seemed it took ten hours. When it came my heart sank.

The door opened slowly. No one was visible. A voice called out, "Rooster, you in there?"

Oh shit! The person who was least likely to show me any compassion was in the building and hunting me. I sincerely hoped he didn't know who he was looking for.

"Rooster," the man repeated.

I had to remember to breathe. First came the muzzle of the machine gun followed by the guard holding it as he peeked around the corner of the jamb. His eyes systematically scoured the room's interior. He said something I couldn't hear, into a radio mounted on his shoulder. I wanted to curse. Help was sure to come. If it was possible, my best chance was to dispose of the man walking through the door, quickly, and get out of the room where I was caged like a rat. The guard didn't take a second look at the area where I hid.

Instead, the man flattened against the wall and focused completely at the cell that I had ripped open and where Ruppert laid unconscious. My decision and action was instantaneous. The guard would be less than thirty feet away, his back toward me when he investigated Ruppert's cell, and I'd be out of his peripheral vision. I hoped. I held the hatchet in my hand and was ready without thinking about it. Noiselessly, I slid from under the table, waited for the man to peer into the cell, then jumped to my feet, and sprinted up to his rear. I couldn't bring myself to use the blade portion of the hatchet on his head, In mid-swing, I altered the blow bringing the flat side of the hatchet down on his head. A mushy *thonk* sound preceded the guard's crumbling to the ground.

I dropped the hatchet and knife. The Uzi submachine was a present from heaven. It seemed that way until I tried to pick it up from the ground. When I lifted it, the strap pulled tight. The strap I'd noticed in the truck hours ago was shackled to his wrist and bolted to the gun. Unless I wanted to become a female Custer, the weapon wasn't any value to me. I yelled, "Shit," ran for the door and looked out. Yellow lights rotated and flashed. The sound of a gong added to the bedlam the buzzer caused. All three large truck doors on the exterior wall on the opposite side of the building stood open. If I could get to one of the ATVs I'd have a chance.

Quickly, I swiveled my head from side to side looking for Rooster or other guards that might bar my way. No one was in sight. I took a deep breath, and raced to the visual cover Rooster's truck provided. Flattening against the box section at the truck's rear, still, no one was in sight. I drew another panicked breath, put my head down, and dashed toward the parked ATVs. When I raised my head I was a third of the way across the warehouse floor and Rooster Cocker stood in one of the open truck doors a hundred feet in front of me. He pulled out his Bowie knife and screamed, "It's you! Okay, cunt, it's my turn!"

Stopping quickly, I reversed my path, running as fast as I could for the opposite wall. Dropping the hatchet and knife was super dumb, but ... I had only one slim possibility of not ending up being Rooster's play-toy and eventually a scabbard for his knife. Sprinting, I targeted the door to the cages that housed the big cats. When I reached the wall, Rooster had narrowed my lead to forty feet.

I turned and faced him standing directly in front of the door. My hand went on the door lever. I flexed my knees to make it appear I was going to run. Rooster was a few steps away when he lunged at me. I pulled the door open. Stepping aside and placing one hand on his back, I pushed him into the big cat room, using the momentum of his rush at me to send him sprawling inside. As soon as his legs disappeared, I slammed the door, placed my shoulder against it, grasped the lever, and held it, bracing against his attempt to force it open.

One Mississippi ... two Mississippi ... three Mississippi.
Nothing happened. *Four Mississippi* ... I felt pressure
against my hand as Rooster pushed down on the lever. I
heard him say, "You damned bitch." Desperately, we
fought each other for control of the lever that would
determine if he or I died. On the opposite side of the door,
he was winning. My fingers felt on fire, they hurt.

Seconds from being overpowered, I heard an ear
shattering roar and a shrill scream mixed together. All
pressure ceased on the lever. Screams of pure terror
repeated, mixed with a low growl. In the time it took for
Rooster to grasp the lever and try to get out, the tiger had
killed him. I hoped he never saw the animal until after he
was half dead. Grateful there was no window because I was
sure I would have looked and would have regretted that
forever. I clung to lever for thirty seconds before placing
my ear to the door. There was silence until I heard a crack
followed by a crunching sound. Bones. The tiger was
eating Rooster. In horror, I released the handle and stepped
back from the door, half disbelieving what I knew just
happened.

My knees shook. partly from the fear I'd just
experienced, partly from the relief of believing I was safe.

"Miss Partin, you're a huge pain in the ass." I turned.
Harlan Mengel and Dr. James Orella, whom I recognized
from his photo in the surgical center, stood twenty feet
from me. Mengel frowned and saw me tense my body to
run. He said, "No, no. Don't try that." Mengel held a SIG
Sauer MPX and Orella held a .45 automatic. Mengel was
calm.

Roars from the tiger froze us all for a couple of
seconds. Mengel said, "Poor Rooster, he was a faithful

man, not necessarily a good one. Do you think he deserved to die in that manner, Miss Partin?"

I couldn't answer him and I don't have any idea what kind of expression was on my face. Whatever was there, amused him. He smiled and said, "Stay completely still if you want an opportunity to stay alive."

I'd never experienced a greater feeling of despair combined with discouragement in my life.

Eighty

"The guard she hit, taken care of?" Mengel asked.

A man I never saw before answered, "Yes."

"Everyone else accounted for?" Mengel looked relaxed.

The alarms continued to sound and lights flashed. I wondered why. I was handcuffed to the arm of the office chair where the guard whose head I'd smashed, sat an hour ago. Was someone else loose? What was going on?

"They will be. All but the guard at the main gate," the man said.

"We'll get him with the phone call." He looked at Dr. Orella. "You go with Ivan. Ivan, is everything ready?"

"There will be nothing left of those things that must be destroyed." The man motioned to the doctor. "Come on, it's time to meet the Baron."

I watched two of the more deplorable humans I've ever seen leave the office and climb into an ATV. They drove out through one of the open bay doors into the night and invisibility. I remained in the presence of the most despicable person I'd ever known. And one of the smartest.

Mengel picked up his SIG Sauer submachine gun from the desk and smiled at me. He said, "You might be foolish enough to try if I leave my gun in front of you. Chambering a shell with one hand, very difficult. But you are tenacious and I want you alive - for now."

Mengel turned his back on me as he approached an elaborate control panel. He pushed a sequence of buttons. Things began to turn off: the gong, the buzzer, the flashing yellow lights, and finally, the flood lights. Peace and quiet returned, but it was the peace and quiet of the graveyard. He looked at his watch, smiled, and said, "We'll see if your friend Chief McGill cares for you a lot or a little. I suspect a lot."

I looked at him sullenly, but said nothing.

"I'll answer the question you'd like to ask, but want to deny me any pleasure I'd derive from it." Mengel checked his watch again. "In a few minutes the phone will ring. It will be Benson McGill. He will ask to speak to you. I'll grant him the privilege. Your voice will confirm you're alive. You will tell him you are unhurt. You will say nothing else." Mengel smiled like a father giving advice to his daughter. "Remember, that following those instructions is a life or death matter. Your life or death."

I nodded. No doubt the man would kill me with less feeling than he would have in mashing a mosquito.

"Good. I see you understand." Mengel returned to the desk, lifted one leg, and rested his buttocks on the surface in front of me. "Chessie Partin. A good name for you. You are commonplace and unusual at the same time. I've met few men or women that are so determined, so clever, and so rash. I genuinely admire your tenacity. Miss Partin, you are causing me problems I am careful to avoid."

"Thank you, I think." I said.

The phone rang. Mengel said, "Remain quiet until I give you permission to speak. Remember your instructions. You will be on the speaker." His eyes asked the question and I nodded in response. Mengel pushed a phone button and said, "Good morning, Chief McGill."

"Good mornin', Harlan." Benson's voice sounded more like he was at a church social than negotiating for my life. "I assume you're going to let me speak to Chessie so we can get on with this."

"Unfortunately, I have one additional, unnegotiable demand to make. You have one of my men in custody. I believe he is still at the gate where he was posted. You'll have to release him back to me. Loyalty and all that. Once he's here and I confirm that to you, our agreement goes into effect." Mengel placed an index finger to his lips as a reminder.

"It will take some time. We've removed him from—" Benson tried stalling, but Mengel would have none of that.

"Come, come, McGill. Our relationship hasn't been clouded with lies. Let's not introduce that now." Mengel smiled at me. "You see, I know three things. One, my man is sitting on the ground in cuffs a few feet from the guard shack. Two, the attempts your people are making to cut electric to the fence at the gate won't be successful. In fairness, their continued effort could very well cause a monstrous explosion. Three, your efforts to get the use of Arcel Threep's helicopter will fail. The sheriff is an expensive, but reliable person. Now, shall we proceed, or shall I place my weapon to Miss Partin's head and end her suspense?"

"Okay." Benson's friendly tone was gone. "I want to talk to Chessie. Now!"

Mengel nodded to me. "Say hello, Miss Partin."

"Hello."

There was a hesitation. Benson said, "I want her to answer a couple questions. You could have recorded one word."

"Hmm, no honor? All right, ask your questions. Keep in mind I'll keep her from answering anything that I don't wish you to know." Mengel looked at me.

"How you are, Chessie? Tell me in your words." McGill wanted something that couldn't be faked.

I answered, "I'm not hurt. Just some bruises I did to myself. I am scared shitless."

The Chief remained silent for a few seconds then asked, "One more thing. How many orchids do you have at your duplex?"

My eyes must have widened because Mengel understood the meaning of McGill's question before I did. He raised his finger to his lips. "Good try, Chief. I'll answer that. I have seventeen besides myself. Now, when can I expect my man?"

"How do you expect us to get him through the damned gate without frying him?" Benson was agitated. I could imagine his face.

"Leave that to me. How do you think I could so accurately give you information about my guard's location? My control is centralized. The five people you sent originally, the two squad cars, and the four additional men will all move back a hundred yards after you uncuff my man. I'll allow my man to enter then recharge the fence. The area where your people are could incinerate if there is an accident. We wouldn't want to kill all those folks, would we?"

"No." Benson talked to someone, was silent for a minute, then said, "He's loose and my people are moving back."

Mengel got up and looked at a screen I couldn't see from my seat. "Fine." Mengel pushed some buttons on the control panel, hesitated, then pushed more buttons. He spoke to McGill, "Chief, it has been interesting. I'd council you to keep your force where they are for a minimum of an hour. It would be safer for them. After our truce expires, tell your men while they're groping around in the woods, we're all trained in special combat skills They try to capture us at their peril. You do understand?" He returned to the desk where I sat.

"Yes." Benson's response sounded hollow.

"Good. Oh, you needn't thank me. You should win your election handily, unless you're far less intelligent than I believe you to be." Mengel reach out and pushed the button disconnecting the phone call. He watched me, expecting that I'd say something, but I had nothing. Finally he said, "Now, we wait."

"For what?" I asked.

"The guard who was at the gate."

"Then what, you kill me?" I didn't believe I'd see the sunrise over the Atlantic again.

"No. No, no, no. Your death wouldn't benefit me. Besides you are a person whose life has merit. What I'll tell you now will disgust you. Frankly my dear, I don't give a damn, to quote old Clark Gable." He smiled. "I believe life is a valuable gift. I transfer it to those who have merit, take it from those that don't or have limited time to use it."

Angrily I snapped, "And make a hell of a profit."

"Absolutely. With great risk comes great reward. If I thought I could have purchased your silence I would have done so. Price would not have been an object. As I said, you are a person who possesses merit."

"Why? You don't have to make yourself rich in this way." I couldn't understand a man with his intelligence and some grip on right and wrong doing what he did.

"I can't explain to you what I can't explain to myself." He smiled. "Let's leave it at you'll live, so will those four you saw in the rooms," he pointed to the area where Ruppert and the rest still lay and added, "They will be my present." He shook his head sadly. "You are causing me a great inconvenience; I liked this area of Florida. Moving again wasn't in my plans."

"Moving again?" My jaw dropped, I'm sure.

He smiled, but didn't answer. Instead he said, "Rooster, not you, caused my problem. His need for forced intercourse finally destroyed him. When he killed the Perez girl and her friend, I knew I'd have to do something, but I didn't realize he'd lost all control until I found about you. It was too late. His death was fitting, but a waste of his organs. Now I move and start over."

Speechless, I shook my head. The sound of gun fire made my eyes open wide. Mengel smiled. "Loose ends."

"You really think you'll get away? Benson McGill is honest and as stubborn as a mule. He'll find you." I stopped talking. I'd said too much.

"No, he won't. He'll try. There will be indignation, activity, machinations of all varieties. Fingers will point … at scapegoats. How high does this go? Local officials? I'll answer that, yes. Feds? Some. Government agencies? How high? Cabinet officials?" He paused. "Even higher? You're welcome to try … at your peril."

The sound of an ATV interrupted his warning. "I see my man has arrived." We watched the man drive up to a few feet of the office door. He swung out of the vehicle and entered the office. His first words were, "Thanks, Colonel. I thought I was toast."

"Where's your weapon?"

"Hell, Colonel, they took it. I couldn't hardly ask for it."

Mengel nodded and said, "We need to leave immediately. I have a couple of things that have to go. Put that in the ATV and come back in." He pointed to a large steel box. The man picked up the case, struggled through the door, and placed it in the ATV. The guard returned, smiled and asked, "Is she going? I think the plane's ready. I heard Ivan revving the engines as I came up."

"No." Mengel raised the SIG Sauer, looked at me, before aiming at the guard's chest. He fired six rounds into the man's lungs and heart. When the man hit the floor Mengel took careful aim and placed one additional 9mm in the man's forehead. I screamed, shook uncontrollably, and was sure I was next.

"A loose end," he said.

"What about me?" I was petrified.

Mengel removed a small tube from his shirt pocket and walked behind me.

I asked, "Are you going to kill me?" Simultaneously I felt the prick of a hypodermic needle puncture my neck. I screamed in anger, not fear. Immediately a strange feeling and drowsiness invaded me. The last thing I remember were his words, "If you wake up, you'll know I didn't."

Eighty One

"They went to see the Baron."

"Chessie." The voice sounded familiar. Vaguely.

The only thing my brain allowed me to say was, "They went to see the Baron."

"Chessie, sweetie, wake up." The voice stopped talking to me. It said, "Go get Reading."

"That's my brother," or at least I thought so. What was that first thing? "Oh yes, they went to see the Baron." I wasn't sure who the Baron was, but something in the muddle that was my thinking process yelled *important*. Would it help to see where I was? Probably. Opening my eyes would be good. My eye lids weighed a ton each. I opened them slowly as I remembered someone was going to kill me. I saw white. White everywhere. Good! There wasn't any fire. I had always thought I'd end up in Hell. A familiar smiling face appeared above me. I asked, "Are you dead too, Reading?" I blinked to be sure he was there.

"You're in the hospital, not heaven." Reading put his hand on my forehead, very unReading-like. He's not the touchy, feely type.

Suddenly, the reason I was in a hospital bed crashed its way into my consciousness. "Mengel!" I tried to rise on my elbows, but my arms wouldn't function. My first directive returned, "They went to see the Baron."

"Baron?" Reading asked.

Things were coming back, but in a jumbled, confused manner. "Yes, the Baron. I'm sure. He has two engines. I mean *it* has two engines." I strained my brain for a few seconds before I could finish what I wanted him to know. "The Baron is an airplane."

"Caralene, get McGill in here, please." Reading looked back and to his side.

I rolled my head on the pillow enough to see the bed rails, tubes disappearing into my arm, Reading's body, and the faces of Lisa Lister and Caralene. The portion of my mind that promotes good judgment wasn't functioning. I examined the two ladies and pronounced, "Caralene, you look tired as shit and Lisa you need to go put your makeup on." Both laughed.

Reading said, "We knew some of them got away in an airplane, but we didn't know what type. That will help."

My memory returned in rushes. "Reading, he killed a man in front of me; *right in front of me*. He shot him. Mengel is a monster. He was kidnapping people and harvesting their body parts. He was getting rid of—" Two more faces appeared above me, one of which turned my blood to lava. I screamed, "Sheriff Threep, you are a worthless son-of-a-bitch."

Threep looked as shocked as McGill looked amused. But the person whose interest was most aroused was Lisa. She scrambled for something to write notes on.

"You knew what he was doing out there. You knew he—"

Chief McGill waved his hand at me, winked, and said, "Not now, Chessie." He put his hand on the sheriff's shoulder and said, "Arcel, let's leave the poor girl rest, she's likely still under the effects of the anesthetic Mengel pumped into her." He steered a shook and frightened Threep toward the door. As McGill left he asked, "Beechcraft Baron?"

Reading nodded, said, "Yes," and he held up his finger to his lips for me. I scowled at him and said, "You look just like that bastard, Mengel!"

"What?"

"Never mind!" Explanations of that nature weren't at the top of *my* list. I asked, "Did you catch him or the others?" Before Reading could answer, I said, "He got away or you wouldn't be wanting to know the type aircraft he was flying."

Reading took his normal seconds to organize his thoughts before telling me, "Yes, we haven't caught him, yet. There are lots of complications. We aren't getting cooperation from some of the government sources we'd hoped. The crime scene has been seized by the representatives from the FBI and Justice Department."

Mengel's words replayed in my memory, *How high does this go? Local officials? I'll answer that, yes. Feds? Some. Government agencies? How high? Cabinet officials? Even higher? You're welcome to try ... at your peril.* I asked, "Did you capture any of them?"

"Yes and no," Reading said. He looked disappointed. "We recovered bodies. The man Mengel shot was in the office where we found you, another was in a room on the other side of the warehouse, and we found seven bodies, six men and a woman shot execution style as a group. Judging from what they wore, we believe they were all part of Mengel's people Dead men tell no tales, I'd guess. Best we can tell, he let some get away. We found an ATV at a back gate. We found four prisoners alive in the—"

"Was Ruppert okay?"

Reading cocked his to the side, "Yes ... You were in there?"

"Uh-huh. Reading, I killed the guard you found in there."

"You shot him?"

"No." I dropped my voice to a whisper. "I hit him with the back of a hatchet."

"He had a bump on his head, but I'd bet the two bullets in his brain were what killed him."

"Did you find Rooster?" I asked.

Reading hesitated. His eyes widened. "We think so, it's hard to tell. You know about that too?"

"Yes."

"What are you talking about?" Lisa asked.

I looked at Reading and he shook his head. He said, "Lisa, that will have to wait."

"Why?" She had a sharp edge to her voice.

Caralene interjected, "You want to jeopardize an active investigation? I don't think so. Chessie, you'll give her the first interview when we give you the approval ... won't you."

"Sure," I said.

Reading asked, "Lisa, I'm sorry, but would you and Caralene leave us for a few minutes? Thanks."

Lisa was disappointed, but allowed Caralene to aim her to the door. As Lisa left she said, "Meet you at your place."

"I have to get some sleep," Reading wasn't in the mood. He looked tired enough to drop.

"Absolutely." In Lisa-ese, that meant once or twice. I giggled like a ten year old. Lisa and Caralene disappeared for several seconds before Reading asked, "Can you remember anything else that might help us find Mengel?"

I closed my eyes and tried to concentrate. "That doctor was with him. Dr. Orella. He lives out on Ocean Drive. There might be evidence—"

"The federal people already have a cordon around it. We can't get close enough to smell a clue." Reading shook his head. "I'm afraid we're going to face this—"

"Again and again." Mengel didn't over-state his power to frustrate attempts to bring him to justice. "What about Rooster's home? The address is on a slip paper next to my lap top."

"I'll check his place out as quickly as I can get someone there." Reading wrote a mental note to himself. "Anything else?" he asked.

"No. Maybe something will come later." I had to ask Reading the question I didn't have an answer for. "Why did he let me live?"

Reading shook his head slowly. "I don't have a clue. A man with a mind like his ... who knows how he's wired." He took a breath. "Don't waste your time wondering why. Spend your time giving thanks he did."

Eighty Two

"I'm so happy you've recovered from your horrible experience, Chessie." Gloria Weiss fawned over me like we were long-parted sorority sisters.

I smiled. "Thank you," I said, trying to remain gracious, albeit uncomfortably.

"I'm not supposed to tell you, but I'm sure you won't snitch on me. You're going to get an invitation from the Vero Beach Junior Women's League. I hope you'll give serious consideration to joining. We need women with your energy and determination."

I hoped my continued counterfeit grin wasn't obvious. "I'm honored. I'll certainly give it the consideration you've requested."

"Oh, I see Mildred waving for me. I have to see her. It so nice you'll be joining us." Gloria walked off, her world floating around her like a cloud.

Suppressing the desire to say, *I wouldn't give a Russian rat's ass for the privilege of joining a bunch of snobs who tell each other how great they are*, I kept silent. I was learning to play the game. How much things had changed. Women who would have changed aisles in the grocery store to avoid saying Hi to me, now were sisters. Attending an event like the one I was at certainly was another.

Robatowski's back room needed just a little oil to complete the comparison of it to a packed can of sardines. I've never seen more people compressed in so small a space, rubbing elbows, trying to keep their mixed drinks in their glasses, while being jostled by well-wishers for the new Sheriff of Indian River County. The act of change and creation is often the product of eons of time. Politics isn't a river or a mountain. I watched Benson McGill bask in his new-found glory. As newly elected sheriff, he'd become the political leader and king-maker in the county.

The assemblage was to thank those who had participated in his successful campaign. After Lisa Lister's series of reports on the sensational nature of Mengel's mass murder and organ black market, Arcel Threep's insinuated, not proven, knowledge and choice to ignore the happenings on the Circle X Ranch, the election of McGill was more accurately described as a nuclear explosion than a landslide. When addressing his admirers, Benson made sure to thank everyone remotely connected, maintain a self-effacing image, and asked for a moment of silence for the unknown number of those who were killed and their parts sold to the highest bidder.

The unvarnished truth … many of us had benefitted from the human tragedy. Benson's elevation was the most obvious. This happened despite not being able to prosecute anyone. The FBI and Justice Department placed a stranglehold on anything and everything to do with the matter. There was CIA rumored involvement. The only comment their spokesperson would make was, "No comment." We were assured we would eventually learn the results of their investigations, but it might take a few years to complete them. Once again I remembered Harlan Mengel's words.

Dr. Mark had happily supported McGill at his speaking appearances. Now, Mark's department had gone from pauper poor to new riche. He was happy. Caralene and Reading moved to the sheriff's organization and received promotions. They were happy. Benson hand-picked his replacement as chief of police and made sure Sullivan made captain. They were happy.

My fifteen minutes of fame came and went. Besides Lisa, there were several reporters a day for a week then a couple more. Thank goodness that was all. I was hired as Mark's assistant, and this enables me to finish my degree at a drastically reduced cost. The taste of crime solving appealed to me so I'm looking into criminology and forensics. I may never leave college.

Of all those who benefitted, Lisa Lister gained and lost the most. Her reporting received national attention. Reading said the few government peons that were implicated were as a result of Lisa's exposés. Scapegoat was Mengel's word for them. After things cooled, insufficient evidence connected them to Mengel and things went back the way they were except for three who lost their jobs. I'd guess it was for other reasons.

Lisa, however, became a hot commodity, and one boob job later she accepted a position with a major network in Atlanta. She left Vero in her history's dust, but at a price. Reading is an Indian River County boy and will never leave home. She spends a portion of her increased salary on airfare. Things aren't the same between them. My bet is that the sun is setting on their relationship.

My relationship with Mark is comfortable, but temporary. It serves our purposes, but Mark is a confirmed bachelor and too old for me; we are from different generations and it shows. My thirty-three and his fifty-three create a gulf of different perceptions that can't be crossed. Besides, I want more than the physical, and that's what we have together.

As I sat in my seat at Robatowski's and listened to Benson McGill conduct his show of gratitude, I wondered about Harlan Mengel. Was he alive? If he was alive, where was he? Would he ever be caught? Would he ever pay for the evil he commits? Every time I hear of an organ transplant I wonder if he had an involvement. I took a couple of large sips of wine as Benson spoke. Most of all, I wonder why he let me live. I remembered the trophies in Rooster's house that belonged to Mengel. Was I some sort of trophy? That was a four sip thought.

Epilogue

"Your mail is on the kitchen table," Reading said as we passed going in opposite directions through our duplex's front door. He stopped, smiled, and added, "Saw Hootie today. He said to wish you happy birthday. He also said he needed a part-time mate on the boat if you needed some extra money. Hootie told me you were the best damned mate he ever had." Reading held his hands out, palms up. "Tell me, Sis, does thirty-five feel older than thirty-four?"

"Not one bit. I just double up on my Centrum Silver," I quipped.

"You're well remembered, Chessie. There's a stack of cards mixed in with the bills." Reading waved and walked toward his shiny new sheriff's department cruiser with Captain Reading Partin freshly painted on the side.

It was nice to know I was remembered by my friends; they made a larger stack than the bills. As I sat at the table, one piece of mail caught my eye, a post card. They have become as rare as they were prolific in the past.

I picked it up. The picture featured a waterfront street that had a European flavor to it, with the royal blue water dotted with rustic fishing boats. The caption read: *Beautiful Majorca and the Mediterranean*. Majorca, I thought, where was that? After several seconds I remembered. Off Spain, near Barcelona. I was pretty sure that was correct. Caralene was vacationing in Europe, I guessed it was from her.

I turned the card over. The message was very short.
Happy Birthday, Miss Merit. I miss parts of you.

About Author DL Havlin

DL Havlin is an eclectic author whose varied experiences and background provide him with a memory chest full of material for writing his novels. He graduated from the University of Cincinnati and attended pre-law at Rollins.

His life has been as varied as his novels. Havlin's occupations have included tasks from systems analyst to world-wide customer service director and from licensed boat captain to football coach. He's in demand as a speaker and seminar presenter for relationship and writing skills.

Havlin's passion for fishing, hunting, Florida's wilderness, and its historical heritage, frequently appear in his writing and his speaking engagements. His tales are just as likely to be set in Kiev, Singapore, London, Saxonhausen or other places in the over eighty countries he's visited. Their people and customs resonate in his novels. Known for creating memorable characters, his interjection of humor, and his carefully crafted plots, reading a DL Havlin book is always a pleasurable experience.

Made in USA - Kendallville, IN
1196408_9781986762366
11.18.2020 0822